——————— ★ ———————

"Neal?" I called. No answer. "Neal Hardy! Where are you?" Still no answer.

I walked around behind the desk, wondering if the old man had had a heart attack when the siren went off. Nothing. Went down the hall where my office and Emmett's office are located. Nothing. Nobody. Checked the bathrooms—both men's and women's. Nothing.

I was getting steamed. If Neal had answered the siren, why wasn't he at the firehouse like everybody else? And if he'd left, why hadn't he locked the door?

I started to open the door to the jail cells with my key, but found it was also unlocked and unlatched, swinging wide when I touched it. I stepped into the hallway in front of our three jail cells. He was in the middle one. Leastways I assumed it was Neal. Seemed to be the same clothes he'd been wearing that morning when I'd let him in and shown him around—khakis, a button-down striped shirt, Reeboks, and the watch he'd shown me. The watch Patrol had given him as a retirement gift. Without those things, I might not have recognized him, because his face had been blown off.

——————— ★ ———————

Previously published Worldwide Mystery titles by
SUSAN ROGERS COOPER

THE MAN IN THE GREEN CHEVY
HOUSTON IN THE REARVIEW MIRROR
OTHER PEOPLE'S HOUSES
CHASING AWAY THE DEVIL
LYING WONDERS
ROMANCED TO DEATH

SUSAN ROGERS COOPER

SHOTGUN *Wedding*

W**O**RLDWIDE.

TORONTO • NEW YORK • LONDON
AMSTERDAM • PARIS • SYDNEY • HAMBURG
STOCKHOLM • ATHENS • TOKYO • MILAN
MADRID • WARSAW • BUDAPEST • AUCKLAND

Recycling programs
for this product may
not exist in your area.

SHOTGUN WEDDING

A Worldwide Mystery/January 2013

First published by Severn House

ISBN-13: 978-0-373-26832-0

Printed in U.S.A.

SHOTGUN WEDDING

ONE

WE WERE GONNA have the wedding in our backyard—a June wedding, with all my wife's flowers in bloom. Which woulda been fine as it started out, with just me and Jean in attendance, the preacher, and Emmett Hopkins, my best friend and chief deputy, and his betrothed, Jasmine Bodine, another one of my deputies. They were the ones getting hitched. But then Jasmine had to invite her family: her mother and father, her sisters Rose, Lily, and Daisy, and her brother, Larry, and their spouses and kids. Of course, Emmett didn't want his side of the yard empty, so he insisted on inviting the entire sheriff's department, and the friends he had left on the police force, which was a political hotbed, meaning he had to invite the entire police force. Since the Methodist minister was officiating, the congregation of the First Methodist, which is where Emmett and his first wife, Shirley Beth, had gone before their boy, J.R., had died, got their noses out of joint so Emmett had to invite all of them, and of course when the Baptists found out I was throwing the wingding and the Methodists were coming, I had to invite them, and because me and Jean take turns going one Sunday to the First Baptist and one Sunday to Our Lady of Perpetual Sorrow, we had to invite the Catholics or rue the day.

It was a good thing we had a big backyard. About the only person who didn't show up was Walden Waylon, the mayor of Longbranch. I'm sure it was out of respect to everyone involved that he declined to come—or perhaps it was fear. Waylon had been mayor back when Emmett had his trouble with the police department, and to say the mayor was not supportive is like saying the sun's warm in August—you know, kind of an understatement. Suffice it to say, his honor wasn't missed.

When the people at the Longbranch Inn, where me and Emmett have eaten lunch every day for the past twenty years, found out about it, they offered to cater the event at a discount and close the restaurant for the day so all the employees could come. Since every one of the shop owners and workers in downtown Longbranch belong to either the First Baptist, First Methodist, or Our Lady, basically most of the town was coming and downtown was shutting down for the day. And on a Saturday to boot.

Jasmine had to have all three of her sisters as bridesmaids (the one closest in age to her was the matron-of-honor—some sort of family tradition, I hear), so Emmett had to come up with a corresponding number of groomsmen. I, of course, was best man, and to get in good with his new in-laws, he got Jasmine's brother Larry as one of the groomsmen and asked Anthony Dobbins, the only African-American deputy in the history of the Prophesy County Sheriff's Department, to be another.

There was some consternation among the older guests when Anthony Dobbins and his wife and new baby showed up, but then when they saw Anthony's parents there (they own Dobbins Dry Cleaning and most of the old white people in town forget they're black), things settled down a bit. Ours is one of those semi-Southern towns where the blacks live in a small enclave in the 'bad' part of town, called the Elms, and the whites live everywhere else. There were a handful of people, like the elder Dobbins and Anthony and his wife, Garrett Douglas, who owns the Chrysler dealership, and Dr Earl Jeffries, a retired professor from OU, who live in the 'white' part of town, but that's tolerated because they're rich—or, in Anthony's case, because his parents are rich. Lately, since the new subdivision opened up, regular black folk have been moving out of the Elms into the rest of the town. Mostly this has been ignored, but I do hear stirrings at the barber shop among the old men who hang out there every day, and Gladys tells me there's some concern among the elderly ladies of the Longbranch Ladies' Garden Club. Change is a hard thing for some people. It wasn't until the outbreak of World War II that the City Council decided to take down the signs next to the city limits signs that read 'No Negroes in Town After Dark'. And that was only because an army battalion was bivouacked here and some of the soldiers were African-American and, unfortunately to the townspeople, were gonna be there after dark by order of Uncle Sam.

But the wedding went off like clockwork. Except for one small incident—when Jasmine's ex-husband, Lester Bodine, showed up drunk and had to be escorted physically back to his car, where I got his new girlfriend to drive him home—it went smooth as glass. The food was good, the beer was cold, and the Baptists watched while everybody else danced, mostly to country-and-western music being spun by a punky-looking disc jockey named Flash.

The new police chief, Charlie Smith, had gotten his newest recruit to hold down the fort downtown while everybody came to the wedding and, since we're a smaller outfit and I didn't have any new recruits, I took a little money out of our coffers and hired a retired Highway Patrol officer who had moved to Prophesy County about six months before, to keep an eye on the county shop. He'd rented a small space on the square in downtown Longbranch where he worked part-time as a mediator.

We were at that point when I, as the best man, was

about to give my toast to the new couple when something happened. Like most small to medium-sized towns in tornado alley, Longbranch is set up with a siren system that blares loud enough to wake up the whole town, and half of those perpetually resting in the city cemetery, when a tornado is coming. We'd been lucky: we haven't used the dang thing for almost two years. But just as I opened my mouth to give my toast, it went off, and even up there on Mountain Falls Road, we could hear it. Everybody stopped what they were doing and stared toward town, then most people, including me, looked up in the sky. There wasn't a cloud in sight.

Me, Emmett, and Charlie Smith looked at each other, then all three ran for our cars. Most of the law enforcement personnel, including the bride, who first ran inside to get out of her wedding dress, headed for their cars. I told Jean to keep everybody else there until we found out what was going on. I know that was putting a lot on my wife, but she's a psychiatrist and I figured she could reason with 'em.

DOWNTOWN LONGBRANCH WAS a ghost town. I drove my Jeep in, Emmett sitting shotgun, Jasmine in back. We all had our service revolvers and Jasmine was loading the shotgun in the backseat. Guess you could say she was *really* riding shotgun. A little humor, folks.

No people roamed the sidewalks; no cars except ours drove the streets. All the stores were locked up tight. Still the siren split the air. It was damn spooky. We went first to the volunteer fire department building, on top of which the siren screeched its bad news. The place was empty. Most of the volunteers were members of the sheriff's department, the police force, and local storeowners. They were all either behind me and Emmett or back at my house.

We went into the switch room where the turn-on for the siren was located.

Billy Johansson, the twenty-one-year-old recruit Charlie Smith hired straight out of the Academy in Oklahoma City a couple of months ago, was half lying in a pool of blood on the floor of the switch room. His back and head were propped against the wall, his long, skinny legs out in front of him. His head lolled and blood seeped from wounds on his chest, left arm, and shoulder. Nothing but a shotgun coulda done that damage. Emmett got to him first.

'He's got a pulse. Call an ambulance!' he yelled out into the crowded firehouse.

Charlie Smith called out, 'Who's got EMT training?'

Brad Taylor, a police lieutenant on the city force, raced into the room, moving me out of the way. I stepped back into the larger room of the firehouse and looked at the newly washed, bright and shiny thirty-year-old fire truck that kept Longbranch and the county as safe from fire as it could. Charlie was getting out his cell phone, probably to call an ambulance.

'Charlie, why don't we use the truck? We got an EMT and a siren. Be quicker than waiting for the ambulance,' I said.

Charlie moved into the doorway of the switch room. 'Brad, can we move him?'

'Yeah,' Brad said, 'and we better do it fast.'

'Guys,' Charlie called out, 'we need a couple of you to move him to the fire truck.'

The two biggest—my deputy, Dalton Pettigrew, and Charlie's officer, Dan Sanchez—moved into the switch room to get Billy.

'Who's gonna drive this thing?' Charlie asked, looking at the huge old fire truck.

'Hell, I drove it from 1978 to 1989,' Emmett said.

'Reckon I can still strip the gears some.' He hopped behind the wheel and we all helped stretch Billy out in the space behind. Brad got on board next to Billy and me and Charlie crawled in next to Emmett.

Charlie yelled out, 'Dan, secure the area!'

And I yelled, 'Dalton, help him!'

After going forward twice when he meant to go backward, Emmett remembered the gears and got us going to the hospital.

'Wonder why Neal hasn't responded?' I said aloud, thinking of the retired State Highway Patrol officer who was manning the phones at the sheriff's department. 'Drop me off there on your way, Emmett.'

'You mean if I can find the brake?' he asked, and I hoped he was joking.

The turn-off to the hospital was less than a city block before the sheriff's department, so he stopped there and I got out and walked in my tux to the sheriff's department. The door was unlocked, but there was nobody behind the desk where Gladys, our civilian clerk, ruled during the week. 'Neal?' I called. No answer. 'Neal Hardy! Where are you?' Still no answer.

I walked around behind the desk, wondering if the old man had had a heart attack when the siren went off. Nothing. Went down the hall where my office and Emmett's office are located. Nothing. Nobody. Checked the bathrooms, both men and women. Nothing. Headed back out to the main desk and beyond, where the door to the interrogation room and the jail cells was located. Nobody in the interrogation room. I was getting steamed. If Neal had answered the siren, why wasn't he at the firehouse like everybody else? And if he'd left, why didn't he lock the door?

I started to open the door to the jail cells with my key, but found it was unlocked and unlatched, swinging wide

when I touched it. I stepped into the hallway in front of
our three jail cells. He was in the middle one. Leastways
I assumed it was Neal. Seemed to be the same clothes
he'd been wearing that morning when I'd let him in and
shown him around—khakis, a button-down striped shirt,
Reeboks, and the watch he'd shown me, the one the Patrol
had given him as a retirement gift, on his left wrist. Without those things I might not have recognized him. His face
had been blown off.

I LEFT HIM WHERE he was and went into the big room to
make the necessary calls from Gladys's phone. Didn't have
to do like Emmett did with Billy Johansson and look for a
pulse; I could tell by looking that Neal Hardy was no longer
with us. Two things were running through my mind. First
was that I felt like shit 'cause I'd talked Neal into coming
in and playing temp for me while the rest of us had a good
time at the wedding. Didn't know the man too well, but still
and all, he wouldn't be dead if I hadn't hired him. Then
there was the other thing: what in Sam Hill was going on?
I didn't have a vehicle with me, or I'd have hightailed it
back to town. Of course, I couldn't leave the body even if
I did have a vehicle… Then I remembered Neal's car was
parked out back. Neal's keys were probably in his pocket.
But even after being an officer of the law for close to thirty
years, I couldn't see sticking my hand in Neal's pocket,
what with his missing face and all. Just didn't seem right.

   I called it in to the coroner's office. Old Doc Watson had
retired last year, and there was a new coroner. Her name
was Rose Church and usually she was an anesthesiolo-
gist (a gas-passer), but had been elected coroner. She was
a friend of my wife's, but for some reason we didn't like
each other much. I'm not sure if I didn't like her because

she didn't like me, or vice versa. You know, a chicken-and-egg kinda thing.

While I was waiting for Dr Church to show up, I tried to remember if I knew whether or not Neal Hardy was married. I needed to call somebody, but I sure didn't want to bring this bad news to a wife. Over the years I've gotten some varied responses from wives when I've told them their husbands had been killed—be it a knifing at the Dew Drop Inn, a wreck on the highway, or a heart attack away from home. There was the one old gal who'd said, 'Thank God!' when I gave her what turned out to be the good news. Mostly there's crying, sometimes screaming. Davey Mercer's wife plumb passed out when I tried to tell her about Davey's wreck on the highway. Nicole Dunlavey slapped my face when I told her Butch had bit the big one at the Dew Drop. I had no idea if there was a Mrs Hardy waiting at home for the extra cash Neal was supposed to be bringing in from his stint at the Sheriff's Department, but if there was, I dreaded having to give her the news.

I went back to my office and looked through my top drawer to find the paperwork Neal had filled out for his temporary job. It showed an address on Stanhope, a street in an older section of town, one of those small-town eclectic areas where you got Victorian semi-mansions next to nine-hundred square foot shotgun houses. The 'in case of emergency, call…' had been left blank. I shoulda checked that, I thought. Wedding plans had been so big in my mind that I guess I didn't look over the application the way I shoulda. That kinda thing can get you in big trouble. Bill Williams, a friend of mine and sheriff of Tejas, one county over, didn't look over an application real good one time and ended up hiring a drunk wife-beater with three DWIs. Just goes to show, you know.

I called Emmett on his cell phone, told him what had happened, and asked him to send some of the guys back.

'I'll be right there,' he said.

'No,' I said. 'You and Jasmine got a plane to catch in the morning. Y'all go have your wedding night.'

Emmett laughed. 'Milt, we been doing that for a while now. We'll make the plane.'

'Charlie there?' I asked, not needing or wanting to argue with him. Help's help, you know?

'Yeah, hold on.'

A couple of seconds later I had Charlie Smith, Police Chief of Longbranch, Oklahoma, on the line. 'Hey, Milt, what's up?'

'How's your boy?' I asked.

'Still in surgery,' Charlie said and sighed. 'His mama's here and if looks could kill, I'd be a dead man.'

'Not your fault,' I said, which is something you say but we both knew it probably was. 'Look, did Emmett tell you about my temp here?'

'Uh-uh,' he said. 'What's up?'

'Looks like whatever happened with Billy happened here, too. Neal Hardy's dead,' I said.

'Jesus H. Christ on a bicycle!' Charlie said. 'What's going on? You think this is Lester Bodine's way of getting back at his ex?'

'Naw,' I said. 'When I poured Lester into his pick-up, I doubt he coulda lifted a .22, much less the fire power that did what I saw to Neal's face. I'd say shotgun, same as Billy's wounds. What I'm thinking, Charlie, is that something went down in Longbranch while we were all up on the mountain.'

'Yeah, I've sorta been thinking the same thing,' Charlie said.

'I know the city's your jurisdiction, but I wouldn't

mind a bit if you came and got me here. I'd be happy to go with you.'

'I'll find me a squad car and be there in about five.'

'Bring one of my guys with you to hold down the fort here, OK?'

'Got it.'

While I was waiting I called home. Jean answered on the first ring. My wife's on crutches due to childhood polio, and she keeps our cordless phone with her most of the time. Smart thing to do with a three-year-old in the house.

'Hey, baby,' I said. 'How things going up there?'

'I haven't been able to keep people here, Milt. Almost everyone's gone,' she said.

'Well, nothing we can do about that.' I sighed. 'You know that new recruit Charlie Smith used to cover while they were all here?'

'No,' she said.

'Billy Johansson,' I said.

'Paul Johansson's son?' she asked.

'How do you know Paul Johansson?' I asked. My wife's a Yankee, not raised in Longbranch, so she doesn't know everybody the way I do. In fact, if it weren't for the hospital, church and my work, she wouldn't really know a soul.

'That's privileged, Milt,' my wife the psychiatrist said.

'Oh,' I said. 'Anyway, we found Billy in the switch room at the firehouse. Been shot. He's at the hospital now.'

'Oh, my God! Do you know what happened?' she asked.

'No, and what's worse, when I got here to the shop, I found Neal Hardy, you know, the guy I hired to babysit the shop?'

'Yes?'

'Anyway, found him dead as a doornail. Somebody blew his face off.'

'Oh, God!'

'Sorry about that. You don't need the details,' I said.

'Baby, you tell me whatever you need to tell me,' Jean said. 'I'm so sorry, Milt,' she continued. 'Do you have any idea what's going on?'

'Hell, I wish I knew,' I answered. 'Look, babe, it could be a while before I get home.'

'Don't worry about it. I'll take care of everything here.'

We said goodbye and I hung up.

Dr Church beat Charlie to the shop.

'Hey, Doc,' I said. 'Glad you could make it. Let me show you where the body is.'

'Natural causes?' she asked, being civil, which is what we generally were with each other.

'Oh, not so much,' I said, leading her back to the carnage in the cells.

'Shit,' she said upon seeing the body. 'Who is it?' she asked.

'Pretty sure it's Neal Hardy, the guy I hired to sit the shop while we were all at a wedding at my house. I didn't touch the body,' I added.

'Well, we can rule out natural causes all right,' Dr Church said. 'And I think suicide, too.'

I nodded. She didn't smile when she said it, so I wasn't sure if she was making a joke or not. Jean said she had a 'dry' sense of humor. Maybe that's what dry meant. 'Yeah, I think we can rule out suicide,' I said.

I heard hollering from the front and left Dr Church to do her thing, and went into the big room. Charlie, Emmett, and Jasmine were standing there.

'You ready?' Charlie asked.

'As a tomcat in season,' I said, heading for the door.

'Well, just don't go humping my leg,' Charlie said.

'I'm coming,' Emmett said behind us.

'Good to have your expertise,' Charlie said, and I was

glad to hear it. He was still wearing his suit, like the rest of us, but at least he didn't have to deal with a tux. His was a nice summer-weight wool glen plaid and looked fairly new. He was a good-looking man, our new police chief—at least that's what I think my wife would say. One of those men born with a rugged face, so it was hard to tell how old he was. Taller than me, skinnier than me (although that's not difficult), with just a little bit of a paunch. His hair was dark with very little gray, cut short with military sideburns. And he had straight teeth, which you could see because he smiled a lot, and it didn't seem to be that smarmy kind of smile some guys give you just because they think it's gonna win friends and influence people, as the saying goes.

Charlie was new, but already he was doing a hell of a better job, at least at politics, than his predecessor, who had been Emmett's second in command when he was police chief, and a backstabbing son-of-a-bitch. He got run out of town when he got caught with his hand not only in the cookie jar (the petty cash drawer), but up the skirt of a civilian employee. Couldn't have happened to a more deserving guy.

'Sheriff?' Jasmine said behind me.

'Jasmine, can you stay here until Anthony or Dalton come? Doc Church is back in the cells with the body. Then you're off-duty for two weeks and if I see you or Emmett anytime in that period you're both fired.' I grinned. 'You got it?'

She grinned back. 'Yes, sir!' she said and gave me a mock salute.

I couldn't help noticing that the change in Jasmine since she and Emmett had gotten together was complete. The droopy Eeyore voice was gone, there was a spring in her step, and you'd have to slap her to get the grin off her face.

We headed out to the city cruiser Charlie had commandeered and, with the lights and siren wide open, sped our way back into Longbranch. The place wasn't as deserted anymore. The shopkeepers and business people had wandered down from my mountain and were opening up, trying to see if anything had happened to their stuff while all this was going on. Charlie slowed down as we got to the square, with the three of us looking out the open windows to see if anybody looked upset. Didn't see much until we got to the Longbranch First National. That's when Katy Monroe, one of the bank's VPs, came running out screaming.

Charlie slammed on the breaks and the three of us fell outta the car.

'Katy! What's the matter?' I asked, then remembered it was Charlie's jurisdiction and stepped back to let him take the lead.

'Oh, my God, we've been hit!' she wailed.

She led us into the bank and back to the vault. The door was standing open. 'How'd they get it open?' Charlie asked.

'They didn't,' Katy said. 'I opened it to check. Look,' she said, pointing inside.

There was a big old hole at the back of the vault, through the concrete, but there wasn't anything else in there. Not a dime.

THE BUILDING HOUSING the First National was built around the turn of the century as a bank. Like most banks at the time, it had a safe where the money and other valuables were kept. Sometime in the twenties, when Bonnie and Clyde and their ilk were running wild, the First National, like a lot of small-town banks, had a vault put in. It was the latest thing at the time: a big concrete bunker with a steel door. Over the years, the door has been replaced many times, keeping up with the latest technology. Unfortunately, the vault is the same one put in back in the twenties. Somehow, whoever did this thing must have known that. They didn't even try the door; instead they went straight for the vulnerable back, just a couple of feet of non-reinforced concrete, ripe for the picking.

Katy Monroe sat in the bank president's office, in one of the visitors' chairs. Charlie Smith sat in the president's chair. I sat in the other vacant chair and Emmett leaned against one of the glass walls.

Dewayne Dickey, president of the Longbranch First National Bank, was the current husband of my ex-wife, LaDonna. I didn't like him and he didn't like me, and that seemed to work for both of us. They were out of town visiting his daughter and her new baby in Oklahoma City. He'd been called and was on his way back. The FBI had been notified, as bank robberies were their jurisdiction, and I didn't envy Charlie Smith's next couple of weeks. I was on my own with the murder that happened in county jurisdiction, unless it turned out to be connected. Somehow I couldn't see how it wasn't.

'You know how much was in the vault?' Charlie Smith asked Katy Monroe. 'Approximately.'

'Close to five hundred thousand dollars,' Katy said.

'That's a lot to keep on hand in a town this size, isn't it?' he asked.

'If they'd hit us on Friday it would have been more like seven hundred and fifty thousand,' she said. 'It's the end of the month and everybody's got payroll. A lot pay on Friday, but with Monday being the first of the month, we got even more employers who pay then.'

'You always keep that much cash on hand first of the month? I'd think nowadays, with direct deposit and such, it would all be just numbers floating around in space, not actual cash.' From the way Charlie asked about the cash, I figured this was the first he'd heard about it. I doubt the departing police chief had had much time to fill Charlie in on the minutia of city policing. What with being rode out of town on a rail and all. Figuratively speaking, of course.

'A lot of people use direct deposit, but most want cash in hand. It's still sorta scary to a lot of folks not to have actual money. And since MedPro moved into the county six months ago, and OnLine Inc. last month, we've had to increase our monthly and bi-monthly cash-on-hand. Last year our end of the month cash was more like fifty to sixty thousand dollars. But MedPro and OnLine have a lot of employees.'

Yeah, I wanted to say, ones they brought with 'em. The honey deal the county commissioners had made with both companies had included no property taxes for five years. This was supposed to be a way of bringing jobs to the community. Instead, both companies had brought their own employees, leaving the job openings for Prophesy County those of janitors, file clerks, and cafeteria employees. Not what you'd call fast-track employment. And I'd bet my next paycheck that after five years, when they were supposed to start paying taxes, both companies would up and move to some other honey deal. At that point, the one benefit our community had received—that of housing being bought right and left for the brought-in employees—would end up as a bunch of houses on the market and nobody to buy 'em. But I didn't say anything. I figured now wasn't the time to vent my pet peeves.

'I shouldn't have gone to the wedding!' Katy wailed. 'Mr Dickey's going to fire me!' She broke down sobbing.

Katy Monroe had been Katy Lydecker until she got married to her college sweetheart straight out of school and moved to Tulsa. That had been seven or eight years ago. Now she was back in town, the ink hardly dry on her divorce papers, not quite thirty, and taking a demotion from being the VP of finance at a large corporation in Tulsa, to being VP number three out of three at the First National. I'm not sure where she'd been living in Tulsa, but something made me think it was nicer than living in her parents' RV in their back driveway.

I'd known Monte and Sylvia Lydecker for a lot of years, and had seen Katy some growing up. She'd been a pretty little girl, a chirpy, sexy teenager, and a hot college girl. Now, nearing thirty, she looked like she'd been rode hard and put up wet. I figured that must have been some bad marriage she'd been in. Monte and Sylvia hadn't said much when she moved back, just that she needed to 'regroup' from the divorce. She'd always been a natural blonde, but sometime over the last few years she musta taken to bleaching it lighter. It had kind of a burnt look about it, and it was almost white. Her eyes were bloodshot, probably from lack of sleep. I'd been divorced and I'm told one of two things happen—you either sleep too little or too much. I'd taken the latter route, but I was thinking Katy was taking the former. She was neat as a pin, though, as befitted a bank vice president pinch-hitting for the president at a wedding his wife probably refused to go to. She had on a light blue silk-looking suit, the blazer-style jacket with no shirt under it, which would normally have showed a little cleavage. On Katy, however, it just showed bony collarbones with a dip at her throat that looked too deep for someone her age. Personally, I wanted to find that ex-husband of hers and beat the crap out of him.

'Dewayne's not gonna fire you,' I said, standing up from my chair and squatting by hers, taking her hand in mine. 'You came to the wedding representing the bank, right?' She nodded. 'Well, then, you did exactly what you were supposed to do. Bank's not open on Saturdays anyway. No one saw this coming. And there's a big sign there, right on the door: FDIC insured, right? And, Katy, the robbery's secondary here. We got one deputy dead and a policeman shot.'

Her crying stopped and she looked up at me with wide, red-rimmed eyes. 'Oh, my God! Milt, I'm so sorry!' she said, gripping my arm. 'Who?'

I shook my head. 'It wasn't one of my regulars, Katy. Nobody you knew, probably. Old retired state trooper named Hardy. Neal Hardy.'

She shook her head, not recognizing the name. Then she looked at Charlie, who said, 'Billy Johansson. Paul and Marsha's boy.'

She put her hand to her lips. 'Oh, Lord! I know them from church. How is he?'

'Still in surgery last I heard.' Which seemed to remind him, because he picked up the phone, said to us, 'Just a minute,' and dialed. He asked after Billy, said a gruff 'thanks' and looked at us. 'He's still in surgery. They don't know how long it's gonna take.'

Katy stood up. 'I—I need to go to the hospital. Marsha's probably frantic.'

I looked at Emmett, who said, 'I'll drive you, Katy, if you can get a ride home. I need to find my new wife.'

She gave a ghost of a smile, and touched Emmett's hand. 'Really bad timing, huh, Emmett?'

'Can't think what would have been good timing for this,' he said.

Katy waved a tentative goodbye to me and Charlie and she and Emmett headed out of the bank. Charlie and I sat for a while in Dewayne's office, Charlie probably contemplating the whole situation, trying to reason it out, while

I, to my discredit, was mostly thinking about how pissed Dewayne Dickey would be when he found I'd been sitting in his office all of a Saturday afternoon. You know, 'petty' only gets that name when somebody else is doing it.

Finally, Charlie said, 'Neal Hardy's your guy, Milt, but his office is my jurisdiction. I'm thinking that hole might go into his office next door.'

I never knew where Neal Hardy's mediator's office was; had no idea it was next door to the bank.

I pointed in that direction. 'His office is over there?' I asked, which was dumb, 'cause he just said that.

'Yeah. Wanna go look?'

'Does the Pope shit in the woods?'

'No,' Charlie said, 'but the bear's Catholic.'

So we got up, leaving Dewayne's office and the bank, and headed to the storefront next door. Sure enough, there was gold lettering on the plate glass window that said, 'Neal Hardy, Mediator, Notary Public, Family Counseling, Passport Photos, Deer Licenses.' Jack-of-all-trades, our Neal Hardy. The door was locked but Charlie impressed me with a little gadget from his pocket and after a few twists and turns of the old door handle, the thing popped right open. 'After you,' he said, so I went in ahead.

There was a small front office with a reception-type desk that looked unused. There was a calendar turned to the first of the year—about six months before—and a cup with assorted pens, pencils, scissors, etc., and a tape dispenser. No pictures of kids, husbands, or boyfriends—or girlfriends, for that matter—no plants, no mementoes or anything else taped to the wall behind. My guess would be that Neal Hardy's office was a one-person operation. Behind the wall was an office of sorts, more homey—or junky to be honest—with a cluttered desk top, diplomas and pictures on the walls of Neal in his Highway Patrol uniform standing next to unknown dignitaries. There was a door at the back of the office that led to a unisex bathroom, and a door to the right that led to a small kitchen. This is where the big hole was that led to the bank vault. It was obviously dug out with shovels and a jackhammer, not blown out with explosives. The hole wasn't big enough for me to get through, not with my gut, but somehow Neal had made it. He was taller, but maybe thinner.

'So how long did you know this guy?' Charlie asked me.

I shook my head. 'Didn't really know him. Met him at a Kiwanis Club meeting couple of months ago. Introduced himself. Told me he was retired Highway Patrol.' I shook my head, wondering at my stupidity. 'And I just took his word for it. But you saw those pictures, right?' I said, pointing back towards Neal's office and the pictures of him in his uniform.

'Easy enough to take a picture wearing whatever you want. They got all sorts of get-ups you can rent at those costume shops in the city,' Charlie said.

'Yeah, I know,' I said, feeling like a total idiot. He said he was retired Highway Patrol, and I said, 'Oh boy, come rob our town when it's totally empty, OK?' I sighed deep and hard. 'Well, at least we know he wasn't in this alone,' I said. 'Somebody killed him.'

'You think it was a shoot-out between him and my boy Billy?' Charlie asked.

'And Billy crawled from my shop to the firehouse with a gut wound?'

Charlie shrugged. 'Just thinking out loud,' he said.

I shrugged, too, 'cause his thinking was beating the hell out of my thinking, out loud or not. Then I did think of something. 'Speaking of Billy crawling, did you see any kind of blood trail at all? Into the switch room, I mean.'

Charlie was still for a moment, then shook his head. 'Nope, sure didn't. Think Billy was shot in the switch room?'

'Sure looks that way. Billy gets away from the perp, runs to the firehouse, gets into the switch room to turn on the siren, perp finds him and shoots him.'

'So why didn't he turn off the siren?' Charlie asked. 'The perp, I mean.'

'Seem to remember that the new system's on a timer,' I said. 'Once you pull the switch the siren blares for a certain length of time, like five minutes or something, before it cuts off. There's another switch you can hit that makes it go until you turn it off manually.'

'You thinking what I'm thinking?' Charlie asked.

'That maybe we should go back to the firehouse? That that's probably the crime scene?' I said.

'You know, you're smarter than you look, Kovak,' Charlie said.

I took it as a compliment.

TWO

CHARLIE PUT A CALL in to the state forensic team, then we went over to the firehouse to look at the crime scene.

We weren't gonna make the forensic guys happy, I can tell you that. Bloody footprints were everywhere. Anybody who'd gone into the switch room had to step in the blood pooling by Billy's body, and that blood was tracked everywhere in the big room. Our two guys had wrapped crime-scene tape around the front of the building and the door to the switch room. But it had been kinda like closing the barn door after the horse is gone.

There wasn't much for us to see; that would be up to the state forensic guys, so Charlie and me went to the sheriff's department to see how things were going there. Dr Church was just finishing up, and the hearse from Marley's Funeral Home was parked by the side entrance to the department. We got out and went in that way, me having to suck my gut in to get past the hearse. Inside, Jasmine was gone, replaced by Anthony Dobbins, still in his tux and good shoes, although the jacket was resting on the back of Gladys's chair and the bow tie was hanging loose around his neck.

'Hey, Sheriff,' he said when we walked in.

'Hey, yourself, Anthony. Where's Church?'

'In with the, ah…back in the cells,' he said.

Anthony was generally a cool guy, nothing much ever ruffling his feathers. But this attack on the sheriff's department had us all spooked. This sort of thing just wasn't supposed to happen. We were the law keepers, and the department building was sorta sacred. You expect almost anything out on the street, but in the building, all was safe. A sanctuary. Maybe you get a guy in cuffs thinks he can headbutt you while you're trying to get him in a cell, but that's just business as usual. But to have a deputy, even a part-time deputy, killed in a who-done-it inside the sheriff's department was just plain wrong.

I patted Anthony on the back, and me and Charlie headed back to the cells. Dr Church was standing up and taking off her gloves when we walked in. Charlie got one look at Neal Hardy and said, 'Woo doggies, that's rough.'

'Yeah,' I agreed, not thinking I could add much to that. Instead, to Dr Church I said, 'Find anything, Doc?'

'The guy's dead,' she said in her deadpan way.

'I kinda figured that,' I said, not appreciating this 'dry' wit of hers.

'A shotgun,' Dr Church said, 'maybe two or three hours ago.'

'That long?' I asked, wondering about the time. 'You sure?'

'No,' she said, frowning. 'After the autopsy I may be able to tell you more.'

'And you'll do it quick and get me the results real fast, right, Dr Church?'

She turned, bent down to pack her bag. 'You'll get the results when I have them, Sheriff,' she said, not bothering to look at me. I couldn't help noticing she had a big ass, but, again, maybe that was just me being petty.

She stood, nodded at me then Charlie, and left, letting the EMTs in to package up the body and move it to the morgue.

After they left, I got my own crime-scene tape and taped off the middle cell. This was where Neal had been shot, but I doubted this was where it all started. No reason for him to be back here. We didn't have anybody in the cells, the whole building was empty except for Neal Hardy and whoever killed him. It had started probably in Gladys's area. Neal's partner had come in, they talked, there was an argument probably, then the partner pulled the shotgun up—he'd been carrying it by his side in my vision—made Neal walk to the cells and unlock the door, put him in the middle one, Neal probably thinking the guy was going to leave him there and take off with the money. Instead, the guy shoots him, taking off his face and part of his shoulder. This had to be before he shot Billy, since Billy had to have rung the alarm almost immediately upon getting hit, or even just before. It was just God's own miracle that Billy wasn't dead. Chalk it up to youth, clean living and a piss-poor aim.

I shared these thoughts with Charlie.

'Makes sense,' he said, staring like I was at the bloody mess where Neal's body had lain.

'You think the forensic guys are at your shop yet?' I asked.

'Probably not. They had to come in from the barracks in Tulsa,' Charlie said.

'Call one of your guys? Ask him to send them over here when they're done?' I asked.

Charlie nodded. 'Already did it. When we left my shop I told Felix to send 'em over here after.'

'Good,' I said, nodding back. 'Real good.'

'So,' Charlie said, sighing long and hard, 'I guess your next order of business is to call the Highway Patrol and see if Neal Hardy really was a patrolman.'

'Yeah,' I said, heaving my own sigh. 'Nothing to it but to do it, I guess. You wanna come with and listen in?'

'Naw,' he said, following me back out to the big room.

'I need to get back home and change out of these good clothes 'fore I get something on them and my wife has a shit-fit. Then it's back to the station for me.'

'Yeah, I need to change too,' I said, looking at the monkey suit I was still wearing. 'Never did like wearing a tux.'

I walked him to the door and we said goodbye, and I watched him walk to his car. This was the first time I'd spent any quality time with Charlie Smith, and I was feeling glad the city council had gone outside the town to find him. I figured we could work together, and that's saying a lot after the last administration.

I went to my office, took off my tux jacket and undid the tie. In my life before Jean, the tie would have been clip-on and no big deal, but Jean wouldn't have any of that. She actually threw out all my clip-on ties the day we got back from our honeymoon, and when I rented this tux for Emmett's and Jasmine's wedding, she told me if I came home with a rented clip-on, she'd burn it. Personally I think that's pretty damned opinionated for a shrink, don't ya think?

After I was semi-comfortable (the black patent-leather shoes were pinching my feet something fierce), I looked up the number for the Highway Patrol main office in Oklahoma City and got myself put through to their HR department. After being transferred around about five times, I got somebody who actually gave me an answer to my question of whether or not they ever had a patrolman there by the name of Neal Hardy.

'I'm sorry, sir,' the woman said, and to me she didn't sound a bit sorry, 'but we don't give that information over the phone. You'll have to put it in writing, on your county's letterhead, and it will need to be notarized.'

'Now, ma'am, ordinarily I'd do just that, but this is special circumstances. This particular retired patrolman I'm speaking of got himself killed today, and I need to notify

next of kin before they find out on the news or something.'
That wasn't going to happen anytime soon, since we don't
have a local paper anymore and the TV stations are so far
away we can barely see 'em without cable, but she didn't
need to know that.

'Sir, we'd be happy to comply with your request, in
writing on your county's letterhead, with a notary seal
and signature.'

'May I speak to your supervisor, please?' I said.

'Sir, I am the supervisor,' she said, and I could tell she
was smiling when she said it.

I hung up the phone and called Charlie Smith's line at
the police station. He answered on the third ring, and I
told him about the runaround I was getting at the Highway Patrol. 'You know anybody there so I can get past all
this red tape?' I asked.

He gave me a name, told me the forensic people were
just finishing up at the firehouse and would be my way
soon, then I thanked him and we hung up. I called the
number he'd given me. The man's name was Harold Wasserman, and he was a captain. I explained who I was and
who had given me his number.

'Charlie Smith? Hey, how's he doing? Man, you tell him
when you see him that I haven't had a good laugh since
Ardmore. He'll know what I'm talking about,' the captain
said and laughed long and loud.

'I'll do that,' I said. 'The reason I'm calling, Captain,
is that I've got a DB down here who identified himself to
me as retired Highway Patrol. I'm just checking up on it
but I can't get anybody in HR to tell me diddly.'

'Yeah, that's HR for you. The Nazis coulda taken les-
sons from those people. Who's your DB?'

'Guy named Neal Hardy.'

'Well, shit! What the hell happened?' the captain said.

'You knew him?'

'Hell, yes! Neal Hardy was on the patrol for thirty years. He was a good man. Got a lot of commendations, but never would take a promotion. Always wanted to stay on the streets. He was a hell of a good man. What happened?'

'Well, sir,' I said, trying to ease into it, 'we had a bank robbery here today while the whole town was empty due to a wedding. Had one cop on duty in town, and Neal was sitting in for me here at the shop. Both got shotgunned. Policeman's in bad condition at the hospital, but Neal got killed. And, well, seems the perps got to the bank vault through Neal's office.'

The captain said, 'You're not thinking Neal had anything to do with this, are you, Sheriff?' His tone wasn't nearly as friendly as it had been.

'Well, sir,' I said. 'The thing is, the hole into the bank vault came from his office. In the kitchen of his office, to be exact.'

'No way. Neal Hardy was the most honest man I ever met. You sure this is the same guy?'

I described Neal as I had seen him last alive, and the captain said, 'Sounds like him. He had a scar—'

'On his nose?' I put in. 'Right side as you look at him, right under the eye?'

'Shit,' Captain Wasserman said. 'Yeah. That's Neal. But I'm telling you, Sheriff, he had absolutely nothing to do with that heist. I'll bet you a hundred dollars!'

'Gambling's against the law in this state, Captain,' I said, 'but I wouldn't take the bet anyway. I'll keep you informed. You have any information on next of kin? Wife or anything?'

'Margaret died of breast cancer about five years ago, I think,' he said, 'but he's got a son and a daughter. Think I got the boy's number.' He gave me Neal Hardy's son's name, Max, and his number in Tulsa. I decided to put off that particular call as I could hear the forensic guys coming in the front door.

I WAS ON MY WAY back up to my mountain when I got a radio dispatch from Lonnie Sturgis, our night-time clerk.

'Sheriff?' he said.

'Yeah, Lonnie?' I said.

'Got a shots fired at the Motel Five out on Highway five,' he said. 'Can you get it, or you want me to call in Dalton?'

I was about five minutes away from the Motel Five, so I said, 'I'll take it,' and rung off.

The Motel Five, not to be confused with its higher number, Motel Six, is not part of any chain. It's an independent run by an Indian family that moved to the county about ten years ago. I'm not talking 'cowboys and…' here; I'm talking all the way from New Delhi. There's a big bunch of 'em: Taj and Lili, and Lili's mama—we call her Mrs G because nobody around these parts can pronounce her name—and Mrs G's sister, Mrs S, and Taj and Lili's daughter, Miranda, and her two kids, and Taj and Lili's son, David, and two of Taj's nephews and one niece, all who work at the motel. They're not big socializers 'cause they work all the time, even Mrs G and Mrs S. The only ones who get out much are Miranda's kids, a boy about eleven named Todd, and a girl about five named Nefira, who go to one of the elementary schools in Longbranch, taking the bus to get there.

When I pulled into the half-full parking lot of the Motel Five, Taj was standing by the door of the lobby area, waiting. He came out to greet me.

'Sheriff!' he said, coming up to the car. He was a small man, always neatly dressed in pressed slacks and a button-

down shirt and loafers. Today the slacks were brown poly-
ester and the shirt was a madras plaid, heavy on the pink.

'Hey, Taj,' I said, getting out of my Jeep with my
weapon in my hand. Since I was still wearing the tux, I
didn't have it holstered. 'Lonnie said you got shots fired?'

He pointed toward the row of rooms to the back and left
of the motel. 'Three! Room 104,' he said.

'Who's registered?' I asked.

'John Smith,' he said.

I nodded and walked to room 104, knocking on the door.
'Sheriff's department. Open the door, please.'

'It's unlocked, I think,' came a male voice from inside.

'Sir,' I said, calling through the door, 'if you have a
weapon, please put it down. If I see a weapon, I may be
forced to shoot you.'

'I don't have a weapon,' said the voice. 'I'm the vic-
tim here!'

I gingerly opened the door and walked in. And what a
sight did I behold! There, on the floor at the foot of the bed,
sat Mayor Walden Waylon, buck naked, his back against
the foot of the bed, his legs stretched out in front of him.
The only thing covering him was blood.

Walden Waylon was a small man, about five foot five,
and couldn't weigh more than one-forty, maybe one-forty-
five pounds. He wore a bad toupee, which was a bit off-
kilter at the moment, and usually dressed in camo and
other macho stylings. At this point, of course, he didn't
look all that macho.

I leaned out the door and called to Taj, 'Call the paramedics.'

'No, now, Milt, don't go doing that,' His Honor said. 'I
don't want this little incident all over town!'

I knelt down by the mayor, donning gloves I keep in my
back pocket, and examined the wounds. All were fairly

superficial, but there were a lot of 'em—three to be exact. Taj had said he heard three shots; looked like the assailant hadn't missed once.

'You wanna tell me who did this to you?' I asked.

'No' was all he said.

'Well, I hope they take real good care of you at the hospital, because we don't have any medical supervision at the jailhouse so you're gonna have to be well when you get there,' I said.

'You're arresting me?' he shouted, a little of his strength obviously back. 'Who in the hell do you think you are, Sheriff?'

'Mayor, you're in the county now, which is my bailiwick, and you seem to be obstructing justice, sir. That's a jailable offense, Your Honor, sir,' I said. OK, I was being a little sarcastic, but if I'd lived in Longbranch, let's just say I never would have voted for the guy.

'They're self-inflicted,' His Honor said.

'Where's the gun?' I asked.

'I threw it away,' he said.

'Where?'

'I don't know.'

'And why's that?' I asked.

'I was distraught at the time,' he explained.

That's when I heard the sneeze coming from the bathroom.

The mayor covered his face with a bloody hand. Not a good thing—made him look even worse.

I got up from my squat, which is an iffy thing at my age, moved toward the door of the bathroom, and pointed my weapon at the door.

'I know you're in there,' I said to the door. 'This is the sheriff of Prophesy County and I have my weapon drawn. Please come out with your hands up.'

The door opened slightly and a female eye peeked out at me. 'I'd rather stay in here,' the woman said.

The eye looked familiar. 'Inez?'

The eye closed for a moment, then opened, and along with the eye came the door. 'Hey, Milt,' she said, coming out, a towel covering the part of her not covered by the flimsy black teddy.

Now here's the thing: Inez Tatum is the choir director of my church. She's married and has seven children. She's a big woman, real big, so the part of her not covered by the black teddy, the part needing to be covered by the towel, was a lot, and the towel wasn't doing that good a job.

I lowered my weapon and turned away, not wanting to see too much, knowing if I did I'd have a hard time following the music next Sunday.

'You shot His Honor?' I asked, my back to her as I strode back to where the mayor lay bleeding on the floor. I heard the ambulance coming into the motel's parking lot.

'No, of course not,' Inez said.

'Then who did?' I asked, still not looking at her.

'I'm not at liberty to say,' she said.

'Milt,' Walden Waylon whined, 'I told you no ambulance! This'll be all over town!'

'Not your call, Waylon,' I said. I was a little pissed. I thought Inez Tatum had better taste than this.

'If somebody doesn't tell me what the hell is going on, I'm taking you both in for obstructing justice, and that's the God's honest truth!' I said.

The door burst open at that moment and the EMT guys came in. Two of 'em: Fred Barnes, full-time pharmacist and part-time EMT volunteer, and Mindy Curlle, full-time beautician and part-time EMT volunteer. They both stopped in their tracks at the sight before them.

'Oh, Lord,' Fred said, who goes to my church.

Mindy just burst out laughing.

'Mindy!' I said, and she stopped. 'Check the mayor. Wounds look superficial, but you need to check it out. Any word of this gets out in town, I'll know where it came from.' I gave them both stern looks and they went to work.

Inez sat down on the king-sized bed. Her weight, which was substantial, rocked the bed, which jostled His Honor, who moaned.

'Sorry, Walden,' Inez said, and by her tone it didn't sound like she was a bit sorry.

'Inez, I'd like to speak with you in the bathroom, please,' I said.

The Motel Five wasn't known for its grand bathrooms with garden tubs. Actually, the bathroom was about four feet by four feet, and since Inez took up a good three by three, that didn't leave very much room for me.

'Talk,' I said, once we were both squeezed inside the little room.

Inez sighed. 'Milt, it was just an accident,' she said. 'Really.'

'I'll be the judge of that,' I said. 'Talk.'

Again she sighed. 'Walden and I were just here talking…' She paused. 'And someone came in and shot him.' She finished this with a smile on her face, like she thought I was going to buy that.

'You two like to meet in motel rooms, you dressed like this and His Honor buck naked, and "talk"?' I asked.

'It's really not what it looks like,' she said.

'Uh-huh. And someone—some stranger, I take it—just walked in and shot him?' I said.

'Exactly.'

'Inez, I've known you a long time. You're not a good liar. Now, if I arrest you, chances are real good Harry—' that was her husband and the father of her seven children

'—is going to find out about this. You tell me what's going on, the truth, and I'll try my damnedest to keep your name out of it,' I said.

Inez sighed and sat down on the toilet. 'It was Candy,' she said.

I sorta suspected that, but I needed someone to come right out and say it. Candy Waylon is Walden Waylon's wife. She almost made it to the Olympics twenty years ago in the shooting competition, she's that good. I figured it had to take a damn good shot to hit the mayor three times and not do any real damage.

'OK, thanks, Inez. Where are your clothes?' I asked.

'Hanging in the closet,' she said.

'I'll hand 'em to you. You get dressed and go home. I'll try to keep this quiet.'

'I appreciate that, Milt,' she said.

I stepped out, grabbed her clothes, opened the door and handed them to her. She smiled her gratitude, and said, 'See you next Sunday.'

I almost said, 'Not if I see you first,' but I curbed the impulse.

Going back to the end of the bed, I saw that Mindy and Fred were patching the mayor up nicely.

'He need to go to the hospital?' I asked.

'Probably needs to go see his private physician tomorrow, get some antibiotics,' Fred said, 'but he's good to go.'

'Thanks, guys,' I said, then watched them pack up their stuff and leave.

I helped Walden up to the bed, found his clothes and threw them to him. He winced and I smiled inwardly.

'I'm gonna go talk to your wife,' I said.

'No, now, Milt—'

'Shut up, Walden.' He did. 'Inez told me it was Candy. Now I gotta go talk to her.'

'I'm not pressing charges!' Walden said.

'I'm not surprised. I still need to talk to her. I can either follow you to your house, or you can stay here for a while—alone,' I said, when I saw him glance at the bathroom door. 'It's up to you.'

'I'll wait,' he said.

The bathroom door opened and Inez Tatum came out, dressed in her usual below-the-knee skirt, feminine blouse and sensible shoes.

She looked at Walden, then at me. Sighing, she said, 'Well, I guess I'll be leaving.'

'I guess you will,' I said.

I waited until her car was out of sight, then got in my Jeep and headed back to Longbranch.

THE MAYOR LIVED IN a long ranch-style house on a heavily wooded half-acre on the north side of town. Candy Waylon's Hummer was in the driveway. I rang the bell and she opened it immediately, as if waiting for someone to come calling.

Candy Waylon was a tall, skinny woman. All elbows and knees, all angles, no curves. After thirty-something years with that kind of body, I could see Walden's attraction to the soft curviness of Inez Tatum. Candy's hair was cut almost boyishly short, and she was wearing baggy blue jeans and an OU sweatshirt a couple of sizes too large.

'Miz Waylon,' I said.

'Sheriff,' she answered. 'Come in.'

She held the door for me and I entered. I'd never been inside the mayor's house before. It looked like a men's club gone amuck. The living room held the largest gun cabinet I'd ever seen, with a huge assortment of rifles. Dead animals of every sort hung on the walls. The couches were covered in cow's hide, and the coffee table was a round piece of glass mounted atop a pair of five-point antlers. I decided it was probably a good thing the Waylons had no children.

I took a seat on a cowhide-covered armchair. 'Miz Waylon,' I began, 'I need to talk to you about the incident at the Motel Five.'

'Yes,' she said, taking a seat on the couch. 'I shot my husband.'

'Uh-hum,' I said. 'Three times.'

'Yes, that's right,' she said, sitting primly, knees together and hands clasped in her lap. 'I didn't hurt him, did I?'

I shook my head. 'No, ma'am. The EMTs patched him up at the scene. He'll probably need some antibiotics.'

'Hadn't thought of that,' she said. 'He could get an infection. I'll make sure he gets them.'

I sighed. 'Miz Waylon, you can't go around shooting your husband.'

'Extraordinary circumstances,' she said. 'And I took careful aim.'

'And I appreciate that,' I said. 'But still and all. Shooting somebody's against the law.'

'Is he pressing charges?' she asked.

'No,' I said.

'Well, then,' she said, a small smile on her face.

'You're not going to hurt Inez Tatum, are you?' I asked.

She looked shocked at the suggestion. 'Of course not!' she said. 'I don't blame Inez. It's hard for women to resist Walden,' she said, and color infused her face. 'He's, well, he's quite sexy, you know.'

Well, she had me there. First I'd heard tell of it. 'Has he done this sort of thing before?' I asked.

'Not to my knowledge,' she said, standing and walking

towards the door. Smiling, she held the door open for me. 'And I don't think he'll do it again.'

I thought she might have a point. 'Well, OK, Miz Waylon. But let's just keep all those guns locked up, OK?'

'No problem, Sheriff,' she said, smiling shyly. 'And thanks for stopping by.'

With that, I just shook my head and headed home.

I GOT BACK UP to the mountain about ten o'clock that night. The big tent was still in the backyard, but all the other catering stuff was gone: the food and equipment, the chairs, the tables. Everything looked spanking clean. Jean told me they'd come get the tent on Monday.

Johnny Mac was already in bed, but I snuck upstairs to check on him. He was sound asleep, his blonde hair mussed, his lower lip sticking out, and his butt in the air. I pulled his Spider-Man comforter up to his shoulders, kissed him on his soft cheek, then slipped back downstairs where Jean waited for me in the bedroom.

This was an experiment, Johnny Mac being upstairs. My house on Mountain Falls Road (it had been mine before Jean married me, and I still kinda think of it as mine, but don't tell Jean because she'd have an issue with that) was a mish-mash, the main structure having been built back in the thirties as a two up/three down little stucco gem. Downstairs were a living room, dining room, and a nice-size kitchen; up were two bedrooms and a bath. Then somebody came along and added a master bedroom and bath downstairs that was entered through the kitchen (not as inconvenient as you might think—great for midnight snacking). Since the original kitchen had stuck out some beyond the dining room, they built a little room in between the dining room and master bedroom. Before Jean I'd used it as a junk room; after Jean, since we knew she was pregnant when we got married, it became a nursery and had stayed such until pretty recently.

The upstairs had been changed at some point; two smaller bedrooms and a bath over the master and what had been the original two bedrooms had been opened up and converted into a big room with walls of windows. I used to just sit there and stare out the windows at the twin peaks of mountains over in Tejas County, thinking bad and lonely thoughts until Jean came along. Now it's Johnny Mac's playroom, complete with indoor slide, a TV and DVD player, a little CD player, and more toys than most daycare centers. There are two big chairs, but the rest of the furniture is fit for the under-five crowd.

About a month ago, Jean decided Johnny Mac, at three and a half, was old enough to have his room upstairs. Me and Johnny Mac disagreed, but Jean slowly started doing it anyway. That's the thing about being married to a psychiatrist—she thinks she knows more than me. Well, she's right, but still and all. Anyway, she fixed the room up with blue walls, painting clouds on 'em and gluing little wooden birds and airplanes and such to the walls. She bought him a fire engine bed and slowly moved the stuff up from his nursery downstairs. Took her a couple of weeks. She'd put him to bed up there, and we'd do our nightly routine of singing songs and reading books, then it would be lights out. She'd put a gate at the top of the stairs, not so much to lock him up there, as he knew how to pick it, but just to slow him down and make him remember that there were stairs beyond the gate. For the first five nights, he'd stay in bed about as long as it took us to get downstairs, then he'd be beating at the gate saying, 'Wanna go to *my* bed!'

Sometimes she let him; sometimes we'd do the nightly ritual all over again. On the sixth night, he didn't come to the gate. He fell asleep in his fireman bed on the second floor. On the seventh night, he came to the gate and Jean told him to go back to bed. And, miracle of miracles, he did it. It's been back and forth that way ever since.

Sometimes, usually on those nights when he refuses to go to sleep in the fireman bed, I wonder what I was thinking, a man my age, getting myself into this situation meant for a much younger man. But then, on nights like tonight, watching him sleep, seeing that beautiful face so graceful in sleep, I want about a dozen more. That's about the only time I'm grateful for Jean's hysterectomy.

When I got down to our bedroom, Jean was sitting up in bed, an AMA journal on her lap, her reading glasses on her nose. She was wearing a blue T-shirt that used to be mine, had cream on her face, and her hair slicked back. She looked gorgeous.

I wrestled out of the monkey suit and crawled into bed in just my shorts.

'Aren't you going to get ready for bed?' Jean asked.

'In a minute,' I said.

She looked at me and raised an eyebrow. 'Are you trying to be sly, Milt?' she asked, grinning.

'Little bit,' I said, nudging my way closer and kissing her bare shoulder where the big blue T-shirt had slid down.

'You actually expect me to put down this article so that you can have your way with me?' she said.

'Uh huh,' I said, pulling the sleeve of the T-shirt down further, getting to the good stuff.

'Weddings do make you frisky, don't they?' she giggled. I noticed the journal had dropped to the floor and her reading glasses were no longer on her nose.

'No, you do,' I said.

'Oh, that was good,' she said, and turned out the light.

THREE

EMMETT COULDN'T FIND his watch. He looked through the tussled covers, under the bed, in the bathroom; it was nowhere to be found. Jasmine opened the bedside table and held up the watch for his inspection.

'This it?'

Emmett grinned. 'You're gonna come in handy as a wife,' he said, pulling her toward him.

'No!' she said, laughing. 'We have a plane to catch!'

Emmett sighed. 'And a long damn trip to the City to catch it, too.'

'I told you we should have driven to Oklahoma City last night and stayed somewhere there,' Jasmine said.

'And disappoint all the good people here?'

They were at the Longbranch Inn, the only people checked into the seldom-used hotel rooms. The management, along with catering the wedding at a discount, had thrown in the room for free.

Jasmine leaned over the bed to zip her suitcase. 'They're all going to be standing out there waiting for us, aren't they?'

'More'n likely,' Emmett said. 'Think we'll finally get pelted with birdseed, since nobody got the chance to yesterday?'

'Yeah, what was that all about anyway? You really think Neal Hardy robbed the bank?'

'Looks that way.' He kissed her. 'But don't worry your pretty little head about it,' he said, getting swatted by his new wife and dodging away, laughing. 'We'll let Milt and Charlie Smith work that out. And probably the Feebies. They're gonna show up, and personally, I'm glad we're going to be out of it.'

'Luxuriating on sandy beaches, drinking tall, cool—'

'Non-alcoholic,' Emmett cut in.

'Non-alcoholic drinks, gazing at the butts of cute pool boys…'

Emmett grabbed her. 'Yeah, you look at one pool-boy butt, and I'll…I'll…'

'What?' Jasmine asked.

'Burst into tears,' Emmett said.

'Oh, you poor old man,' she said, kissing his eyes. 'I'll be good.'

They got their luggage and headed out the door. Emmett had called it: the entire staff of the Longbranch Inn and many of the staff of neighboring businesses were lined up at the front door of the inn, the line going out into the streets, and birdseed and bubbles were plentiful.

It took over an hour to drive to Oklahoma City, another hour to park in long-term parking, check their luggage, get their boarding passes, and wait to board the plane. They didn't really notice the time, though. There was too much talking, too many plans to make, too many stories to tell, to pay attention to time.

'So if it's a girl we'll name her Magnolia,' Emmett said.

Jasmine snorted. 'Magnolia! That's horrible! Where did that come from?'

'Jasmine, Rose, Lily, and Daisy. What else is there?' Emmett said, grinning at his new bride.

'Ugh. You have no idea how we hated those flower names growing up! I will not do that to a child. And Magnolia? That's just awful. Worse than what my mother came up with! And besides, we shouldn't talk about names yet—it's too early,' she said.

'You're superstitious?' Emmett asked. 'Didn't know that. Um, interesting the things you find out about a woman after you marry her!'

Jasmine pinched his arm. 'I'm not superstitious. It's just not done, is all.'

'So then should we discuss your place or mine? We still haven't come up with an answer on that one yet,' Emmett said.

'Well, see, that's a problem,' Jasmine said. 'Your place is paid for but my place is bigger.'

'So we sell both places and buy our own,' Emmett suggested.

'One of those houses in that new subdivision?' she asked. 'Where we get to pick out the carpet and paint and cabinets and everything?'

'Why not?' Emmett said. 'With selling both houses, we should have enough equity to put up a good down payment and still have some left to pay for this honeymoon.'

They were sitting in the plastic chairs of the airline waiting area. In her excitement, Jasmine jumped up on her knees in the chair. 'A brand-new house! Our house! Oh, Emmett, let's do it! Your house is all profit and my house should have some good equity—'

'You gotta share any of that with the asshole?' he asked, mentioning their private nickname for Jasmine's ex-husband, Lester Bodine.

'Not if he wants what's left of his Johnson,' Jasmine said.

Emmett held up his hand like a traffic cop. 'Don't go there,' he said. He smiled, putting his hand to the back of her neck and bringing her close for a kiss. 'Let's do it,' he said. 'Brand-new life, brand-new house, brand-new baby.'

'And brand-new furniture!' Jasmine added.

Emmett groaned as the first call for their flight came over the loud-speaker system.

They boarded a non-stop to Miami, where they would change planes to San Juan, Puerto Rico, and from there catch a ferry to a private island called San Isabella, where they would spend their leisurely honeymoon.

At least, that had been the plan.

NORMALLY I WOULDA BEEN getting ready for church on a Sunday morning, but I had to contend with just watching Jean and Johnny Mac get ready. Today was our day at Our Lady, and Jean liked to dress up Johnny Mac for the service. He was wearing navy-blue slacks and a white button-down collar shirt, and a little clip-on tie. Why he got to wear clip-ons and I didn't was something she'd not yet been able to explain to me properly. He had on sissy-looking navy-and-white dress-up shoes and his blond hair was slicked back with water. By the time it dried it would be sticking up all over the place, but Jean did her best while refusing to use chemicals on it. Jean looked gorgeous in a springy-looking white dress with pinkish flowers on it. I was in my work clothes.

As we went outside to the cars, Johnny Mac said, 'Daddy, you're not dressed for church.' He was frowning at me, hands on hips.

'Gotta work, honey,' I said. 'Can't go to church today.'

'God's gonna be mad wid you,' he said, frowning harder.

'I think God'll forgive me, John. He agrees with the work I do,' I told my son.

'But I want you to go to church wid us!' he wailed, his face scrunching up as the tear works started.

'Mama's gonna be with you, Big Guy,' I said, leaning down to his level. 'You'll do fine.'

'Her don't play wid me like you do!' he wailed.

Well, that was true. Johnny Mac usually sat between Jean and me during church and he and I played hand games when the service got fairly boring, which, for Johnny Mac, meant anytime they weren't singing. Well, for me, too, but don't tell Jean. We played finger-puppet hand jive, a little rock-scissors-paper, thumb wars, and whatever else I could come up with to keep the two of us occupied. Jean, needless to say, did not approve.

'Son,' I said, looking as serious as I could, 'you're just gonna have to buck up. You gotta be a man.'

'I don' wanna be a man!' he wailed. 'I'm just a little boy!'

'Well, you gotta be a big boy and help your mama. You'll need to open doors for her and help her get to her seat,' I said.

The tears stopped.

'Can you do that? Open doors for her?'

He nodded his head.

'Can you help her find her seat in church?'

He nodded his head.

I smiled. 'You are one big boy, you know that?' I said.

He smiled at me. 'Yeah, and I'm gonna make her sit where I say, and I'm gonna open the doors for her, and I'm gonna tell her what to do and her's gonna do it, too! Right, Daddy?'

I looked at my wife. She raised an eyebrow. Looking down at my son I said, 'You betcha! You're in charge, Big Guy!'

I kissed him goodbye and, as he took his mother's hand, I heard him say, 'You can drive, Mama.'

I said goodbye to my family at the car, as Jean buckled

Johnny Mac in his car seat and I got in my Jeep to drive
to the sheriff's office.

Our weekend deputy, Lonnie Sturgis, who, along with
Dalton Pettigrew, had been an usher at the wedding, had
three pink while-you-were-out slips waiting for me, all
from Charlie Smith, starting at about seven a.m. I called
him at nine thirty, identified myself, and heard him say,
'Yes, Sheriff Kovak, we've been waiting for you. Could
you come by my office, please?'

'What's up, Charlie?'

'The Bureau would like to discuss the events of yesterday with both of us, um hum,' he said.

'Oh, shit, the Feebies are there?' I asked.

'That's certainly true. Anything you can add?'

'I gotta come?'

'Absolutely, Sheriff. Thank you for your time.'

Then he hung up.

Before I had time to slip out the door, however, Agnes
Shorewalter came running in the front door, yelling, 'Sheriff! Sheriff! Look what I found!'

Now, Agnes is about three hundred pounds, so running
is not top on her agenda of things to do today. She was
dressed in her usual brightly colored caftan, her gray hair
in a long braid down her back, Birkenstock sandals taking
a beating. Agnes is our local hippy, having moved here
from California thirty-something years before. I remember
the day she came into town, driving a beat-up Volkswagen
van with flowers painted all over it. She was a seriously
pretty thing, wearing skin-tight jeans with flowers on the
pockets, and a tie-dye T-shirt that showed off breasts men
have written songs about. She wore her hair in a braid
then, too, reaching almost to her butt, but it was a pretty
butter-scotch color, and the sun danced off it like that was
what the sun was meant for. Agnes has a little singlewide

trailer on a piece of land left to her by an uncle, the reason she moved here in the first place. She raises goats
and vegetables, and has a little stand by the road that runs
past her place, where she sells goat cheese, fresh, organic
vegetables, hand-made candles, and any other new-age,
hippy kind of thing you might want to think about buying.

But what she was holding in her hand wasn't one of
her home-made hippy things, not unless she'd changed
religions from worshiping Mother Earth to the guy un-
derground.

'Whatya got, Agnes?' I asked, moving to see what had
excited her so.

'I found this out back of my place by the old railroad
track,' she said. 'It's an upside-down cross!'

'How you know you're not just holding it upside-down?'
I asked.

She looked at me like I was a complete idiot, which I
suppose I often am. 'It's got a base, Milt! And the base is
on the bottom!'

'Hum,' I said. 'That means something, don't it?'

'It means I had some devil worshipers on my property
is what it means!' she said, getting all excited. 'Now I believe in all sorts of freedoms, Milt, but not the freedom to
burn babies on my property!'

'Huh?' I said. 'Burned babies?'

'There was a fire ring in the shape of a pentagram,
Milt, and there were bones in the middle of that fire ring!'
She leaned forward and whispered, 'Human bones!' Tears
stinging her eyes, she said, 'Tiny little human bones!'

Now Agnes Shorewalter is an excitable lady, especially
since—and don't you women get all excited now, 'cause it's
the truth—but especially since she started going through
the change. I'm not saying all women get excitable when
they go through the change, so nobody sue me, I'm just

saying Agnes Shorewalter got excitable when she started going through the change, OK?

I turned to Anthony, because delegating is a thing I do real well, and said, 'Anthony, call Doc Church and have her meet you over at Miz Shorewalter's, and follow her on back to her place, will ya? See what this is all about, then call me. I'll be on my cell.'

And with that, I headed over to the police department to deal with the Feds.

FIFTEEN MINUTES LATER I walked into Police Chief Charlie Smith's office. I'd been there before, of course, when Emmett had been police chief, but it still galled me that it was about twice the size of my office, had leather chairs, and was carpeted. Me, I got half the size, cloth chairs and linoleum. But this time, more than the size, the leather, and the carpet, I noticed that Mulder and Scully were sitting in two of the three leather side chairs. The guy was tall and lanky and wearing a stupid tie and the gal was short and redheaded. What would you have thought?

'Milt Kovak, Sheriff of Prophesy County,' Charlie Smith said, 'meet Special Agents Michael Whysmith and Luanne Carmody.'

We shook hands all around, then I took the only seat that was left. I noticed Charlie had three visitors' chairs, while I only had two. Once again, the city doing better for theirs than the county did for mine. I had to keep telling myself it was only a chair. And carpet. And leather. But, you know, it's the principle of the thing.

'Had a little excitement around here yesterday, huh, Sheriff?' Special Agent Whysmith said. He had no discernible accent—obviously wasn't from around here.

'I had a deputy killed in the line of duty,' I said stiffly.

'Yes, we checked this man out, this—' he looked at

a paper in front of him '—Neal Hardy. Seems like the real deal.'

'Yes, sir, far as I can tell from talking with the State Patrol, he was who he said he was. And they claim he was as honest as the day is long.'

'Yet the hole into the bank came from his office.' It was a statement, not a question. So far Scully—I mean Carmody—hadn't said a word.

'Appears so, yes,' I said.

'Hard to believe he never noticed it,' Whysmith said.

'Have to agree with that,' I answered.

'How well did you personally know Mr Hardy?' Scully asked. OK, Carmody.

'Not well at all. Met him a couple of months ago at a Kiwanis meeting, and got to talking, him being retired law enforcement. He gave me his card, and when this thing yesterday came up, I called him, asked him to watch the shop.'

'Am I understanding this correctly?' Whysmith said, looking from me to Charlie. 'The entire downtown was deserted, no police presence except one rookie policeman and a retired gentleman playing deputy? All so the lot of you could go to a wedding?'

The boy was getting my hackles up. 'It wasn't just *any* wedding, Special Agent Whysmith,' I said. 'And the "retired gentleman",' I went on, my quotation marks pretty damn obvious, 'wasn't playing deputy. He was duly sworn in and had the training for the job.'

'What made this wedding so special, Sheriff?' Carmody asked.

I looked at Charlie, who shrugged. 'The groom was the former police chief and the bride was one of my deputies.'

'And that made it special enough to close down the entire downtown area?' Whysmith asked.

I squirmed a little. How much to get into with the Feebies? Wasn't any of their business, really. On the other hand, I didn't want to seem as if I was hiding anything. 'I guess you could say the entire county was excited about the union. Both of them had had their share of heartache, and it was a blessing to see them find each other.'

'How romantic,' said Whysmith, with more than a hint of sarcasm. 'I guess I don't really understand small-town life.'

'I guess you don't,' I shot back, then regretted it. I don't like Feds in general, and was beginning not to like Whysmith in particular, but you gotta talk the talk and walk the walk with these people, or find yourself and your county getting shorted come Federal-spending time. And since I lived in a county that hardly had a pot to piss in, Federal money was our bread and butter. So I said, 'Getting back to the bank robbery, Special Agent—'

'Call me Mike,' Whysmith said. 'And this is Luanne.'

'I'm Milt,' I said, trying on a smile.

'Charlie,' Charlie said, trying on his own smile. It looked as pitiful as mine felt.

'Yes, Milt, let's get back to the bank robbery. As I understand it, one of the bank personnel discovered the robbery?'

'Yes, sir, Katy Monroe, one of the VPs. After all the commotion, she went to check on the bank, opened the vault and found the hole and the money gone.'

'Five hundred thousand sounds like a lot for a small-town bank to have on hand,' Carmody said.

'Yes, ma'am,' Charlie said, 'but Ms Monroe explained to us that that was first of the month payroll for two new companies that just came to town. Big outfits. Lot of employees.'

'So they usually don't have that much cash on hand?' Carmody asked.

'Not until the last few months. One company just opened shop like a month ago, the other's been here maybe six months. So this was probably the first month they had that much cash in the vault,' Charlie said.

'So somebody knew that,' Whysmith mused.

'Yeah,' Charlie said, 'like the whole town. Maybe not the exact amount, but it stands to reason that that many new people in town gotta get paid. Wouldn't take a genius to figure out the bank would be where the money was.'

I was liking Charlie Smith more and more.

'Your patrolman—' Carmody started.

'Billy Johansson,' Charlie furnished.

'He's still in a coma?'

'He's unconscious,' Charlie said, frowning, obviously not liking the word 'coma'. 'Only been a day since he was in surgery. They had him in there for hours.'

'Has the doctor given you any idea how long he's likely to be unconscious?' she asked.

'No, ma'am.'

'Seems to me your patrolman should have a story to tell,' Carmody said.

'I'm sure he does, ma'am,' Charlie said stiffly, 'and as soon as he wakes up, I'll find out what it is.'

'We'd like to be in on that interview, Chief,' Whysmith said.

'That'll be up to the doctor,' Charlie said.

Whysmith smiled. 'I'm sure you can influence him, Chief.'

'You'd be surprised how ornery small town doctors can be,' I said. 'I know, I'm married to one of 'em.'

Whysmith stood up and Carmody followed suit. When she stood up, me and Charlie, both being gentlemen, stood up, too. Whysmith smiled. 'As you both know, bank robberies are under federal purview, and since your patrolman appears to be our only possible witness to this, we will be speaking to him immediately upon his awakening.' He stuck out his hand to Charlie, who reluctantly shook it, then to me. I did the same. Then we went through it with Carmody. 'Chief,' Whysmith said, nodding goodbye, then to me. 'Sheriff.' With that, they picked up identical brief-cases and left.

I sank back down in my chair while Charlie quietly shut the door to his office.

'I hate the goddam Feds,' he said, sitting down.

'Don't they just make you wanna spit?' I said.

'I don't want them harassing Billy. That boy's not gonna be in any condition to be harassed by the goddam Feds.'

'Sure enough,' I said. Then I smiled. 'Got an idea.'

'What's that?' Charlie asked, an expectant look on his face.

'Stick Billy's mama on 'em. You'll have plenty of time to talk to Billy while they're trying to get away from her.'

Charlie smiled. 'Now that's a plan.'

'Oh,' I said, hand on the door to leave, 'forgot to men-tion—that Highway Patrol captain, Wasserman?'

Charlie nodded his head. 'You talked to him, right?'

'Yeah. And he said to tell you hi and to tell you he hasn't had that good a laugh since Ardmore,' I said. 'So what happened in Ardmore?'

Blood filled Charlie's face and he grimaced. 'And I thought Wasserman was an OK guy.'

I could feel something good coming. 'Oh, man, now you gotta tell me!' I said, shutting the door and sitting back down.

'None of your business, Kovak!' he said.

I settled back in my chair, crossing my legs. 'Not mov-ing,' I said, grinning.

'It was stupid,' he said.

'So many things are,' I agreed.

He sighed. 'I had a little too much to drink.'

'Uh huh,' I encouraged.

'It was a conference in Ardmore on new police procedures,' he said, then stopped.

'That's so?' I said.

He sighed. 'We went out afterward, me and Wasserman and a couple other guys.'

'Yeah?' Talk about pulling teeth.

'And this lady asked me to dance,' he said, the red of his face getting deeper, almost purplish.

'Dancin's no biggie,' I said.

'No, not usually. Not until I saw her Adam's apple.'

We both just sat there and then I burst into laughter.

'You're an asshole, Kovak,' he said.

I stood up and headed for the door. 'My lips are sealed,' I said, and left.

I was walking to my Jeep when my cell phone rang. I answered the call, then heard Anthony say, 'Sheriff, just finished up at Miz Shorewalter's.'

'So we got burnt babies or what?' I asked.

'No, sir. Dr Church said they were rodent bones. But there was definitely a pentagram, and some of the rocks had what Dr Church confirmed to be blood on 'em, like they drew pictures in blood of pentagrams and upside-down crosses, and wrote "Satan Rules" on one rock.'

'Satan Rules?' I asked. 'Sounds like kids to me. Did Dr Church say if it was human blood or rodent blood?'

'She took some samples back to her lab with her. But, Sheriff, this could get out of hand. Miz Shorewalter's neighbors were all over the place, like she called 'em before she left, or maybe she called 'em on her way back. All I know is there were about ten people there and they were all excited about Satan worshipers.'

'Shit.' I sighed. 'Just come on back to the house. You take pictures?'

'Yes, sir,' Anthony said.

'Well, come on back and we'll try to squash this thing before it gets out of hand.' And here I was, forgetting all about Murphy's Law and not even knocking on wood.

EMMETT AND JASMINE got into Miami around noon eastern time, and had to run to catch the plane to San Juan. They were the last on, and had to climb over a very large man to get to their seats. Jasmine got the window seat, leaving Emmett sitting next to the large man. Which normally would have been fine, except the large man was a retired cop from Boco Raton, Florida, on his way to visit his Internet girlfriend in San Juan, and he and Emmett talked cop shop the entire way to Puerto Rico. So Jasmine, being Jasmine, and hormonal to boot, fumed, deciding finally that Emmett had planned it that way. So, the hour and a half it took to get to the ferry port and wait for its arrival was spent arguing.

'Why aren't you talking to me?' Emmett said after fifteen minutes of silence.

'You don't want me to talk to you,' Jasmine said, her teeth gritted.

'Why, yes I do,' Emmett said, trying to be playful.

'If you wanted to talk to me, Emmett,' she said, not looking at him, 'I believe we could have done that on the airplane.' She turned and stared him in the eye. 'Oh, gee, I forgot, you spent all your time talking to that fat ex-cop!'

'Oh, Lord,' Emmett said under his breath.

'I heard that!' Jasmine said.

'I'm sorry if I talked shop when I should have been paying attention to you,' Emmett said, trying to take her hand.

Jasmine pulled it out of his reach. 'I thought we were on our honeymoon!' she said, tears stinging her eyes.

'Honey, we are, I think you're just being hormonal—' Emmett started, which was his second mistake of the trip.

'How dare you accuse me of being hormonal after what you did!' Jasmine said, and burst into tears.

Emmett took her in his arms. 'I'm sorry,' he said. 'I really shouldn't have done that. Please forgive me.'

Jasmine nodded her head. 'Maybe,' she said. 'In an hour or so.'

He kissed the top of her head. 'That'll work,' he said.

Once they got on the ferry and were staring out at the blue Caribbean, Jasmine gave it up, folding into Emmett's arms.

It took two hours for the ferry to reach San Isabella. They had three other stops at other small islands, then a long stretch of nothing but blue Caribbean before they got there. But when the ferry docked, they were both overcome by the beauty of the place. Bright white beaches rolling uphill into palm trees, palmettos, huge elephant-ear plants, bougainvillea and azaleas as far as the eye could see. Two open-air buses with striped and fringed canvas tops pulled up to meet the ferry. Jasmine, Emmett, and twelve other people got off.

The resort hotel itself seemed to spring from the very earth of the island. Its white stucco walls seemed an extension of the white sand, and the hotel flowed through the trees like a living thing.

Before they even got off the bus, the driver called their names. 'You the honeymoon couple?' he asked, grinning.

Emmett blushed and Jasmine asserted that they were.

'You already checked in, mon,' he said. 'Part of the honeymoon package. I take you to your secluded cabin.'

Their driver, a dark-skinned, self-proclaimed 'islander',

explained that there were almost one hundred cottages strung out on either side of the main hotel, but Emmett couldn't see them. When they got to theirs, they found out why: all the cottages were basically hidden behind trees and vegetation, and the quaint thatched roof of the cottage blended in with the growth around them.

Like the hotel, the cottage was white stucco, mimicking the sand around them. Inside were a sitting room, kitchenette, bedroom, and bath. Outside was a secluded pool and hot tub. Jasmine waited for their escort to leave before she jumped Emmett, literally.

Arms and legs entwined around him, she said, 'Oh, baby, you did good! This is beautiful.'

'Yeah, well, I wish I could take the credit, but you gotta thank Anthony when we get back. He found it on the Internet.'

'But did you turn on the computer for him?' she asked, grinning.

'Why, yes, yes I did,' he said, grinning back.

'Then you're my hero,' she said, then hopped down and led him to the bedroom.

FOUR

ON MY WAY BACK to the shop, my mind started going in weird directions. I couldn't help but remember what my wife had said when I'd told her the young rookie that got shot was Billy Johansson. She'd said, 'Paul Johansson's son?' When I asked how she knew him, she'd cited 'confidentiality'. Which meant only one thing: Paul Johansson was a patient of my wife's. More than likely.

Which meant what? That Paul was nutso? Now, being married to a psychiatrist, one tries not to think along those lines—at least that's what I'm told I'm not to think. Going to a psychiatrist does not necessarily mean someone's a nut-case. Lots of reasons for someone to go see a psychiatrist.

Like maybe he was depressed, just like ninety-seven percent of the population over forty in the United States. So why didn't he get his anti-depressants from his GP, like everybody else? GPs were giving the damn things away like they used to give away suckers to their kid patients.

Then I had to think about why a father would shotgun his son. Being a father myself, it was inconceivable to me, but then again, it happens. Not every day, but it happens. Fathers killing sons, daughters, wives; mothers killing daughters, sons, husbands. Even a cousin or two if truth be known, and don't forget grandma and grandpa. It happens.

But Paul Johansson didn't seem the type. Then again, I thought, neither did Ted Bundy. Jeez, that man had a lot to answer for. We could no longer think of serial killers or other bad guys looking like the scum they were; then we had Susan Smith, killing her own kids, so we could no longer believe a mother when she says, 'Somebody took my child'. We gotta check her out. Then there was that asshole in Boston who killed his pregnant wife—can't even believe a Yuppie anymore.

But maybe that wasn't it. Maybe Paul Johansson had a reason to shoot his son—or thought he did. Maybe Billy was a bad guy—hey, it could happen. Maybe Billy was so out of control his dad thought he had no other recourse but to put him out of everybody else's misery.

Then what would that have to do with Neal Hardy? And the money being gone from the bank? Not a damn thing, I told myself, glad I'd kept all these musings to myself and not said 'em out loud to Charlie Smith or anyone else— like the Feebies.

I finally got to the office, having come to no conclusions, to find a surprise waiting for me. It wasn't the packaged and beribboned kind though; it was the son and daughter of Neal Hardy kind. I came in the side door that leads straight to my office so I didn't see 'em sitting out in the bullpen being watched over by our Dalton Pettigrew. But Dalton heard me come in and buzzed me before I had a chance to sit down in my good chair.

'Ah, Sheriff,' he said, his voice stiff, which clued me in that something was going on. 'You've got visitors out here, sir,' he said. He never called me sir. Another clue.

'And they are?'

'Mr Hardy's next of kin,' he said.

'Shit,' I said. 'I'll be right out.'

Well, I figured Captain Wasserman musta called Max Hardy, 'cause I sure didn't, which I shoulda. I shoulda done that right away. I was feeling pretty guilty when I walked out to the bullpen. Max Hardy looked like he'd be a nice-looking young man if he didn't have a scowl on his face. He was at least six feet tall, slender in build but you could tell he worked out, had sandy brown hair neatly trimmed, and wore casual clothes. His sister, whose name I didn't know, was shorter than me, but not by much, maybe five-eight or five-nine. She had that frosted type of hair that looked like stripes, and was probably pretty when her faced wasn't puffed up from crying. She too was slender and looked like she worked out. Your typical thirty-something urban professionals with good genes.

I held out my hand and said, 'Mr Hardy, Ms Hardy.' He didn't take my hand, just kept scowling at me. His sister took it instead and shook with a firm but slightly shaky grip. 'I'm so sorry I didn't call you myself—'

'Pretty fuckin' inconsiderate, Sheriff!' Max Hardy said.

'Max!' his sister said, gripping his arm.

'Why don't we go down to my office?'

'Yeah, let's do that,' Max said, and led the way.

I hurried to catch up and ushered them into my private sanctum. I offered the two visitor chairs, but it seemed Max Hardy preferred to stand. His sister dropped into one, as if exhausted.

'Ma'am,' I said, addressing the sister, 'I'm afraid I didn't get your name...'

'You didn't bother to check my father's paperwork? See who his next of kin was?' Max said, his voice rising.

'Yes, sir, I did,' I said, 'but your father didn't fill out that part. Again, I'm sorry you found out the way you did, rather than from me. But that's water under the bridge. Maybe we can start fresh here, OK?'

The sister pulled her brother down to the other visitor chair, at the same time saying, 'I'm Elise Hardy, Sheriff. Please excuse my brother; he's very upset. As am I.'

'Believe me, ma'am, I totally understand. This has been a shock to all of us.'

'What in the hell was my father doing here anyway?' Max Hardy asked, his voice again a little loud for the small room. 'He's retired! He had that silly little business of his, but that had nothing to do with you! When did he come to work here?'

'Let me try to explain,' I said, then told them about the wedding and about hiring their dad for the day to watch the shop. I told them about Billy Johansson and the bank, the Feds, and what we planned to do. And then I told them about the hole in the wall of their daddy's office that went into the vault of the bank next door.

'Are you trying to tell me you suspect my father of robbing the damn bank?' Max Hardy exclaimed, jumping up from his chair.

Elise pulled at his arm, trying to get him to sit back down; it didn't work. 'Are you out of your minds!' he yelled.

'Sheriff,' Elise said, 'my father didn't rob the bank. Besides the fact that he was an incredibly honest man, he had no need to.' She sighed. 'Dad won the Texas lottery about two years ago. Seventeen point five million dollars. We incorporated as a family for tax purposes, and after taxes, we each got a yearly annuity of one point two million. Dad put most of his in CDs and high-interest accounts, and decided finally on his second career as a mediator. He was always good at communications. He was the one the rest of the patrol got for any domestic disputes they ran up against. Daddy used to say he could talk a preacher into sinning or a sinner into preaching,' she said, her voice breaking.

Max took up the story. 'In other words, Sheriff, there's no way in hell our dad was involved with this bank robbery. If he knew anybody was using his office that way,

he would have arrested them himself, retired or not. He
believed in the law, Sheriff. Like it was a religion.'

The picture I was getting from both Neal's kids and
Captain Wasserman of the Highway Patrol jibed with the
first impression I had of the man. An honest, upstanding
law enforcer, retired. And after finding out about the lottery winnings, I was at even more of a loss as to why Neal
Hardy would have had anything to do with a bank robbery
in Longbranch. But that wasn't my jurisdiction.

'Look, Mr Hardy, Ms Hardy, I'm handling your father's murder, but as far as the bank robbery goes, that's
out of my hands. It was committed within the city limits
of Longbranch, which initially makes it a city police matter, and, since the bank was FDIC insured, that makes it a
federal matter, which brought in the FBI. They're lead on
this.' I sighed and stood up. 'Tell you what we should do,
I'll drive you two into town and introduce you to the police chief. He's a good man. Name of Charlie Smith. He'll
help you with the FBI. What you told me about your dad is
something they need to know. If your dad wasn't involved,
then they're working bad leads and need to change their
investigation.'

'There's no "if" about whether or not my father was involved, Sheriff,' Elise Hardy said, standing up. 'He wasn't.
And you can take that to the bank.' She stopped a moment,
then a small grin played across her face. 'Well, maybe not
the bank in Longbranch,' she said.

AFTER I DROPPED Max and Elise Hardy off with Charlie
Smith, and after grudgingly getting a key to their dad's
house from Max, I went over there to investigate.

Like I said before, the houses on Stanhope Street were
eclectic, from big almost-mansions to little shotgun houses.
But all were neat and tidy, with healthy lawns and fresh

paint. It was a nice street. Neal Hardy's place was an almost-mansion. I was sorta expecting that since Elise Hardy told me her dad had bought an old Victorian and had spent a small fortune fixing it up. Not that it seemed to bother his bottom line.

The house was a beaut. Two and half stories of Victorian gee-gaws, painted a classy muted blue with white and maroon trim. There were two white rockers on one side of the front porch and a white two-seater wood swing on the other. Hanging plants hung from the trim of the front porch. Well, that's where the decorating stopped. Once inside it was kinda like nobody lived there much. There was fresh paint everywhere, each room painted a different color, but the living room (painted a brilliant blue with white trim) had only a much-loved and much-abused recliner sitting in front of a large-screen TV. The only other furniture in the room was a gun cabinet with several rifles and a shotgun inside. I put on rubber gloves and immediately took the shotgun into custody. I laid it by the front door and went across the foyer to what should have been the dining room. It was painted a muted dark red shade with natural wood trim at the windows and doors, and had a real classy-looking chandelier hanging from the middle of the room. The electricity used up by that chandelier could probably take care of my whole house for a month. The only furniture in there was a computer table and a good leather executive-type chair and a computer. I unhooked the computer like Anthony had shown me and put it with the rifle by the front door.

The kitchen was in back of the dining room, with what looked like a den or family room coming off that. That room was freshly painted, too, the same shade as the dining room, but empty of everything but a few boxes. Rifling through them, I discovered nothing more than old

clothes, mostly women's—probably his late wife's stuff
that he hadn't been able to throw away yet. The kitchen,
painted a buttery yellow, was a bachelor's mess, with a
box of cereal on the Formica table, crumbs spilled next
to it, and a bowl, spoon, and coffee cup in the sink. The
automatic coffee pot had about a half a pot left in it, but
it had been turned off, probably as he left to come to the
sheriff's department.

Trudging upstairs I found four good-size bedrooms.
The largest was obviously Neal's. Like the rooms downstairs, it was freshly painted, in a dark, avocado green with
white trim. The bed was neatly made, but there were some
shorts on the floor, and a shirt crumpled on the bed. His
night-stand held a roll of toilet tissue (Neal's idea of a box
of Kleenex—I used to use that, too, before Jean came into
my life), a lamp left turned on, a W.E.B. Griffin novel, a
roll of Tums, and a bottle of Maalox. In the top drawer
were some prescription bottles, most of which I recognized as stomach remedies. The ones I didn't recognize
I put on the bed to add to my haul downstairs. Under the
prescription bottles was the latest issue of *Playboy*, which
made me smile. Happy to know you never get too old for
that kind of pleasure.

The bottom drawer held socks rolled into little balls.
There were three single socks that didn't seem to match.
I've got a drawer with those myself.

The bureau drawers held undershirts and shorts, all
neatly folded, a drawer of golf-type shirts and Bermuda-
type shorts, and a drawer of pajama bottoms—no tops. A
small drawer on the top of the bureau held the usual male
minutia: a box with tie tacks and cufflinks, a Swiss Army
knife, a couple of money clips, an old pocket watch, a
string tie with a turquoise-and-silver clasp, and a rubber-
banded stack of letters. I took those out and opened the

first one. It was a love letter from his wife, addressed to an APO in California. I'd check, but I was assuming Neal had spent some time overseas in the service, Vietnam maybe. I only read the first few lines, embarrassed to be prying into an old love affair, checked the rest of the letters to make sure they were all of the same ilk, and put them on the bed with the unidentified prescription bottles. I'd have to check the letters out more thoroughly, but I'd do that myself. No reason for everybody in the sheriff's department to know about Neal Hardy's past love life.

The closet held one good suit, never worn: the label was still on the sleeve and the pockets were still sewn shut. He must have bought that with his winnings, I thought, and hadn't gotten around to wearing it. There were a couple of decent sports coats, a couple of old sports coats, one nice brown leather sports-type coat, about ten button-down collar shirts, two bathrobes—summer and winter—and assorted pairs of pants—one pair of blue jeans, a hanger with ties draped across it, and one with belts. There were shoes on the floor of the closet, three pairs of dress shoes, two pairs of slip-ons, a pair of cowboy boots (Noconas with ostrich hide tops and leather bottoms, half-inch heel, in a dark brown), and a pair of Reeboks exactly like the ones he wore the day he died, except these were older and more scuffed up. It made me kinda proud that he'd worn his good Reeboks to come to the office.

The top shelf of the closet held a beige Stetson with a brown leather hatband. I could see Neal now, all decked out in his blue jeans, the brown leather sports coat, the Noconas, and the Stetson. He woulda been, as my mama used to say, a fine figure of a man. Also on the shelf was a lockbox with a key taped to the bottom. I used the key to open the box and found his service revolver from his Highway Patrol days. I had to wonder why he didn't bring that with him when he came to the sheriff's department yesterday. It mighta saved his life.

Also on the top shelf was a woman's hatbox, all bedecked with flowers and rhinestones and gee-gaws. I brought it down and opened it up. I hadn't noticed much paperwork in his dining room/office; that's because he kept it all in his wife's old hatbox. It was crammed full of receipts and paid bills and other such stuff you keep around for tax purposes. I took it and the lockbox to the bed, put the prescription bottles and the love letters in the hatbox, took both out to the landing and then checked out the other three bedrooms.

One was set up as a guest room, with nothing personal in it whatsoever. The other two bedrooms were basically empty, except for some boxes of old taxes and a broken lamp or two. All three bedrooms, however, were newly painted: one a pale green, one a peachy shade, and the guest room pale blue. The bathroom looked like it had original tile: small squares of black-and-white coming up to shoulder height along the walls and the back of the claw-foot tub, the same tile on the floor. The walls above the tile were crisp white. Other than that, the room gave up nothing more than the fact that Neal Hardy was a Gillette man, used Old Spice deodorant and aftershave, Dial soap and Pearl shampoo. There was a hamper in the bathroom full to overflowing with dirty clothes. I went through it and found nothing—except dirty clothes.

I took the stuff I'd confiscated downstairs and hauled it and the other stuff to my car, locked up, and went back to the police station, handing the clerk on duty the key and a list of the things I'd taken, asking him to be sure to return it to Max Hardy. Then I took my loot to the sheriff's department.

Where, unfortunately, Lonnie Sturgis handed me ten while-you-were-out slips.

'Phone's been ringing off the hook!' Lonnie said, all excited like.

''Bout what?' I asked, gingerly taking the slips.

'The Satan worshipers!' he said.

'There are no Satan worshipers in Prophesy County,' I said, heading back to my office.

I sat down and looked through the slips: six ordinary citizens, two city council members, a county commissioner, and the mayor. Since I answer to the county, I called the commissioner back first.

When I finally got him on the phone, I said, 'Luke, Milt Kovak returning your call.'

'About damn time,' he said. Luke Mayhew was a Republican and he didn't like me much since I was a Democrat and had supported his opponent rather openly during his recent campaign.

'What can I do for you?' I asked, pretty sure I already knew the answer.

'What are you doing about these damn Satan worshipers?' he demanded.

'Looking into it,' I said.

'How's it connected to the bank robbery and the murder of your deputy?' he asked.

Well, that threw me. 'I don't know that it is, Luke,' I said.

'How can it not be? We go along forever with nothing much happening in a negative way around here, then in a week we get a bank robbery, a murder, an attempted murder and Satan worshipers! Coincidence? I think not!' he said.

'Well,' I said, in an attempt to placate him, 'I'll certainly look into that angle.'

'You damn well better. And, Milt…'

'Yeah, Luke?' I asked.

'Don't let the media get a hold of this. Bad for the county image,' he said and rung off.

Media, I thought. What media? The 'Shop and Save' was the only paper in these parts, and it didn't do articles, only ads. The nearest TV station was in Ardmore and we could barely get that without cable. I doubted they'd give a big goddamn if we were having Satan worshipers in Prophesy County. They sure didn't seem interested in the bank robbery or murder.

I crumpled up the slip of paper with Luke Mayhew's message, and picked up the next one, from Mayor Walden Waylon. I was surprised he was up and about, to tell you the truth.

'Mayor,' I said, when I got him on the line, 'this is Sheriff Kovak. What can I do you for?'

'Tell me what you're doing about these Satan worshipers!' he demanded.

'I'm thinking it's just a teenage prank, Mayor,' I said.

'Prank my ass! Killing babies! Where'd they come from? The babies, I mean?' he demanded, almost screeching.

'They weren't babies,' I said, trying to keep my patience. 'They were rodent bones.'

'Rodent bones? Like rats, mice, that sorta thing?' he demanded. We have a very sharp mayor, or have I mentioned that?

'Yes, sir, like a rat or a mouse. And I'm looking into it.'

'Well, you better,' His Honor said, ''cause I got about a hundred calls this morning about this and I don't know what to tell 'em.'

'Just tell 'em Sheriff Kovak is on the job and you have

every confidence he'll get this cleared up as soon as possible,' I said.

'In other words,' the mayor said, 'you want me to lie?'

'That about sums it up,' I said and rang off.

IT STARTED RAINING as Emmett and Jasmine unpacked. The first clap of thunder surprised Jasmine's stomach into rebellion. She started vomiting and the wind picked up, blowing the palm trees almost horizontal. Emmett discovered a leak in the cute thatched roof, right over their bed. When he picked up the phone to call and report it, the line was dead. He hurt his back pushing the bed away from the leak. The lights went out, and with them the air-conditioning. The room became so stuffy that Emmett went to open the windows, only to discover they were painted shut. Opening the front and back door, he discovered why there was mosquito-netting hanging over their bed. Jasmine shuffled out of the bathroom, holding her gut, saw Emmett batting at mosquitoes almost as big as her cat, and went back in, shutting the door behind her.

WHEN I GOT THROUGH answering all my while-you-were-out slips—and yeah, they were all regarding the Satan worshipers, which you would think people had more sense than to worry about—I told Lonnie to hold my calls unless it was my wife or Charlie Smith, then closed my door and opened Neal Hardy's wife's hatbox. I put the love letters to the APO address and the prescription bottles on my desk and went through the rest of the box. Bank statements and canceled checks, receipts from restaurants and one from a motel in Dallas, and sundry other crap one keeps just in case the tax man decides he can use it. The receipt for the motel in Dallas I kept for the case file, just in case that was some kind of connection to this whole thing.

After I'd gone through the receipt mess, I sat down with the stack of love letters and read 'em.

My darling Neal,
You should see my stomach! I'm huge! If you get home before this baby's born, I hope you decide you like fat women!!! I miss you so much. I see all those things on TV they keep showing, and I die a little each day. I pray for you every night, that you're safe, and healthy, and that you stay that way. I don't know what I'd do without you, my love. I don't want to even imagine. Sometimes at night I pretend we're back in that little motel in Honolulu, and I can smell the jasmine outside our door and feel your arms around me, smell your wonderful scent, feel the touch of your skin. Come home to me, my darling. And I'll never let you leave again.
Your wife,
Emma

I felt like a voyeur, reading these letters from a dead woman to a dead man. It didn't seem right to be reading them, and I didn't know how in the world they'd help now, forty years after they were written, but if there was a hint to Neal Hardy's persona in here, then I needed to know it. At least that's what I kept telling myself.

My darling Neal,
Okay, buster, you need to get home and DEAL with your son! God, honey, he's so cute I can hardly believe it!! He's got your eyes, like I told you, but the nose seems to be changing. It's beginning to look like my uncle Walter's! Hopefully little Maxwell will grow into it!

I know you didn't want to, but I've begun calling him
Max. I can't help myself. Maxwell is just too big a
name for such a little guy! I can't wait until you get
home and the three of us are a real family. Daddy is
doing what he can to be a 'male influence' on little
Max, but you know he'd rather just read his paper!
Ha, ha! I am glad, however, that you talked me into
moving home with my parents. I really don't know
what I'd do right now without my mother's help. One
little baby takes up so much time and energy, you
just wouldn't believe! When you get home I'm going
to let you have twelve whole hours of 'quality time'
with him! I heard about 'quality time' on TV. I think
it's a way of making rich parents feel it's okay to
abandon their kids to nannies and such as long as
they spend an hour a day playing with them! Ha, ha!
Gee, honey, can you believe the little girl you left
behind is a mother now! I feel so grown up! I can't
wait to see you as a father! You're going to be great!
I miss you, my darling! Please write. I need to hear
from you and I need to know you still love me. I did
lose the extra weight, by the way. Think you can still
love your skinny girl?
Your wife,
Emma

After reading the second one straight through, I just
started reading the first paragraph and the last one to make
sure there was nothing sinister in there. I felt like less of
a perv that way.

An hour later, having found nothing of value—at
least to my investigation—in forty-year-old love letters, I
checked out the shotgun to find it hadn't been fired prob-

ably in a year or two, and gave Anthony the computer to check out.

Then Lonnie got a call and turned to me. 'Eighteen-wheeler jack-knifed on Highway five at the Switchback,' he said. 'Multiple car involvement.'

'How many?' I asked, while he got on the radio to find out.

Anthony was getting out of his seat to go deal with it, but I told him to stay put. 'I need you on the computer,' I told him. 'Me and Dalton'll take the wreck.' I looked around and saw Dalton Pettigrew already standing by the front door.

'Ready when you are, Milt,' he said.

We headed toward the highway, sirens blaring. When we got there we found a real mess. The 18-wheeler trailer was on its side, spilling its contents all over the highway. All I knew at this point was that the contents were liquid. The volunteers from the fire department showed up same time as us, as well as the ambulance.

The trucker was standing by his cab, holding something bloody to his head when I walked over. 'Whatya got in the trailer?' I asked him.

'Corn syrup,' he said.

'What?' I asked, just as I saw Dalton step in it. Picking up one foot, I saw the sticky mess adhering to his boot, saw Dalton trying to shake it off, then lift the other foot, putting the first one down, back in the syrup, and on and on. I figured he'd be occupied with that for a while.

'It's not gonna blow up, right?' I asked the trucker.

He shook his head, then winced. 'Not hardly,' he said.

'How bad's your head?' I asked him.

'I'm gonna live,' he said. The he nodded toward one of the cars in the pile up. 'I ain't so sure about her, though.'

An older woman had two young children sitting on the

grassy verge of the highway, while the volunteers were using the jaws of life on the front driver's door. I hurried over to survey the damage. The back door on the passenger side had popped open on impact, which was how the two kids made it out. He was about five, the little girl about three. Both had been in car seats.

'They OK?' I asked the older woman, who I recognized as Mrs Impaca, the Methodist preacher's wife.

She smiled. 'They're just fine, aren't you, guys?' she said, touching the little girl's head but looking at the boy.

'Is Mama gonna be OK?' the little boy asked.

'Looks like the firemen are taking real good care of her,' I said, looking in the passenger side front window. It didn't look good. The engine of the mother's little Ford Taurus was in her lap and the guys working it were having a hard time.

'Son,' I said, 'can you tell me where your daddy is?'

'He's at work,' the boy said.

'What's your name?' I asked.

'Christian Taylor Metcalf!' he said loudly.

I smiled at him. 'Well, Christian Taylor Metcalf, you know where your daddy works?'

'At his job,' he said.

'What kind of job does your daddy have?' I asked.

'He sells cars, but not enough of 'em, that's for sure!' the boy said. 'That's what Mommy says.'

'Y'all live in Longbranch?' I asked the boy.

He shrugged his shoulders. 'We live at 7131 Hazelnut Street.'

I looked over my shoulder to see that Dalton had finally gotten out of his sticky situation. 'Dalton!' I called. 'Check the directory in the car, or call Lonnie, find out if Hazelnut Street is in Longbranch, and—wait.' I looked again at the boy. 'You know your daddy's first name?'

At that point the little girl piped up. 'Daddy!' she said, like I was a complete idiot.

'Mike,' the boy said.

'Is not!' the girl cried out. 'It's Daddy!'

'It's Mike!' the boy shouted back, but I left the bickering for Mrs Impaca to deal with.

'Dalton, see if there's a Mike Metcalf works at the Chrysler dealership. Talk to Garrett Douglas himself. Don't ask for Mike. We'll go get him. You understand?'

'Which you want me to do first, Milt?' Dalton asked. 'Call Lonnie or call Mr Douglas?'

'Call Douglas first,' I said, then turned back to the kids.

That's when I noticed a big knot on Mrs Impaca's head. 'Ma'am,' I said, 'your car involved in this?'

She nodded, then pointed at a silver Buick, its tail end crumpled and the whole car turned sideways on the highway. I noticed then that no one had stopped the flow of traffic on the highway, slight as it was, and there were now cars heading toward this mess.

I got up from where I was with the kids, grabbed a man who seemed to be in good shape and said, 'Come with me. We gotta direct us some traffic.'

He was obviously a businessman, traveling the highway between Tulsa and Ardmore, and someone I didn't know, but he came along politely enough. We set up cones on both sides of the highway, slowing down the traffic and moving the southbound into one of the northbound lanes, as all the southbound lanes were tied up with broken vehicles.

Dalton wandered over while we were in the middle of this.

'Milt?' he said.

'Yeah, Dalton?' I asked, stopping what I was doing to give him my full attention. That was about the only way to get Dalton's full attention back.

'I found Mike Metcalf,' he said, making it sound like a question.

'Yeah?' I said. 'He at Douglas's dealership?'

'Yeah,' Dalton answered.

I handed him my stack of cones. 'Finish up here,' I said. 'Get a ride into town with the volunteers if I'm not back in time. I'm going in to get Mike Metcalf.'

'OK,' Dalton said. 'And, Milt?'

'Yes, Dalton?' I said, getting impatient, which I try not to do with Dalton. After all, he's doing the best he can. At least that's what my wife keeps telling me.

'You want I should do just the one lane or you think we need to do both?' he asked.

'Just one lane, Dalton,' I said.

'OK, Milt,' he said, smiling at me.

I took my Jeep back into town and to the Chrysler dealership. Garrett Douglas's dealership was an official Chrysler dealership, but you could get just about any car you wanted from Douglas, from a brand-new Dodge truck to a brand-new Jaguar. And he had about twenty acres of used cars on top of that. It being a Sunday and all, the dealership would usually be closed, but they were having some kind of promotional thing and there were flags and balloons and a sign offering free hotdogs. That I could get behind.

As I mentioned before, Douglas was an African-American and had owned this dealership for about as long as I could remember, but he didn't call attention to himself. He hired mostly white employees and stayed locked up in his office most of the time. I'm not saying that was right, I'm just saying that's how Garrett Douglas dealt with being one of the few African-American business owners in a small Oklahoma town.

I found him in his office and he immediately stood up when I entered, extending his hand, which I shook. 'Sheriff,' he said. 'I understand there's been an accident with Mike Metcalf's family?'

'Yes, sir,' I said. 'Have you talked to him?'

Douglas shook his head. 'No, no,' he said. 'I understood you wanted to talk to him first.'

I nodded. 'Could you get him in here?' I asked.

Douglas nodded and went to his desk, sitting back down and turning on an intercom. 'Julie, please have Mike Metcalf come to my office,' he said. Then added, 'Thank you,' and rung off. To me, he said, 'Can I get you anything? Coffee, soda?'

'No, I'm fine, Mr Douglas,' I said. 'But thank you.'

As we stood there awkwardly, he ventured, 'So how is Anthony Dobbins working out?'

I smiled. 'Real good,' I said. 'Only one in the department knows a thing about computers for one thing,' I said. I was saved from having to continue by the door opening and a man walking in. I could only assume it was Mike Metcalf. He was late twenties, early thirties, with close-cropped sandy brown hair, and the same dimples I'd seen on the face of his son—the kind where you didn't have to smile to get 'em, they just stayed there all the time. He looked fit and trim and was wearing slacks and a button-down shirt.

'Mike,' Douglas said, which meant I'd assumed right. 'Please have a seat.'

Seeing me, Mike Metcalf didn't sit. Instead he said, 'What's going on?'

'Mr Metcalf,' I said, 'there's been a pile-up on Highway five—'

At this point Mike fell into the offered chair. 'Darla?' he said. 'The kids?'

Douglas and I sat down with him, Douglas reaching out to touch Mike's arm. 'The kids are fine, Mr Metcalf,'

I said. 'Your wife is alive. She's stuck in the car at the moment, and the fire department is trying to get her out. From what little I could see, looked like the engine is pressing up against her,' I said, omitting the part where it look like it was in her lap. He didn't need to know that. I could be wrong.

Metcalf jumped up. 'I gotta get out there!' he said.

'Your kids are being watched by the Methodist preacher's wife,' I said. I smiled. 'Can't get a better babysitter than that. But I'll drive you out there now.'

Metcalf looked at Douglas who said, 'Go, Mike. Call me on your cell, tell me where you want your car delivered. I'll have one of the guys take it to your house, or the hospital, or wherever you need it.'

Metcalf reached in his pocket and handed Douglas his keys. 'Thanks, Garrett,' he said, and we headed out the door.

People handle things differently. I've never particularly liked to hear someone say, 'If I can do this, anybody can,' or 'He sure didn't act upset,' or anything like that. Everybody's different; everybody's got their own baggage, their own strengths, their own weaknesses. Just 'cause Joe Blow can pull himself up by his bootstraps from an impoverished childhood and become a millionaire at thirty, doesn't mean everybody can. Just because Sally Sue cried like a baby when such-and-such happened, doesn't mean everybody does. Like I said about telling wives about their husband's dying, I got a lot of different takes on the subject.

Mike Metcalf talked the entire way to the wreck.

'You like this Jeep?' he said, not waiting for an answer. 'Seems to be getting a little old. Maybe you should think about trading it in for a new Dodge truck—got some good four-doors for a family man. You a family man, Sheriff? Seem to remember you are. I'm a family man. Oh, you know that. Nelson, that's my boy, he's five, and Tierra, my daughter, she's three-and-a-half.' He laughed. 'Can't forget the half! Hey, I think she might be in the same class as your boy, is that right, Sheriff?' Again, not waiting for an answer. 'Me and Darla, we've been married eight years, but we've been going together since high school. She's a real good mom. Always knew she would be, but we waited for a while to have kids. Probably shouldn't have done that. Probably should have started out right away. You seen Darla? No, I guess not. Not except…Darla's really pretty, prettiest girl in school. Darn lucky, that's what I am! Tierra looks just like her mama…'

When I pulled the Jeep up to the scene of the jackknife, the paramedics were just getting Darla Metcalf out of the car. She didn't look good. Mike Metcalf ran to the car. When the kids saw him, there wasn't much Mrs Impaca could do to keep them away from their parents. Holding his daughter in his arms, his son holding on to his mother's stretcher, the Metcalfs moved as a family into the back of the ambulance.

I left Dalton there to deal with traffic and headed back to the department.

FIVE

LATER THAT EVENING, before heading home, I went with Charlie Smith to Longbranch Memorial to check on Billy Johansson. Longbranch Memorial is not a big hospital, but we got some good doctors and they browbeat the city and the county into coming up with the money for some good equipment. Our ICU is one of the best in our part of Oklahoma, rivaling the best in Tulsa or Oklahoma City. So there had been no need to air-flight Billy out of Longbranch to a bigger city. The flight would have been risky in his condition, and Longbranch Memorial was more than equipped to handle his trauma.

I got stopped by three nurses, an orderly and an excitable intern before I got to the ICU waiting room, all of 'em asking if it was true we got Satan worshipers in Longbranch. I told 'em all it was just kids being kids, more than likely, but they didn't want to believe that. The fantasy of Satan worshiping teams roaming the woods was a lot more fun than the reality of a bank robbery and murder.

The ICU waiting room was full when we got there. I noticed Beth Gilmartin, my next-door neighbor when I was married to my ex-wife, sitting in a corner with her two daughters. I excused myself and went over.

'Beth,' I said, 'you OK?'

She looked up at me with dull eyes. Finally recognition hit and she said, 'Milt. Hey.' She stood up and hugged me. 'What are you doing here?'

I pointed over to where Charlie sat with Mr and Mrs

Johansson. 'Here about the policeman who got shot yesterday.'

She nodded her head. 'Heard about that. Sorry.'

'You?' I asked.

Craig Gilmartin wasn't with his wife and girls, and that worried me. 'Craig had a heart attack this morning,' Beth said.

'Oh, God,' I said, and hugged her again. 'How bad?'

'They're trying to get him stable enough for surgery tomorrow. A quadruple bypass. What they call a full cabbage.'

I nodded my head. 'Yeah, I've heard of that. He conscious and everything?'

'Yes.'

'You know, they're doing wonders nowadays with this kinda thing. He's gonna come out of this smelling like a rose,' I said.

She smiled. 'From your mouth to God's ears,' she said.

'Mind if I come by for a minute when I go in to see Billy?' I asked.

'He'd like that. You know, we were both on your side when you split up with LaDonna.'

I grinned. 'Good to know that. When he gets out, me and my new wife, Jean, are gonna have to have y'all over for a barbeque.'

'Long as it's skinless chicken,' she said. 'When I get him out of here, there'll be no more chicken fried steak and cream gravy, I can tell you that!'

The way she said it, I believed her. Poor Craig. I hugged her again and went over to where Charlie Smith sat with the Johanssons. I couldn't help looking at Paul Johansson a little longer than I did at his wife. The only crime I could think Paul Johansson was guilty of was seeing a psychiatrist, namely my wife and, even in southern Oklahoma, that's not really a crime. I tried not to stare.

On the other side of Mrs Johansson sat Katy Monroe, the bank VP who'd discovered the robbery. She'd changed clothes since the wedding, but, if anything, looked worse. There were bags under her eyes and the jeans and shirt she wore looked like they belonged to a much larger woman.

I shook hands with Mr and Mrs Johansson and asked after Billy, then took a seat next to Katy, taking her hand in mine. 'How you doing?' I asked her quietly.

She tried a smile, then said, 'I'm fine, Milt, thanks for asking.'

She didn't look fine. 'Dewayne giving you any shit?' I asked.

She shook her head. 'No, no, he's been fine. He's naturally upset about the money, but we're insured. Payrolls will go out on schedule tomorrow.'

'That's good,' I said. 'Be a real hardship on more'n half the town if they didn't.'

'We have a commitment to the community,' she said, as if it were something she'd learned by rote, 'and we stand by our commitments.' I thought maybe she was studying to do commercials for the bank.

I squeezed her hand and let it go. 'You been in to see Billy?' I asked.

She shook her head. 'No. He's still unconscious and the visiting periods are so short I think his parents should have the whole time.'

'True enough,' I said, 'though me and Charlie need to get in there for just a minute. Won't take up much of their allotted time.'

'How are Emmett and Jasmine?' she asked. 'Did they get off OK?'

I smiled. 'Yeah. I made sure they didn't stick around.

They should be having a grand old time in the Caribbean right now.'

Katy smiled. 'Doesn't that sound great?'

THEY HUNKERED DOWN under the shower curtain Emmett had taken from the bathroom, and ran toward the main building of the hotel. The wind whipped the curtain from their hands before they'd taken more than a few steps away from the door of their cabin. It was pitch black outside, and only a few lights from the main building led them in the right direction. Emmett held on to Jasmine for dear life as the wind whipped at their clothes and the blowing rain stung their faces raw. It seemed to take forever to get there. For every step forward they took half a step back, moving into the wind. When their feet touched the flag-stones of the covered patio of the main building, Emmett let out a sigh.

'We're here!' he yelled to be heard over the noise of the storm. He pushed Jasmine forward toward the door. It was locked and a paper sign, stuck to the door with scotch tape, was blowing sideways. Emmett straightened it to read: 'Closed for the Season'.

'What the hell?' he said, then started hammering on the door. Jasmine joined him.

Finally, after three or four very long minutes, a young man came to the door. He appeared surprised at seeing them, then wrestled with the lock to finally open the door and allow them in.

'Hey!' he said. 'What are you guys doing here? I thought everybody left on the last ferry!'

'We just came in on the last ferry!' Emmett said.

'Oh, man,' he said, 'they weren't supposed to let any-body else on the island. We got a storm coming.'

'Coming?' Emmett shouted. 'What the hell is that?' he said, pointing outside.

'Oh,' the kid said. He giggled. 'Looks like a storm.'

'Other people got off the ferry when we did,' Jasmine said.

'We made 'em all head back,' the kid said. 'Them and all the employees 'cept me. I'm the skeleton crew.'

'Are you kidding me?' Emmett demanded. 'You're the only one here?'

'Well, no, you guys are here, too,' he said, confused.

He was in his early twenties, skinny, with long blond hair tied in a ponytail at the back of his neck. He had leftover acne on his face, with scars from those that had healed, and crooked teeth. His baggy shorts hung below his navel, with plaid underpants showing above. A jersey that would have been large on a linebacker hung from his skinny shoulders. And as far as Emmett could tell, the kid was stoned out of his mind.

'Why did they leave you here?' Emmett demanded.

'Somebody's gotta watch this place for vandalism. 'Sides, I like hurricanes.'

'Hurricanes?' Jasmine exclaimed. She looked out the window. 'This is a hurricane?'

'Oh, no, not yet,' the kid said. 'Right now she's just a tropical storm,' he said, smiling dreamily, 'but she's gonna make it to hurricane status, I just know she will. She's early, but she's gonna be a hummer.'

'I thought hurricane season wasn't until later in the summer!' Emmett shouted over the rush of wind from the still-open door.

'Yeah,' the kid said, grinning. 'This is cool, huh? They're calling her Annie. Weather service doesn't think she's got the right stuff to make it to hurricane, but I believe in her! Just look at her blow!'

Emmett and Jasmine turned around to stare at the storm

outside. The wind was bending small trees and the rain was so heavy you could barely see past the end of the portico.

'We need to get off this island,' Emmett said, turning back.

The kid shook his head. 'No more ferries until she passes. Probably in a day or two. Oh, man, I'm being so rude!' He stuck out his hand to Emmett. 'I'm Leon McKerry,' he said. 'Welcome to my hurricane party!' And he giggled.

Grudgingly Emmett introduced himself and Jasmine. Then Jasmine said, 'I'm starving.'

'She's pregnant,' Emmett clarified while Jasmine shot him a look.

'Oh, man, we got the best groceries in town,' Leon said, turning and motioning for them to follow. He went into the bar area of the hotel restaurant where a small feast was laid out. 'This is all the stuff they were making when we found out about Annie.

'She came up real quick, see. We'd barely heard about her when the ferry landed. Don't know how they missed you guys.'

'We didn't check in,' Jasmine said. 'Someone took us straight to our room. Said we were already registered and checked in.'

Leon nodded. 'Yeah, they do that for honeymoon couples. They musta forgot. Sorry about that. Maybe the hotel will comp your stay.'

'You bet your ass they'll comp our stay!' Emmett exclaimed. He watched his new bride head to the buffet spread on top of the bar.

'Yum,' she said, 'wings!'

THE HOSPITAL VISIT was depressing and gave us nothing. Billy Johansson was just lying there, tubes going in and tubes going out, eyes closed, breathing with a respirator. He didn't look good, even though all the doctors said he was doing pretty well.

After we left the cubicle where Billy was, I excused myself from Charlie for a minute and peeked in on Craig Gilmartin. Beth and the girls were already in there, surrounding the bed. Craig's complexion was the same color as the starched white sheets.

'Hey, Craig,' I said, 'I was here at the hospital on county business and saw Beth. She told me 'bout you deciding to take a vacation.'

'If I laugh it'll kill me,' Craig said, straight-faced.

'Well, then, did you hear the one about...' I started, and we all laughed. I went to the bed and shook his hand. 'I already told Beth I'm gonna have y'all over to sacrifice some chickens to the barbeque gods, but she said yours has gotta be skinless. I thought I'd serve it along with a carrot.'

'Can you put cream gravy on a carrot?' Craig asked with a wan smile.

'Funny as a heart attack,' his wife said, and me and Craig groaned.

'Look, buddy,' I said, patting his shoulder, 'you hang in there. I hear these quad bypasses are a piece of cake nowadays. You just get better and I'll sneak you in a pizza while you're recouping.'

'Italian sausage and mushrooms,' Craig said.

I squeezed his shoulder again and left. Two cubicles down I saw Mike Metcalf. Mrs Impaca was still with him, sitting in the corridor right outside the cubicle with both children on her lap, a storybook in her hand. I walked up to Mike.

'How's she doing, Mike?' I asked.

He turned, startled at the interruption. He stared at me for half a minute, then I saw recognition in his face. 'Sheriff!' he said. He shook my hand, a tired smile on his face. 'She's doing great!' he said. 'Concussion, broken femur, shoulder dislocation and some internal bleeding, but she's gonna be OK. They're just keeping her up here until a bed's open in the normal rooms.'

I grinned at him and slapped his shoulder. 'That's great,' I said. 'I'm so glad to hear it.'

'Thanks for everything, Sheriff,' he said.

'Hey, it's my job. Mr Douglas get your car to you?' I asked.

'Yeah, a couple of the guys brought it over a while ago.' He looked into the hall at his children. 'My mom's on her way in from Dallas. Ms Impaca's helping until she gets here.'

'Well, you get some sleep when you can, Mike. You look exhausted.'

He shook his head. 'I'm just relieved, Sheriff.' Tears stung his eyes. 'I thought it was all over, you know?'

I squeezed his shoulder and left, finding Charlie and heading out of the hospital.

Fifteen minutes later, Charlie Smith and me sat over coffee and blueberry pie at the Longbranch Inn. I shoulda been home hours ago, but what with Neal Hardy's kids and the hospital visit, the wreck on the highway, another round with Mulder and Scully and, of course, having to defend my county from Satan worshipers, the day had gotten away from me.

'Notice how much those two Feds look like Mulder and Scully?' I asked Charlie.

'Who?' he said.

'The Feds,' I said.

'Look like who?' he said.

'Mulder and Scully,' I said.

'Who are Mulder and Scully?' he said.

'Are we doing "who's on first" here?' I said.

'What?' he said.

'Never mind,' I said. I couldn't help thinking Emmett woulda got both references. 'Anyway,' I continued, 'I'm beginning to think Neal Hardy didn't have anything to do with this whole thing.'

Charlie shook his head. 'Sometimes kids have an elevated opinion of their parents,' he said. 'My daughter thinks I walk on water.'

'How old's your daughter?' I asked.

'Five,' he said.

'I hear their opinions tend to change when they get to about thirteen,' I offered.

'Don't want to hear it,' he said. He shook his head. 'Thing is, what I'm saying, Max and Elise Hardy have an opinion of their old man that might not jibe with reality.'

'Nicely put,' I said. 'My wife couldn't have done a better job. But we got a fact here, Charlie, not just opinions. Neal Hardy won the lottery; he got more money in a year from the lottery than was in that bank. Why would he do it?'

'Bored?' Charlie offered. 'Worked hard all his life, then had that amazing windfall, found out too much money meant too much time on his hands. I understand he didn't have all that much mediation work. Decided he'd try something a little different for a change.'

'Like rob a bank?' I said, pretty sarcastically. 'I think you took one too many psych courses when you were in the city.' I held up my coffee cup to Loretta, my favorite Longbranch waitress, indicating another shot. It was decaf. 'A man doesn't change his whole philosophy just because he gets bored, Charlie. If he was that bored, he woulda taken a job with you or me.'

'Then how'd the hole get in his kitchen?' Charlie asked.

Well, he had me there. That was another fact: there was

a hole from Neal Hardy's office kitchen into the bank vault. It didn't look blasted, it looked dug out with a jackhammer. There was no getting around that. And jackhammers are noisy. I'd checked, and Neal hadn't been on vacation recently, hadn't hired anyone else to work with him.

'I don't know,' I admitted. 'But something's just not right here. I'm not ready to ruin a good man's reputation just yet.'

Charlie shook his head. 'May not be up to you, Milt. Or me. The Feds seem pretty happy to hang this on Neal Hardy.'

He was right about that. Our conversations earlier with Whysmith and Carmody sure seemed to be going that way.

'We're doing a search right now,' Whysmith had said, 'for all associates of Neal Hardy's. I think we should look at his arrests, too. Being a State Highway Patrol officer he had plenty of opportunity to meet some unsavory characters. And with the money he had from the lottery, he had ample opportunity to pick and choose who he hired to help him. Unfortunately for him, I think he chose wrong. Somebody didn't want a share of the loot or the amount Hardy was going to pay him for the job; he wanted the whole thing. That's why Neal Hardy's lying on a slab in your morgue.'

'And speaking of the morgue,' Carmody cut in, 'we got the autopsy results on your Mr Hardy,' she said.

That had pissed me off. He was my vic in my jurisdiction, and the Feds had no jurisdiction over Neal Hardy's murder—only the bank robbery. So why had they gotten the autopsy reports before me? I thought at that point it might be prudent to have a conversation with Dr Church.

'Those should have come to me,' I said.

Carmody ignored me. 'Pretty straight report,' she'd said. 'Shotgun blast to the head. Some slugs penetrated the brain. Your Dr Church said she thought Hardy probably died instantly. No surprises.'

'Pretty healthy for a man his age,' Whysmith added, pissing me off even more as Neal Hardy was just a few years older than me. But I let it go.

Since they'd interviewed the Hardy children too, I'd tried the same theory with them that I was trotting out to Charlie now. Worked about as well.

Coming back to the present, I finished my fourth or fifth or whatever cup of coffee, and said to Charlie, 'Gotta get back up the mountain. My wife's probably filing abandonment papers as we speak.'

'Yeah,' said Charlie, finishing his own cup, which wasn't decaf. 'Me, too. But I gotta stop by the station first. I got paperwork up the ass, and I don't wanna have to face it in the morning.'

As we walked to our respective cars, Charlie said, 'So what's going on with the Satan worshipers?'

Et tu, Charlie, I thought. 'Kids, I reckon,' I said.

He nodded his head. 'Usually is,' he said.

We said good-night and I drove home. It was eleven o'clock when I got there and naturally my boy was sound asleep. I gave him a kiss then went downstairs to the bedroom me and Jean shared. She was fast asleep, too. It's amazing how lonely you can feel when everybody you love is asleep. But it's a good lonely. It's the kinda lonely where you wish you had someone to talk to, but you know in a few hours you will. Not the kinda lonely I had been when I lived in this place by myself, when I knew the only people I'd have to talk to would be the ones at work, and not the kinda lonely I'd felt when I lived with LaDonna, my first wife, when, even with her sitting in the chair next to me watching TV, I felt alone.

I crawled in next to my wife, not touching her, but still

feeling the warmth radiating from her body, and reassessed my thoughts. This isn't lonely, I told myself. This is just right.

'WAKE UP!'

Emmett shot up in bed, reaching for the gun in the drawer of his bedside table. It wasn't there.

'Emmett, you awake?'

Emmett glared at the kid—Leon, he remembered—who squatted before him, bare-chested and wearing only boxer shorts with Tweety Bird imprinted on them. They were such a bright yellow he could see them in the relative darkness.

After Jasmine had eaten everything she could hold at the bar the night before, Leon had used his master key to let them into one of the first-floor rooms. It wasn't as nice as their cabana, but it didn't leak and the bed was a king size. It hadn't taken long to wash off in cold water—the water heaters had gone out with the electricity and the back-up generator only had enough juice for a few security lights—and hop into bed.

Now here it was, still dark outside, and the skinny, pock-faced kid was waking them up.

'What?' Emmett demanded, using his outside voice.

'Shhh!' Leon said, holding his finger to his mouth. 'Pirates!' he whispered loudly.

'What?' Emmett demanded again, still talking like a normal person.

Leon slapped his hand over Emmett's mouth, and whispered, 'Pirates! I heard a noise and looked outside and saw their boat pull up. They'll be inside in a matter of minutes!'

'Leon, there's no such thing as pirates. You had a bad dream—'

'How long have you been in these waters, Emmett?

Well, I've been here four years, and let me tell you there *are* such things as pirates, and they board pleasure craft, kill everybody aboard, and steal the boats. That's what they do. I'm not talking Long John Silver, here, Emmett; I'm talking some real mean *hombres*!'

Hearing noise beyond the rage of the storm, Emmett got up and went to the window. What he saw didn't look like pirates; they just looked like your ordinary, run-of-the-mill, bad-news psycho killers. 'Shit!' he whispered.

'Get Jasmine!' Leon whispered. 'We gotta get out of here!'

'Where the hell we going in this storm?' Emmett demanded, also whispering.

'Don't worry, I got a plan,' Leon said. Which didn't make Emmett feel that much better.

MONDAY MORNING dawned with overcast skies and the threat of rain. I got Jean up to date on what was happening with the case, while we fed Johnny Mac his breakfast (Cheerios with banana slices and a glass of apple juice), made his snack lunch (peanut butter and jelly sandwich, apple slices in a baggie, and baby carrots in another baggie), and got him and us dressed.

'Daddy,' he said, while we both ate our Cheerios.

'Yes, son?' I said.

'You carry a gun!' Johnny Mac declared.

'Yes, sir, I do,' I agreed.

'You shoot bad people!' he declared.

'No, not really, son,' I said. 'I try never to shoot anybody. Shooting people's not nice.'

'I shoot bad guys!' Johnny Mac announced. Then held his hand out in an approximation of a gun and yelled, 'Bang, bang! Dead bad guy!'

'The best thing to do with a bad guy,' I told my son, 'is lock 'em up in the jail house.'

'And trow away da key!' Johnny Mac sang.

I laughed. 'That's right, big guy! Throw away the key!'

'Daddy?' he asked.

'Yes, son?'

'You're amazing!' my son said.

I smiled and tousled his hair. 'So are you, my boy. You are amazing.'

'Daddy?' he asked.

'Yes, son?'

'You think Mama's pretty?' he asked.

'I think your mama is beautiful,' I said.

'Boo-ti-ful,' he said musingly, trying out the word.

'That's even better than pretty,' I told him.

'Mama!' he called to Jean who was packing his lunch at the kitchen counter.

'Yes, John?' she said.

'You are boo-ti-ful!' he yelled.

Jean turned around, smiling. 'Why, thank you, John,' she said. 'You're pretty handsome yourself.'

My son grinned at me, always happy to make his mama smile. Let me tell you about my son.

His daycare had had to make a special class for Johnny Mac and two other kids. They were all three-year-olds, but they were bored with the stuff the three-year-old class was doing, but weren't quite ready for the four-year-old class. So they'd come up with an advanced three-year-old class, and I'm proud to say my son was in it. I'm not so proud to say the reason they had to do it was that Johnny Mac and the one other boy and the girl in this new class had been terrorizing the other three-year-olds out of sheer boredom. Johnny Mac was the gang leader. I'm not proud of that, but he *was* the leader. What can I say? I just hope we can turn his evil ways towards truth, justice, and the American dream. I'm kidding—he's three, get over it.

I got to the shop around eight, and Gladys was already in and the coffee made. I can say what I want about Gladys, but she does make a mean cup of coffee.

'The jail cell's a mess, Milt, and I'm not cleaning it up,' she said by way of greeting.

'Call somebody to come clean it, will ya?' I said, grabbing a cup of coffee and heading for my office.

'And who am I supposed to call?' she yelled after me.

'I don't know! Figure it out!' I yelled back.

'Well, I never!' she said.

I thought she probably had, but I let it go. Charlie Smith had talked about doing his paperwork the night before; I shoulda followed his lead. My desktop was heaving with it. You wouldn't believe who wants reports on every little thing there is—from how much time each deputy spends in a squad car to how much paper we use a month in the Xerox machine. The county, the state, the Feds, and special interest groups all got papers to fill out, and you'd think I had nothing better to do.

I'd been at it for about half an hour when Anthony Dobbins knocked on my door. 'Sheriff? Got a minute?' he asked.

I gratefully put down the form I was working on. 'Sure, Anthony,' I said. 'What's up?'

Anthony came in, shutting the door behind him, and sat in one of the chairs in front of my desk. He had a stack of papers in his hand. 'I was going through Neal Hardy's computer,' he said, 'and I found the usual stuff. He had two email accounts, one he used to talk to his kids, and one he used for Match.com and other computer dating sites.'

I grinned. 'Well, good for him. Can you tell if he found anybody?'

Anthony shook his head. 'Looks like he talked to a couple of women just a few times each. I guess they weren't his type. But I did find something else,' Anthony said.

'OK,' I said by way of encouragement.

'Seems Mr Hardy was looking into somebody's background, and using the Highway Patrol's ID system to do it,' Anthony said.

This piqued my interest. 'Who?' I asked.

'The name Mr Hardy put in was Wilson Everett, which brought up a few other names, like Everett Wilson, a.k.a. William Evers, a.k.a. Evan Wilson, and so on and so forth.'

'You know why he was checking out this guy?' I asked.

Anthony shook his head. 'No, sure don't, Sheriff. But the guy doesn't look all that good, whoever he is. Several arrests but no convictions.'

'Arrests for what?' I asked.

'Fraud mostly. Hot checks. Falsifying state and federal records. Sounds like a scam artist to me,' Anthony said.

I nodded my head. 'Sure does. Wonder if someone decided to try to talk Neal out of his lottery winnings?'

Anthony shrugged his shoulders. 'Might be,' he said.

'Anything else?' I asked.

'Not really. Most of the sites Mr Hardy visited were just Google hits, looking up stuff in general. Nothing terribly interesting.'

'Why don't you run the names of the women he was talking to on the dating sites, see if any of them have records? Just in case.'

'Will do,' Anthony said and left my office.

I was sitting there thinking about this Wilson Everett, a.k.a. whoever, when the phone rang. I picked it up, said, 'Sheriff Kovak,' and heard Charlie Smith's voice.

'Get to the hospital,' he said. 'It's bad.' Then he hung up.

It took me less than ten minutes to get there, longer to find a parking place and wade through the corridors and the elevators to get to ICU. Marsha Johansson was in her husband's arms, bawling her eyes out. It didn't take a rocket scientist to know that Billy had taken a turn for the worse.

The very worst I found out when Charlie saw me and hurried over. 'Billy's dead,' he said.

'Ah, shit,' I said. 'I'm sorry.'

He took my arm and pulled me as far away from the Johanssons as we could get and still be on the same floor. 'And it's fishy. The doctor said he was doing OK, had just regained consciousness late last night.'

'Did he say anything?' I asked.

Charlie shook his head. 'They gave him a sedative and he went back to sleep. When the nurse came in this morning, he was dead.'

'What kind of sedative did they give him?' I asked.

'The nurse swears it was what the doctor ordered. Just a light sleeping pill. But Dr Church has Billy's body down in the morgue now doing a rush autopsy. She sent out for a tox screen, top priority. Said we might get it back by noon.'

'You tell the Feds?' I asked.

'Yeah, I called them at the Longbranch Inn where they're staying. Said they'd be over quick.'

'Charlie, if this wasn't some kind of freak accident…' I said.

'If somebody murdered him…' Charlie said.

'Then whoever did this…' I said.

'Or whoever Neal Hardy's partner was…' Charlie said.

'Is somebody Billy knew,' I finished.

'Yeah,' Charlie said.

We both stared down the hall at the Johanssons, inconsolable in their grief. I'm not sure what Charlie was thinking, but my thoughts were rooting around who Billy knew. Billy Johansson had been born and bred in Prophesy

County; the only time he'd left the county for any long
period was when he went to Oklahoma City to the police
academy. So, basically, everybody he knew was everybody
I knew. Point being, somebody I knew had killed Billy, and
therefore Neal Hardy. And, therefore, had robbed the bank.

We got unsavory characters in Prophesy County, just
like anywhere else, but most of 'em weren't bright enough
to rob a bank. A Saturday Night Special and a convenience
store, yeah, but coming up with a real plan and digging
into the vault? Most of the guys I've arrested over the years
woulda picked the wrong wall and ended up in the street.

By and large, criminals are a stupid lot. They get stoned
on their drug of choice and do something dumb and get
caught. I've had a few who-done-its over the years, but
they've been the exception to the rule. I'm not saying that
whoever robbed the bank and killed both Neal Hardy and
Billy Johansson wasn't a dumb-ass, I'm just saying that he
was a clever dumb-ass, or we'd have caught him by now.

I was in the middle of this reverie when Whysmith
and Carmody showed up. They were both wearing suits,
black ones, and both looked spic and span. The Feebies
are a clean lot, by and large. You rarely see a pudgy Feeb
or one with his shirt tail hanging out.

'What happened?' Carmody asked, both of 'em walking by the grieving parents without a glance.

Looking at the parents, I couldn't help wondering how
this was gonna affect Paul Johansson's therapy with my
wife. If he was seeing my wife. But, then again, it was none
of my business. Confidentiality and all that. Still and all, I
felt a little guilty having had those thoughts about Paul and
his boy Billy, now that Billy was dead. Didn't make those
thoughts any less valid, just made me feel a little bad, is all.

'We don't know for sure,' Charlie said, answering Carmody's question and bringing me out of my reverie. 'The

medical examiner is doing the autopsy now, and she's sent specimens out for a tox screen.'

'Do the doctors think it had anything to do with his injuries?' Whysmith asked.

Charlie shook his head. 'Don't look like it,' he said.

Whysmith looked at me. 'And how is this your jurisdiction?' he asked.

'I called Milt in for a consultation,' Charlie said, getting his back up. And I appreciated it.

'Seeing as how all this is related,' I added.

'Yes, it is related,' Carmody said with a smug smile. 'That's why we'll be taking over both murders—Hardy and Johansson.'

'Say what?' I said, getting my own back up.

She handed me and Charlie papers signed by a judge saying that the bank robbery and both murders were now FBI jurisdiction. 'We'd appreciate all the cooperation we can get from the two of you, of course,' Carmody said.

Whysmith added, 'And do you see any way these Satanic rituals are involved?'

I sighed. Not them, too. 'No, I don't,' I said, and left the hospital.

With my nose out of joint and my tail between my legs, I went back to my shop. I had paperwork and a county to oversee; I didn't need handouts from the Feds. Hell, it was a blessing they were taking over the Neal Hardy mess. I had enough to do with wrecks on the highway and knife fights at the Dew Drop Inn. I didn't need a who-done-it plaguing me. This was good news.

Trying like crazy to convince myself of this, while still being pretty pissed off about the whole thing, I threw myself into the paperwork, pretending I was interested in how much toilet paper our department used a month.

I'd barely settled in my good chair when Gladys rang to

tell me I had a call from Dr Church on line one. I picked it up, wondering what in the hell she wanted. 'Sheriff Kovak,' I said.

'Sheriff Kovak?' she asked in her brusque way. 'This is Dr Church. I have the autopsy report on Billy Johansson.'

She was supposed to have called me with the autopsy report on Neal Hardy; instead, she'd called the Feebies. Now that she was *supposed* to call the Feebies with Billy's autopsy report, she calls me. I coulda straightened her out. Coulda told her where she'd gone wrong. Actually, shoulda rather than coulda. Can't say I felt really guilty when I didn't.

'Whatya got?' I asked.

'His injuries from the shotgun blast were healing nicely after the surgery. That is not what killed him. What killed him was an overdose of methamphetamine.'

'Meth?' I said.

'Methamphetamine,' she corrected.

'Guess you should call the FBI about this, Doc,' I said, now that I knew what they were gonna know.

There was silence on the other end of the line. When she hung up without another word, I figured she figured out her mistake. I also figured Dr Church didn't like making mistakes—or at least didn't like getting caught making one. I smiled as I hung up the phone.

And sat there thinking. We'd had a meth lab in the county, but we'd busted them a couple of months ago. Couple of guys had been moved to the district jail to await trial. Meth was an up-and-comer in Prophesy County— the redneck drug of choice. A couple of six packs of Bud Lite and a couple of hits of meth made for a fun Saturday night. Except meth's a killer. When it doesn't blow up the lab and kill the makers, when it actually gets to the streets, or the roads in our case, you end up with real skinny, real mean people who don't sleep much. Which makes 'em even meaner. The longer somebody's on meth, the worse it gets. You ever seen meth sores? It's like the worse case of acne you ever saw, but open and full of pus. It's downright disgusting.

Which brought me to the conclusion that somebody in Prophesy County was either making meth again, or had access to it. Which, when you get right down to it, was a real bad thing.

SIX

'YOU KNOW HOW to use a weapon?' Leon asked Emmett.

'I'm a cop,' Emmett said. 'So's my wife.'

Jasmine was awake, and not quite believing what was going on.

'Here,' Leon said, thrusting two twelve-gauge shotguns at them. 'They're for skeet, but they work—double barrel, over and under, extra ammo,' he said, thrusting a box of shells at Emmett.

'What about you?' Emmett asked.

Leon grinned and showed them a .357 magnum handgun. 'Found this in the manager's desk. Knew he kept it there. Had to break the lock, but I figured what the hell. I was looking for a job when I found this one.'

'Pirates?' Jasmine said for the third time.

'If you wanna look out the window, Jas,' Leon said, 'be my guest. Just hope they don't see you. They don't treat women nice.'

Jasmine shuddered and moved closer to Emmett.

Emmett asked, 'Where's this hiding place you were talking about?'

'Follow me!' Leon whispered, and led the way.

As far as they could tell the hotel hadn't been breached yet; at least not in any of the common areas. Everything appeared locked up tight. Leon led them down the hall to the front desk, behind it to the other side, then quickly across a short hall to the dining room. Weaving between the tables, they were headed for the kitchen when they heard the glass shatter in the foyer of the hotel.

'Shit!' Leon whispered. 'Come on, quick, into the kitchen!'

They were moving fast when Emmett accidentally hit one of the tables, rattling the glassware and silver. The three of them stopped dead still and listened. They heard talking from the foyer, a man's laugh, but no sign that the pirates, or whatever, had heard the table being jostled over the sound of the storm.

'Come on,' Leon whispered, his voice as soft as a breath now. Bent almost double, the three crept to the kitchen door, opening it only slightly to slither through.

There was no security light in the kitchen. To Emmett's eyes, it was pitch black.

'Jas in the middle,' Leon whispered, 'hold hands and follow me.'

They crept through the kitchen, trying not to bump into anything. A pan rattled and they stopped, waiting for a reaction. There was none, so they crept forward. Finally, Leon brought them to a wall. 'Here,' he said, feeling his way up the wall. He opened a door and the three of them moved inside. It wasn't until the door closed behind them that a flashlight shone full in their eyes.

'Oh, shit!' Leon said, throwing up his hands, the .357 dropping to the floor.

Emmett lifted the twelve-gauge and pointed it at the flashlight. 'I'm taking somebody down!' he said.

'Whoa, now!' came a voice from behind the flashlight. 'Don't you be shooting nobody, man.' The flashlight was one of those fancy rigs that was a flashlight at one end and a lantern in the middle. The man flipped it to lantern light, which lit up most of the small room.

'Leon?' said the man holding the lantern. He was at least

Emmett's age, late fifties, his graying hair kinky and cut close to his head. In the weird light of the lantern his skin looked almost black, making the whites of his eyes and his teeth iridescently white.

Leon put down his arms. 'Patch, that you?'

'Yeah, man.'

'Shit,' Leon said. Turning to Emmett and Jasmine, he said, 'It's OK. He's with the hotel. Who you got with you?'

'This here's Mr and Mrs George Thomas,' Patch said, indicating an old and frail-looking couple, looking to be in their late seventies, early eighties. Mr Thomas was wearing Bermuda shorts, a Hawaiian shirt, and black dress shoes with black socks. His wife was wearing a turquoise muu-muu and orthopedic shoes. Emmett couldn't help thinking he'd rather have a twenty-something couple consisting of a weight lifter and an aerobics instructor as back-up. Patch said, 'They come to the island to celebrate their sixtieth wedding anniversary.'

'Whoa, that was a bad idea, huh?' Leon said. Pointing toward Emmett and Jasmine, Leon said, 'These two are on their honeymoon.' Both Leon and Patch laughed.

'It's them damn Internet ads,' Patch said. 'Makes people think this is a place they'd actually wanna be.'

'How'd you get stuck here? I thought you went with the ferry?' Leon asked.

'Planning to,' Patch said, 'but Mr and Mrs Thomas here were a little slow getting their shit together.'

'Please don't curse in front of my wife,' Mr Thomas said.

'Ah, folks,' Emmett said, 'we're gonna have a lot worse than cussing if we keep standing here talking. The pirates, remember?'

'Man, I hate them dudes,' Patch said. ''Member summer before last, Leon, when they took that big ol' boat anchored right off Point Sunset? Shit, and me and Lurel had to go clean up that mess. Dead bodies everywhere!'

'OK, just shut up!' Jasmine said. 'Either you guys are playing some really stupid game with the four of us, or we're all in serious trouble here. And I want to know how we're going to get out of it.'

'We hide in here,' Leon said.

'Where are we?' Emmett asked.

'The walk-in freezer, but with the electricity off, we won't freeze.'

Jasmine took Patch's hand, moving the lantern to illuminate the walls of their hiding place. There were packaged foods everywhere, some beginning to leak fluids.

'I hate to rain on your parade, Leon, but wouldn't any self-respecting pirate loot the freezer pretty quick for food?' Emmett asked.

'Well, see, that's the thing,' Leon said, jumping up and down and reaching for the ceiling, 'they'll just come to this part of the freezer. Not the back-up.'

Finally his hand caught what he'd been aiming for: a rope hanging from the ceiling that brought down an extendable ladder leading to another room above the one they were in.

'Emmett, you wanna go first and help the ladies up?' Leon said, grinning his snaggle-toothed grin.

'Ah, Patch, the flashlight?' Emmett asked.

Patch turned the lantern off and the flashlight on, and handed it to Emmett who was already climbing the stairs. Once at the top, he hoisted himself into the room and flashed the light around. It was indeed a back-up to the walk-in freezer below. But where the bottom held packaged foods, the top held defrosting carcasses of meat— chickens hanging by their necks, half a steer, a couple of lambs, three baby goats. He could only hope the 'pirates' or whatever they were wouldn't stay long.

'Mrs Thomas,' he called down, keeping his voice low. 'You come up now.'

The lady looked at her husband, who walked her to the stairway and held her elbow while she started up the ladder-like steps. Emmett held his hand down to her. 'Here, ma'am, be careful now. Just grab my hand.'

'I'm trying to, young man. Just hold your horses.'

It seemed an eternity before he got her to the top and into the room. Seeing the carcasses hanging around her, she said, 'Oh, my.'

'Jasmine,' Emmett called down. 'You're next.'

Instead, Jasmine had Mr Thomas by the elbow, escorting him to the steps. 'Mr Thomas will go next,' she said.

'No, he won't!' Emmett all but shouted. 'Damn it, you're pregnant! Get your butt up here!'

Mr Thomas stopped and looked at Jasmine. 'Young lady, do as your husband says.'

Jasmine gritted her teeth and started up the steps. Grabbing Emmett's hand, she said, 'Don't think of this as a precedent, Mr Thinks-he-can-boss-me-around! I *do not* come on command!'

'I don't want pirates raising my baby!' Emmett said, which shut her up enough to get her up and into the room.

'Oh, God!' Jasmine said on seeing the meat. 'This is gonna be fun!'

It took a good ten minutes to get everyone up and the door closed. 'Patch,' Emmett said to the last one up, 'bring that rope in with you. Let's not give 'em any ideas.'

'Good thinkin',' Patch said, pulling the rope inside.

They'd no sooner gotten the trap door closed before they heard the outer door of the main walk-in freezer open.

'Hey, lookie here, blokes!' said a very English accent. 'Got enough vittles to feed a small army.'

Jasmine whispered in Emmett's ear, 'Sorta sounds like a pirate, huh?'

San Juan, Puerto Rico

DYLAN 'PICK-ME' WEBSTER was a scion of *the* Websters and a distant relative of Daniel Webster. His particular branch of the family had settled in Rhode Island where his great-great-grandfather had made a fortune off the backs of itinerate workers. His grandfather had trebled that fortune, managing to hold on to almost all of it during the 1929 crash, and his father had managed to invest wisely, quadrupling the family fortune while not actually doing anything.

Pick-Me was doing his best to squander it all. A fourth generation Yalie, he had done his best at school and earned a bachelors in something so esoteric even he couldn't remember exactly what it was. He was recruited in the spring of his senior year at Yale by the CIA, who thought of Yale as their own undergraduate program. After a brief training period with the Company, it was at a meeting of new recruits that Pick-Me acquired his nickname.

The supervisor was describing an assignment, telling the thirty-odd new recruits that only three would be picked for this adventure, being led by a more experienced senior operative. At the outset, Dylan Webster thrust his arm high in the air and, like a grammar school kid at the beginning of a dodgeball game, shouted out, 'Pick me! Pick me!'

Thus the nickname, now pronounced 'Pikme'. Few people were still alive who knew the actual origin of the name.

On this particular day, Pick-Me sat at the bar of the Casa Con Aqua with a fourteen-year-old hooker under one arm and her twenty-seven-year-old hooker mother under the other arm. Pick-Me was on what he believed to be his third day of a drinking binge; in actuality it was his third week, but no one had the heart to tell him.

The two hookers, Maria and her daughter, Lola, liked Pick-Me because he paid well and often, usually forgetting that he'd already paid them, fed them good food, and always fell asleep before anything was required of either of them. They had been with him now for the entire three-week bender and had no desire to go back out on the street. Being with Pick-Me was always a good gig.

Pick-Me was a man of many talents, as could be ascribed to by any of his three ex-wives, all of whom were the recipients of bits and pieces of the Webster family fortune. Unfortunately, Dylan 'Pick-Me' Webster believed in true love; he did not, however, believe in pre-nups.

His first wife, Anna Louise Boudreaux Webster, a former stripper at the Meow Kitty Klub in Baton Rouge, Louisiana, could tell you of her courtship by Pick-Me of midnight runs through the bayous on airboats and watching her beloved shoot alligators, calling out the shot like a pool shark.

His second wife, Mary Jane Champion Webster, a librarian he met at a charity function in Philadelphia, where he paid over ten thousand dollars for a dinner date with the blonde beauty, could tell you about *her* courtship by Pick-Me of midnight flights in a glider plane and ocean-crossing trips to Paris for dinner.

His third wife, Margaret 'Missy' Sheridan Webster, the teenaged daughter of one of his father's golfing buddies, could tell you of prospecting for gold in Argentina, of digging for ruins in Egypt, and of diving for treasure off the coast of Australia.

None of these young ladies, however, could tell you

anything about Pick-Me's work for the CIA. None of them even knew that he worked for the CIA. This was Pick-Me's one and only true secret. The only thing he never told anyone.

Except, of course, anyone who claimed to be with his or any other American, British, Australian, French, Italian, German or Russian agency.

On this particular evening, Pick-Me sat at the bar of the Casa Con Aqua with his two hookers under his arms and tried to ignore the blasting of the soon-to-be hurricane against the mud walls of the bar. Pick-Me wasn't crazy about storms, especially ones with lightning and thunder. They wouldn't let you fly when there was lightning and thunder, and Pick-Me didn't like anything that made it so he was unable to fly. Nowadays, flying was the only thing that Pick-Me really wanted to do.

ALTHOUGH I WAS out of it, been told I wasn't needed, I did have a bit of information the Feds didn't have. Namely, the existence of Wilson Everett and Neal Hardy's interest in same. The Feds were looking for a connection between Hardy and an evil-doer, and there was a slight possibility I had that connection.

I had Anthony run a further check on Wilson Everett and his aliases, and it came back that he was currently living in Oklahoma City. For some reason, the address he was living at seemed familiar. I didn't know why. I hardly knew anybody anymore in Oklahoma City, so I didn't understand why the address was familiar, until I spied the slip of paper where I'd written down Neal Hardy's next of kin's names and addresses. The address the computer had for Wilson Everett was the same address Elise Hardy had put down as hers.

I suppose I shoulda given this information directly over

to the Feds. OK, no supposing about it: I shoulda. But I didn't. I called Charlie Smith, asked if he was alone, then told him what I'd found out.

'Need to give that info to the Feds,' Charlie said.

'And what if it's nothing?' I said.

'Then they'll find it out,' he said.

'Then we'd be having the Feds chasing worthless leads and not doing the work they should be doing. That would be a waste of taxpayers' money,' I reasoned.

'Uh huh,' Charlie said. 'And your point is?'

'Well, I was just thinking we could save them some legwork and you and me take a trip to the City, see what's what?'

'Just so we won't have the Feds chasing a wild goose?' Charlie said.

'My point exactly,' I said, grinning from ear to ear at Charlie's quickness.

'Well, I got nothing much to do here,' he said, 'what with the bank robbery and Billy's murder out of my hands.'

'My point exactly,' I said again. 'I got nothing to do either except fill out stupid forms, now that Neal Hardy's murder is out of my hands.'

'So we'd really be doing the Feds a favor, going to the City and checking out this Everett fella?' Charlie said.

'That's what I'm saying,' I said.

'You're a good man, Milt Kovak,' Charlie said.

'I do my best,' I said humbly and rang off.

Mrs Thomas slept fitfully against her husband's shoulder, while Leon laid on his back on the floor, snoring loudly. When it got too loud, either Patch or Emmett would roll him to his side to keep the noise level down. Jasmine rested her head against a portion of the wall that wasn't too close to the hanging carcasses. The small room was getting hot and the meat was beginning to smell. Jasmine had already vomited twice, as far away from the others as she could, apologizing profusely.

It seemed to have taken the pirates, or whatever they were, a very long time to loot the freezer below them. It had been quiet for about an hour now, but Patch assured Emmett they hadn't left.

'Not till they get ever last thing not nailed down,' he said. 'And they'll want to wait out the storm here, too. We could be up here a while.'

'When they find our stuff and the Thomas's stuff in our rooms,' Jasmine asked, 'won't they know we're here?'

Patch shrugged. 'Could go either way. These guys ain't rocket scientists, ma'am. They pretty damn stupid.'

'I've got a question,' Emmett said. 'How do they get the meat up here? And then back down? This doesn't seem very practical.'

From his position on the floor, Patch pushed aside a slab of beef to show a mechanical contraption next to the wall. 'See that? It's programmable from the kitchen. You tell it what you want—you know, beef, chicken, lamb— and the hook connects to the correct carcass and brings it down through a dumb waiter.'

'Well, shit!' Emmett said. 'Why don't we use that to get to the kitchen?'

'Don't work manually. Just with the computer. The head chef got real pissed off when they installed the damn thing and it didn't have any manual controls. Electricity goes off all the time on an island like this—can't tell you the number of times we've had to serve the guests a veggie meal 'cause they couldn't get to the meat.'

Not totally believing Patch, although he couldn't come up with a reason why he'd lie about it, Emmett went to the dumb waiter and tried to open it. It didn't budge. He kicked it, used implements; nothing worked. Patch just watched, and when Emmett sat back down, exhausted, Patch said, 'Man, I ain't no liar.'

'I didn't say you were,' Emmett said, panting.

'Whatja call trying to open that damn thing when I just tole you it was impossible? That's calling me a liar in my book,' Patch said.

Emmett just shook his head and leaned back against the wall.

Sweat was beading up on his face, back, and underarms, and after his exertion he was finding it hard to breathe.

He could smell Mr Thomas, a sickly odor of sweat and disease. He didn't know what afflicted the old man, but knew there was something. He'd hung around hospitals too long when J.R. was dying not to recognize the smell.

Mrs Thomas moved fitfully in her sleep, gasping occasionally for air. Which began to worry Emmett. They were in tightly sealed freezer units. Were they going to run out of breathable air?

At some point Emmett slept. By his watch it was late afternoon when he awoke, his fingers and toes numb. It took him a moment to realize he was cold. Very cold.

Using the flashlight to look around, he saw the others lying on the floor or leaning against wall space. All appeared asleep. He flashed the light on the hanging carcasses; they were frosting up.

He jumped up and began waking his fellow inmates. 'Leon, Patch, wake up! The electricity's back on! We're fixin' to freeze to death!'

It didn't take long in Charlie Smith's squad car, with lights and siren running, to get to Oklahoma City and, because Charlie had lived in the City for a while, it didn't take long to find Forest Lane, the street on which Elise

Hardy lived. It was a house in a newer subdivision, maybe built in the 1990s, and what trees had been planted originally were showing some healthy growth. The house that fit the number Elise Hardy had put on the slip of paper was a two-story white-brick number with green shutters and trim. The front yard held two good-sized trees, one of which had to have been there longer than the subdivision judging by its size. The yard was green and well trimmed, and there were neat round-topped shrubs along the front, all clipped to look a lot like mushrooms. The front had a long porch with a painted green porch rail, and the double front door was oak with beveled glass side windows and a beveled glass fan window at the top. Real pretty house on the outside.

I rang the bell, and in just a minute Elise Hardy came to the door. She was dressed casually in blue jeans and a knit top, her frosted hair pulled back in a ponytail and wearing little or no make-up.

'Sheriff!' she said, surprise in her voice. 'Chief?'

'Hey, Miz Hardy,' I said, and I woulda doffed my hat if I had one. 'Wonder if the Chief and I could come in for a minute? Got a couple more questions.'

She held the door open wide. 'Of course,' she said, ushering us in. 'Should I call my brother?' she asked.

'No need at this point, ma'am,' Charlie said. 'Unless, of course, you want to.'

Elise laughed slightly. 'No, I don't need my big brother's protection, Chief.' Looking at us quizzically, she said, 'Or do I?'

'Not on our account, ma'am,' I said, following her into her living room.

The interior of her house was as different as night and day from her daddy's. Where his had been empty of furniture or anything personal, his daughter's was full to the brim. The living room held two full-sized couches, two love seats, and two easy chairs, both with ottomans. The mantel was crowded with a collection of commemorative plates: china plates from different states, silver plates with Elvis's visage adorning it, or the moon walk, or 9/11. There were a bunch of tables sitting next to every couch, love seat and chair, all with a different style lamp and holding more knickknacks than you could shake a stick at. Glass-fronted bookcases covered one wall with more knick-knacks and a few books. She seemed to collect everything from the plates on the mantel to salt shakers to salt spoons to shot glasses to Fabergé-type eggs.

'Lovely room,' Charlie Smith said, and I hoped he was just being polite.

'Thank you,' Elise said, obviously pleased at his comment. Sitting down on one of the couches, she said, 'How can I help you, gentlemen?'

Charlie sat down on one of the love seats and I took the other, both of us facing Elise. 'Well, ma'am,' I said, 'I came upon something in your father's computer that I hoped you could clear up. Do you know a man by the name of Wilson Everett?'

For a second Elise looked taken aback, but then she smiled and said, 'Yes, I do. He's my fiancé.'

'Can you tell us where he is right now?' I asked.

'In Houston, on business,' she said, no longer smiling. 'May I ask why you're looking for him?'

Being in law enforcement as long as I've been, I knew the best technique for a question like that. Ignore it. 'And what kind of business is Mr Everett in?' I asked.

'He's in antiques and collectibles,' she said. Smiling again, she pointed to the glassed-in bookcases behind her. 'He specializes in antique salt spoons and Fabergé eggs,' she said. 'That's how we met.'

'When do you expect him back from Houston?' I asked.

'In a couple of days,' she said, then frowned. 'What is this about, Sheriff?'

'Ma'am, like I said, we found your fiancé's name on your father's computer. Seems he was checking Mr Everett out.'

Elise Hardy laughed. 'Checking him out? What do you mean?'

I looked at Charlie and he looked away. As if to say, 'This is your party, pal.' Well, I guess he was right about that. 'He discovered some things about Mr Everett that possibly you're not aware of,' I said, trying to gentle my way into this.

'Like what, for instance?' she said, and her voice was getting a might unfriendly.

'Like Wilson Everett isn't his real name. Near as I can tell, his real name's Everett Wilson. You know, he just switched it around.'

'Lots of people in his line of work will use a more...' She searched for a word, finally came up with, '...interesting name. So he switched it around. I don't understand the problem.'

'He's used a lot more names than just those two,' I said. 'And he's got a record under several of his names.'

Elise Hardy's posture had gotten stiffer and stiffer as I talked, and now she was sitting on the couch ramrod straight. 'What kind of record?' she asked.

'Mostly fraud, check-kiting, running confidence scams,' I said, ashamed and embarrassed having to tell this nice lady such news. Shoulda left it up to the Feds, I told myself. That'll teach me to get tricky.

Elise Hardy began to shake her head. 'I don't understand,' she said.

'Ma'am,' I said, 'did your dad ever meet Mr Everett?'

'Yes, of course! At Thanksgiving. And Christmas. And we went for a visit a couple of weeks ago. No, maybe more like a month. Late February, early March.' She took a deep breath, her shoulders slumping. 'I don't understand any of this,' she said.

'Well, ma'am, worst case scenario, he had something to do with the bank robbery and your father's death. Second worst, he maybe targeted you because of your lottery winnings,' Charlie Smith said.

I wanted to kick him, but it was the right thing to do.

Elise Hardy stood up quickly. 'I think you need to leave now,' she said, her eyes brimming with tears.

Charlie and I both stood up. 'Ma'am, we'd appreciate it if you didn't say anything to Mr Everett about our visit. If he was involved—'

'Get out!' she screamed at us, already at the door with it open. 'Just get the hell out!'

We walked to the door. I tried to touch her on the arm but she drew back. 'Ma'am, I'm so sorry—' I started, but she didn't let me finish.

'Get out!' she said, her teeth gritted.

Me and Charlie left.

EVERYBODY AWOKE TO Emmett's command, except Mrs Thomas. Her husband bent over her, rubbing her hands, shaking her. But nothing was happening. Emmett knelt down beside her. She was cold all right. Dead cold.

'Naomi?' Mr Thomas kept saying. 'Naomi, dear, wake up!'

Emmett pulled the distraught old man away from his wife. 'Mr Thomas, I'm sorry, but she's gone.'

'No!' he shouted.

Emmett quickly put his hand over the old man's mouth, and everyone stood very still, waiting for some sign from below that they'd been heard. After a couple of minutes, Emmett removed his hand from Mr Thomas's mouth.

'I'm sorry, sir, I really am. But we've all got to get out of here—'

'I'm staying with Naomi,' Mr Thomas said. 'You all go on without me.'

Patch and Leon looked at each other and nodded, thinking that was the best idea they'd heard in a while, but neither Emmett nor Jasmine agreed with it.

'Mr Thomas,' Jasmine said, taking his cold hands in hers, 'George, she's at peace now. She doesn't have to run and hide from these people any more, but we do. You do. You have to get out of here so you can tell the authorities how your wife died and who's to blame. You can't stay here, George. You have to go with us. You have to be the one to tell your children.'

He nodded at that. 'Yes,' he said. 'The kids. They need to know.'

Emmett turned to Leon and Patch. 'Can we use the dumb waiter now?'

Leon went over to it, looking at it. 'It makes a hell of a racket,' he said. He frowned, looking at Emmett. 'What if they're in the kitchen? Or even in the hallways outside the kitchen? They'd hear it for sure.'

'What other choice do we have?' Emmett asked.

'Well, I've been looking at that vent up there,' Leon said, pointing to a large vent. 'I think that's part of the regular air-conditioning system, not the freezing system. This used to be something else before they turned it into another freezer. It's been blocked off but we should be able to open it.'

'Then what?' Emmett asked.

'Then we crawl through to someplace else,' Patch said. 'These vents go all over the hotel. Just like in the movies. I doubt if they're as big as in the movies, but I think we can make it. We just gotta be quiet is all, so the pirates don't hear us.'

Emmett looked at Jasmine, who shrugged. 'Better than any idea I've come up with,' she said to her husband.

Emmett nodded. 'OK,' he said to the hotel employees, 'let's get that sucker open.'

ME AND CHARLIE WERE real quiet driving back to Long-branch. No sirens or lights this time. Charlie dropped me off at the shop around three in the afternoon and I sat down at my desk, determined now to stay the hell out of the investigation. I didn't need to have a thing to do with it, and messing with what wasn't my business just got me all jacked up. I felt horrible about Elise Hardy and the damage we'd done her, but still and all, it was something she needed to know.

Charlie called me around four p.m. and told me the insurance money was coming in that day and that the Feebies had asked for the full force of the police department to watch over the transfer from the armored car to the bank, and for guards to be placed there throughout the night. I told him that sounded like a good idea.

'Yeah, and what about the rest of the town while this is going on? It's gonna be the wedding all over again, Milt. My whole force will be at the bank, so what are they gonna hit this time?'

'You wanna borrow a deputy?' I asked.

'No, I wanna borrow you. You and me, bro, we're gonna keep an eye on the rest of the town. Money's coming in this evening at six o'clock. My guys have to be in place by five. So the town's gonna be defenseless from like five to seven. Plenty of time to do damage.'

'Where?' I asked. 'There's no money in town except at
the bank, Charlie.'

'What about Quibbies?' Charlie demanded, referring to
the local grocery store, which used to do a mostly cash and
carry business until the bank started issuing debit cards.
So I mentioned that.

'Not everybody in Prophesy County's got a checking
account, Milt,' Charlie protested. 'Lots of people still use
cash. And what if they hit a lot of stores? Not just Quibbies? We don't know how many are in this gang. Could
be a bunch of 'em. This ain't right, Milt! I'm telling you,
something's gonna happen!'

So I called Jean and told her I'd be late getting home
and not to hold supper for me. I figured if I had to stay in
town, I might as well have dinner at the Longbranch Inn,
having missed lunch while in the City. Me and Charlie
could chow down once his men were back in place. 'Sides,
it was Monday, which is vegetarian day at our house, and
the thought of a rare steak with a side of baby back ribs
at the Longbranch sounded a lot more appetizing than
going home. If I remembered correctly, tonight's menu
had something to do with roasted beets with asparagus
and lentil soup. It was a shame, a real shame, but I guess
I was gonna have to miss it.

Come five o'clock, me and Charlie drove around in his
car, keeping an eye on every shop in town. People closed
up, pulling in sidewalk display stuff, pulling down security gates, generally heading home. Nothing else happened. Nobody slinking around the back alleys in a black
turtleneck and ski mask, no alarms, silent or otherwise.
Just business as usual—or no business, as usual.

The transfer of funds went smooth as glass, Dewayne
Dickey locked up the bank tight and waved goodbye to
me and Charlie and his troops. One police officer stayed

inside the bank, while another stood guard outside. The rest, four of 'em, went back to the shop, two to go home, two to stay on duty.

That's when I suggested me and Charlie go to the Longbranch for some supper. 'Best idea I heard all day. Wife's got me on a diet,' Charlie said. 'I go home, all I'll get to eat is carrot sticks and celery.'

'Sounds as bad as my house. I'm thinking a steak. Rare and juicy, with hash browns and some black-eyed peas.'

'Sounds like a plan,' he said, and we headed for the Longbranch. The first person I saw on entering the restaurant part of the inn was Agnes Shorewalter, the hippy lady with the Satanic cult in her backyard. I tried keeping my back to her as me and Charlie found a table, but she saw me anyway and came over to the table.

'Miz Shorewalter,' I said, standing up when she accosted me. She was wearing another bright-colored muumuu-caftan thingy, and her gray braid was wrapped around her head like an old German lady in a storybook.

'Sheriff!' she said by way of greeting, and I noticed her usual happy-looking face was missing. The face she presented me was anything but happy.

'Yes, ma'am?'

'You've got to *do* something!' she said, taking an empty chair and sitting down. 'I've got throngs of people traipsing through my garden! How organic can my produce be when it's got footprints all over it?'

'They trying to find the Satanic site?' I asked.

She threw up her hands. 'Yes! I wouldn't even have told you about it if I thought it would cause all this ruckus! Have you found these Satan worshipers yet?'

I didn't mention that *I* didn't tell anyone; *she* did. That would have been tacky, and I try never to be tacky. I answered, 'No, ma'am, haven't found out anything about that yet. This whole bank robbery thing has taken up most of my time.'

'Well, they're probably related,' she said.

'How so?' I asked.

She looked at me like I was a slow learner. 'Bank robbery? Satan worshiping? You don't see the connection?'

'No, ma'am,' I said, trying to keep a straight face as Charlie Smith rolled his eyes behind Agnes Shorewalter's back.

'They need money for their cause! Believe me, I've been involved with enough causes to know, you need money! Not that I've ever been into Satan worshiping. In my humble opinion, that's just silly. But each to their own, I say. Unless you trample on other people's rights. Like mine! They came on my property to do this and now I've got everybody and their sister traipsing through my land to get a look at it! I just can't have that, Sheriff. I want you to post my land and have a deputy there around the clock!'

'I'm afraid I can't do that, Ms Shorewalter,' I said. 'We're running low on deputies. Don't have enough manpower as it is.'

'People power,' Agnes said.

'Excuse me?' I said.

'You said "manpower". That's misogynistic, elitist and just plain wrong. You should say "people power".'

'Oh,' I said. 'OK. I don't have enough people power as it is.'

'Well, you have to do *something*! I just can't have this!'

'I'll look into it,' I said, as Loretta brought our menus and set-ups.

'You better do more than look into it, Sheriff!' she said, standing up, all three hundred and something pounds looming over me like the Angel of Death.

I pushed my chair back and stood up, like my mama

taught me to do in the presence of a lady. But then my mama never said anything about a lady threatening me, which is what I think Agnes Shorewalter just did. 'Ma'am,' I said, 'I'll do my best.'

She made a sound that sounded like 'humph', then turned and stalked off.

Charlie, who'd stood up when Agnes did, just like *his* mama taught *him*, said, 'I think you're in serious trouble, Milt.'

We both sat down and picked up our menus. 'Tell me something I *don't* know,' I said, and stuck my nose in amongst the fried chicken livers and chicken fried steak.

SEVEN

I DIDN'T GET HOME 'til around nine. And believe me I was some surprised when I saw a big old Lincoln town car sitting in my driveway. The vanity tag said 'Banker', so I knew without going inside that either Dewayne Dickey or LaDonna, or both, were here. Which would be the first time we'd ever been so blessed. I thought about turning around and going back to the office, but then I thought of what my wife would say to that, so I parked the Jeep and got out.

Dewayne Dickey sat in the living room with Johnny Mac on his knee. I thought my son had better taste than that, but he was busy laughing at Dewayne and pulling at his ear. When Dewayne saw me, he sat Johnny Mac on the floor and stood up.

'Milt,' he said.

'Dewayne, to what do we owe this honor?' I said.

'Hi, honey,' my wife said, coming over to pretend to kiss my cheek. Instead she whispered in my ear, 'Be nice.'

'Can I speak to you in private, please?' Dewayne said.

Well, since he said please. I looked at Jean who said, 'Time for John's bath. Nice to see you, Dewayne.' She took Johnny Mac's hand and headed for the stairs.

'You, too, Jean. You take care now, John,' he said.

'Bye, Mr Dick,' my son said. Boy, did he have that right.

I waved Dewayne to a chair and took one myself. 'What can I do for you, Dewayne?' I asked.

I noticed Dewayne's face kept changing from too pale

to too red. 'I've got something to tell you, Milt, and it has to be in strictest confidence. You can't tell anyone, and until I have that promise from you, I can't say anything.'

Keeping secrets with Dewayne Dickey wasn't my idea of a fun evening, but I promised just the same.

After I did, Dewayne took a huge gulp of air and said, 'They got LaDonna.'

'Who's got LaDonna?' I asked, visions of Satan worshippers tying my ex-wife to a sacrificial alter dancing in my head.

'The bank robbers,' Dewayne said, and started to cry.

I moved my chair closer to his and touched his arm. 'Hold on, now, Dewayne. Tell me what happened. Start from the beginning.'

He gulped in air and tried to steady himself. 'I…I got home right after I left y'all at the bank. All the lights were on, just like usual. But LaDonna wasn't in the kitchen. Instead, the kitchen was all messed up. Dishes on the floor, food on the floor.' He looked at me, his eyes pleading. 'You know LaDonna, she keeps a real neat kitchen.'

'Yes, sir,' I agreed, 'that she does. When was the last time you talked to LaDonna?'

'Right before I left the bank. I called to tell her I was on my way home. She was fine, Milt. I swear she was. She asked me to stop and get some margarine on the way home, but I reminded her we had some in the freezer. And she laughed. Milt, she wouldn't have laughed if they had her then, would she? And she said, "You're right, I remember now".'

'How do you know the bank robbers have her? Hell, she mighta cut herself and drove herself to the hospital—'

''Cause they called me, that's why!' he said, almost shouting. 'They called me,' he said more calmly. 'They said they had her and that they'd kill her if I didn't bring them the money the insurance paid off! They said if I told anybody they'd send me an ear in the mail! They said if I didn't get it to 'em by midnight tonight, I'd get an ear in the mail! They said if I didn't come alone I'd get an ear in the mail!' The tears were running freely down his face. 'Milt, what am I gonna do?'

'We gotta call the Feds,' I said.

'No!' he shouted, standing up. 'You promised me! You promised you wouldn't tell anyone! They said if I told the cops they'd hurt her, Milt! For God's sake, do you still hate her that much?'

I stood up and put my hands on his arms. 'Calm down, Dewayne. You know I don't hate LaDonna. We drifted apart, we didn't have some big fight or cheat on each other or anything. I'm real glad LaDonna has someone like you in her life, Dewayne. Someone who loves her this much.'

He crumpled in my arms, crying. I patted his back and said, 'If we can't call the Feds, then we gotta do this ourselves, right?' I could feel him nod against my chest. 'You got any ideas?' I could feel his head shake. 'OK, we gotta get that money out of the vault, but it's gonna be kinda hard with two policemen guarding it. Sure would be easier if we could at least get Charlie Smith in on this. Then he could call off the guards and we could get in there.'

Dewayne backed away from me. 'No! No police. No Feds! Just you! Milt,' he said, his eyes haunted, 'you're the only one I trust.'

Lord Almighty, that was a low blow. Dewayne Dickey just put my ex-wife's life in my hands. It woulda been better if he'd just poured boiling water over my head.

Jean came down the stairs. Me and Dewayne both looked up. 'I'm sorry,' she said, taking Dewayne's hands. 'I heard. I shouldn't have been listening, but I did just the same.'

'You can't tell—' Dewayne started.

'I won't,' she said.

I was relieved. I didn't like to lie to my wife, and if she hadn't already known what was going on, I woulda had to. And I was relieved for another reason. Jean's a smart woman. She's a psychiatrist. She knows how people think. I could sure use her input on this.

'What do you think?' I asked her.

'I think we need to do exactly what they say,' Jean said. 'This group has already killed two people—Neal Hardy and Billy Johansson. I don't think we need to pretend that they won't hurt LaDonna.'

'Oh, my God, oh, my God,' Dewayne said over and over under his breath.

'Dewayne, do you want a sedative?' Jean asked. 'I can get you something.'

'No, no,' he said, shaking his head. 'I gotta stay alert. I gotta get LaDonna back.'

'That's your call,' she said. She used her crutches to come into the room and sit down. 'They said they want the money by midnight, right?'

Dewayne nodded.

'Where's the drop-off?' Jean asked.

'County Road seventeen, the old Maxwell place. Supposed to leave the bag in a bucket in the old well, then lower the bucket down. Then get back in my car and go home.'

'Nobody's living out there anymore,' I said. 'Place has been abandoned for years.'

'No neighbors for miles,' Dewayne said. 'Fields are still wide open though, no place for you to hide,' he said, looking at me.

'Chances are they've had someone there since they

called you,' Jean said. 'So it wouldn't do any good for Milt to go out there now. They'd see him.'

'Best thing would be to hide in Dewayne's car,' I said, looking at my wife.

'Then what? Jump out and say boo?' she asked me.

I shrugged. 'I'm working this by the seat of my pants, Jean,' I said.

'I'm not criticizing,' she said. 'Just trying to help you think it out.'

I nodded. 'Yeah, I know.' I sighed. 'I'm trying to think of the layout of the Maxwell place. Dewayne, isn't there a mimosa tree by that well? Pretty big one?'

'Yeah,' he said, thinking. 'Pretty sure there is. Always thought that was dumb, planting a mimosa by a well. All that crap that falls off a mimosa all the time.'

'Did they say where you were supposed to park?' I asked him.

'Next to the well, is all,' Dewayne said.

'Then we pull up next to the mimosa, I roll out and hit the ground, stay low, between the well and the tree. They won't see me.'

'Then what?' Jean asked.

'Then I grab 'em when they come for the money.'

'And how does that get LaDonna back?' Jean asked. 'I doubt they'll have her with them. They never do in the movies.'

I thought about it. She was right. It was a dumb idea. Then I thought of something. It just might work, but it would mean breaking my promise to Dewayne.

THERE WERE MEAT HOOKS hanging on the walls of the freezer unit that worked as well as any crowbar in removing the boards from the vent. Beneath the boards was the air-conditioning vent cover, which was also fairly easy to remove. The problem was going to be getting everybody up there. They didn't have the luxury of an extendable ladder like they'd had getting into the upper freezer unit.

'OK,' Emmett said, eyeing the hole into the venting system. 'Let's do Mr Thomas first. Sir, if you'd come over here—'

'We have to take Naomi with us,' the old man said.

'Sir, we can't,' Emmett said. 'She'll be better off here. When the authorities show up, we'll get her down and transport her home with you, OK?'

'I want to take her with me,' the old man insisted.

Patch, arms akimbo, said, 'Look, old man, it ain't gonna happen. Jest give it up.'

'Patch!' Jasmine said. Turning to the old man, she put her hand on his arm and said, 'George, we have to leave Naomi here. But it won't be for long, like Emmett said. There's just no way we can drag her through those vents, George. It would be cruel to do it.'

He nodded his head. 'You're right,' he said. 'I know you are, but I just can't… We've been together for so long, I just can't abandon her here like this.'

Jasmine looked at the rest of the group. Leon was wearing nothing but his Tweety Bird boxers, Emmett had on a white T-shirt and striped boxers, and she was just wearing one of Emmett's T-shirts over her panties. Only Patch and Mr and Mrs Thomas were fully clothed, and Patch was wearing an extra large Hawaiian shirt.

'Patch,' Jasmine said, 'give me your shirt.'

'Say what?'

'Now!' she said.

Mumbling under his breath, Patch took off his shirt, revealing a skinny, hairless chest. 'Whatja want my shirt for anyway?' he asked.

Jasmine took it and placed it over Mrs Thomas, covering her face and most of her chest. She looked up at Mr Thomas. He nodded and headed for the vent.

'I'm ready now,' the old man said.

It took Emmett, Patch and Leon all three to heft the old man up to the vent. His upper-body strength was greatly limited, and Emmett and Patch put their hands together to lift Leon up to help the old man into the venting system. There was a lot of grunting from the old man, a lot of cursing from the younger one, and a couple of 'ouches' and 'watch what you're doings' from Emmett and Patch, but they got him up there, with Leon right behind.

Emmett and Patch got Jasmine up, then Emmett boosted Patch up, leaving Emmett below. Emmett handed up the two twelve-gauges, the .357 and the lantern/flashlight. With no one to help lift him into the vent, all Emmett could do was try to jump to reach the outstretched hands from above. But just as he was about to, he heard the door to the freezer unit below open.

Everyone stopped what they were doing, waiting. Emmett motioned Leon and Patch back further into the vent, while he laid on the floor, trying to listen and to see through the small crack around the extendable ladder. The light from the open doorway to the freezer illuminated the men below.

'I thought we got all we was gonna get outta here,' said the same English voice they'd heard earlier.

'Yeah, well where's the meat?' came another voice, either Australian or New Zealand.

The first said, 'Where's the beef?' and laughed like crazy—crazy being the word that scared Emmett the most. 'Remember that Yank ad on the telly? Where's the beef?'

'Shut up, you wanker,' said the second voice.

'Wanker? Who you calling a wanker?' And the first man shoved the second man.

The second man pulled a knife, shoving the first man against the wall, the knife at his throat.

The first man laughed uneasily and said, 'Terry, me boyo, it was a joke. Just a little joke.'

'I don't got a sense of humor,' the Aussie, the man called Terry, said.

The door opened and a third man joined the fray. Dark with a drooping black mustache, the third man had a decidedly Hispanic accent when he said, 'Whatja doing, guys? Huh? We got shit to get here and you guys are fucking around—'

'There weren't no meat,' Terry said. 'There should be meat. I ain't ate nothing but fish in three months! I want some red meat! These fancy hotels don't serve nothing but fruits and vegetables. Where's the meat?'

'Where's the beef?' the Hispanic man said, hitting the first man in the ribs and both laughing.

'I don't watch the fucking telly and I don't know shit about where's the fucking beef!' Terry shouted. 'I want some meat! It's been months since we had any red meat, goddamn it, and I want some fucking red meat!' To emphasize his desire for protein, Terry shoved the knife into the wall, less than an inch from the first man's ear.

The Hispanic man laughed. 'Hey, Kev, he almost took your ear off! You be like that painter with only one ear!'

Then the one named Terry, obviously ignoring the art history reference, looked up, and as far as Emmett could tell, stared straight at him. Emmett jerked back, afraid he'd been seen.

'Lookie here, you assholes,' Terry said. Emmett could see him point at him. 'There's a trap door up there. I'll be a dingo's pecker if there ain't meat up there! Oz,' he said to the Hispanic, 'give me a lift up!'

Leon and Patch were back at the vent hole, waving their arms at Emmett and mouthing, 'Get up here!'

Other than jumping, which would make a noise loud enough to be heard from below, even with the storm still raging outside, Emmett could think of no other way to get up. Then Leon pointed at one of the sides of beef. 'Climb it!' he mouthed. Then, 'Hurry!'

Emmett pulled on the side of beef hanging from a hook in the ceiling of the room. It seemed secure. He put his arms around the top of the slab, got a foothold in the bottom, and lifted himself up. That's when he heard the sound of meat tearing.

The slab of beef came down, Emmett attached, and crashed through the trap door to the freezer room below.

IT WAS CLOSE TO eleven o'clock before Charlie showed up. It had taken some mighty convincing to get Dewayne to agree to call Charlie in, and it had taken more convincing to get Charlie to come to the house without telling him why. Making him go to the police station to pick up some equipment for me took even more convincing.

'What the hell's going on?' Charlie asked when I opened the door to his knock.

'Come on in, Charlie,' I said, ushering him into the living room. 'You remember my wife, Jean, and Dewayne here.'

'Of course,' he said, shaking hands with Jean and then Dewayne. He then shot me a look.

'Something's come up, Charlie. You better sit down,' I said.

'Would you like a cup of coffee?' Jean asked. 'I've got a pot of decaf made.'

'Yes, ma'am, thank you,' Charlie said. While Jean left the room, he took one of the easy chairs and said, 'What's up?'

'Well, here's the deal,' I said, then looked at Dewayne. He just looked at me, not saying a word, so I said, 'We've got a bit of a problem.'

'You said that,' Charlie said.

'Right. Well, while we were all at the bank, like you suspected, something else was going down,' I said.

Charlie shot up out of his seat. 'I told you!' he said, too loudly. I hushed him, pointing upstairs to where my son hopefully slept. Somewhat more quietly, Charlie said, 'Didn't I tell you they'd try something?'

'Yeah, Charlie, you sure did,' I said.

Sitting back down, a smug look on his face, Charlie said, 'So what'd they steal?'

'My wife!' Dewayne said, then sat down himself, head in hands, and started bawling. Hey, I'm a liberated man, sort of, and I have no problem with a man shedding tears, but I have to admit Dewayne was getting on my nerves. There's such a thing as manly sniffles, a far cry from girlish slobbering, which is what Dewayne was up to.

Charlie looked from Dewayne to me then back again. Finally, looking at me, as it was a little embarrassing to look at Dewayne, Charlie said, 'Huh?'

'While your guys and Dewayne here and the Feebies were securing the bank, and you and me were out checking out the rest of the town, the bad guys were out at Dewayne's house kidnapping his wife, who happens to be my ex-wife, in case I never mentioned that,' I said.

'No, don't believe you did ever mention that,' he said, looking at Dewayne. 'They kidnapped his *wife*?' Charlie stage-whispered to me. I nodded my head. 'Sweet Jesus!' he muttered under his breath. 'We hear anything from the perps?'

'Yeah,' I started, but Charlie's mind had gone on.

'I told you! Didn't I tell you? I said something was

gonna happen when everybody was at the bank! Shit, we were just guarding the wrong places!' He slapped both hands to his knees. 'Well, we gotta call the goddam Feds,' he said.

'No!' Dewayne said, jumping up. 'I told you! I told Milt! I wasn't supposed to tell anybody and now three people know and two of 'em are cops! Oh, my God! They're gonna kill her! You can't call the Feds!'

I looked at Charlie. 'We can't call the Feds,' I said.

'We're not equipped to handle a kidnapping, Milt! You know that!'

'I got a plan,' I said.

But before I ever got the plan out of my mouth, there was a knock on the front door. I looked at Dewayne, who looked at Charlie, and then we all turned to look at my wife who was just coming out of the kitchen.

'It's not me,' she said, finagling the tray of coffee cups and such.

'I'll get it,' I said. Still in my work clothes, my service revolver was still holstered at my side. I took my gun out, holding it behind me, and went to the door, peeking through the peephole.

I'm not sure who I expected to see, but it sure as hell wasn't Max Hardy, Neal Hardy's son.

I shoved the gun back in my holster and opened the door. 'Mr Hardy?' I said.

He brushed past me into the foyer. 'What the hell did you think you were doing? Huh? You had no right to bother my sister that way!'

'Whoa! Hold on now, Mr Hardy. We interviewed your sister on official police business, following up leads in your father's murder. I thought the two of you might be happy to know before she marries Wilson Everett that he's a con artist!'

Looking past me at the people in the living room, he said, 'Is there someplace private we can talk?'

The little room between the dining room and the master bedroom that had been Johnny Mac's nursery had been converted into a home office that Jean and I shared. It wasn't that big, so Jean had bought an antique partner's desk (don't even ask how much that cost!) and put in a love seat against the wall. I took one of the two office chairs and indicated Max Hardy take the couch.

'Mr Hardy,' I said. 'I'm sorry if we upset your sister, but your father obviously had plans to tell her about this fiancé of hers. He's a con man, plain and simple. Your sister's got a shit-pot full of money from the lottery winnings, more now what with your daddy dying and all, so I'm sure that's why she was targeted. Her getting more money because of your father's death makes him a suspect in your father's murder.'

'Look, I know Wilson Everett and, believe me, he hasn't got the brains to rob a bank. I'm not disputing that he's a scumbag and the fact that he's a con artist doesn't really surprise me. What surprises me, Sheriff, is that you would so cavalierly drop this bombshell on my sister!'

I was puzzled. 'Why wouldn't we, Mr Hardy? She's a grown woman and it's her business. Not yours. I shouldn't even be discussing this with you.'

He shook his head and for once I saw real concern on his face. 'Look, I know I'm an over-protective big brother, but Elise has been through hell and gone, OK? Her long-time boyfriend, high school and college, was in the Gulf War. He came back without legs. Elise tried to stand by him, said she loved him, that it didn't really matter to her, and you know, I really don't think it did. She would have done anything for Brett. But he called off their wedding, refused to see her. But she still went over to his mother's house every day. He wouldn't see her, but she did for him; washed his clothes, helped cook his meals, anything she could do. Then, six months after he got home, he killed himself. Shot himself. She was alone in the house with him at the time. She found him.'

'Ah, Jesus, Mr Hardy. That's awful. I'm so sorry,' I said.

As if not hearing me, he continued, 'Then, three months later our mother finds out she's got breast cancer. Elise nursed her for over a year. That was five years ago. Elise didn't even date. She didn't want anything to do with any-one, until she met Wilson Everett. I knew he was a scum-bag, but I couldn't tell her. You understand? I just couldn't tell her!'

'Of course you couldn't, Max,' I said, moving to the love seat to sit beside him, patting him on the back. 'You didn't have any facts to back it. I had facts, Max. I gave her those facts. Better she finds out now before she gives him all her money and he runs off on her.'

He nodded his head. 'I know, I know,' he said, head hanging low. 'God, we used to be such a normal family. Ozzie and Harriet, Leave it to Beaver. That was the Hardy family. Then one tragedy led to another and now Dad—and that asshole Wilson!'

'Look, you think he could be involved in what's hap-pened here? You think he knew your dad was looking into him?'

Max Hardy shook his head. 'I don't see how. But I don't know really. I tried to stay out of Elise's business, only met the guy a few times. She invited my wife and I over for dinner and we had to reciprocate, although I couldn't stand the guy first time I met him. Very...' He thought for a moment, then said, 'Smarmy. Know what I mean?'

I nodded. 'Look, I'm in the middle of something here,

something to do with the bank robbery, and I've got to leave. I hate to ask you to leave right now, but…'

'If it's got something to do with the bank robbery, then it has something to do with my father's murder. I'll go with you.'

'Ah, not a good idea, Max.'

Max Hardy stood up. 'I won't get in the way, I promise.'

This thing was getting a little out of hand. From the other room we could hear the beginning of a commotion, then words got to our ears.

'You can't call the Feds!' Dewayne shouted. 'They'll kill my wife!'

'Ah, you see, Max,' I started, trying to distract him from what was going on in the other room. He held up a hand to shush me, just as Charlie Smith said, 'It's a kidnapping, Dewayne! That's Federal!'

Max turned and looked at me. 'Somebody's been kidnapped. You don't want the FBI to know for some reason. That's what you're up to.'

'Maybe we can discuss this later—' I started but Max Hardy was shaking his head.

'Uh uh,' he said emphatically. 'This has got to do with the bank robbery, right?' He didn't wait for an answer. 'Whatever y'all are doing, I'm in on it.'

'Now, you see, Max, you're a civilian—'

'Who can very easily go to the FBI and tell them what you're doing,' he said.

I threw up my hands in disgust. This was getting way out of control.

SEVERAL THINGS HAPPENED when Emmett and the side of beef fell through the trap door into the bottom freezer unit. Kev, the Englishman, screamed; Oz the Hispanic and Terry the Aussie, who'd both been hit by the side of beef, scrambled out from under and grabbed their knives; and, like manna from Heaven, the .357 Magnum fell into Emmett's lap. Emmett grabbed the gun, sat up with his back against the wall, and pointed it at the three men staring at him.

'*Buenos dios*!' the Hispanic said, crossing himself.

'Who the fuck are you?' Terry said.

'Shut the door!' Emmett said to Kev, the one standing closest to the freezer unit door.

Kev did as he said.

'I asked you a question!' Terry shouted.

'One more shout out of you,' Emmett said, 'and I'll blow off your kneecap!'

'He's a bloody Yank!' Kev said.

'You work here?' Terry asked.

'How many more of you are there?' Emmett asked.

'There's three of us here, asshole, and only one you and one gun. We rush you, you might take one of us but two of us is gonna gut you like a fuckin' chicken!' Terry said.

Emmett moved the gun slowly between the three of them. 'OK,' he said. 'Which one of you wants to commit suicide?'

I CAME BACK INTO the living room, followed by Max Hardy. 'We got a problem,' I said.

My wife stood up. 'Another cup of coffee?' she asked.

I looked at Max who said, 'Decaf?'

Jean said, 'Of course,' and left the room.

Charlie stood up and Dewayne just sat where he was, head in hands, mumbling under his breath.

'What's up?' Charlie asked.

'Mr Hardy here thinks he should be involved with what's going on,' I said.

Charlie looked at me like he would at a two-bit felon

going down for the third time. 'Milt,' he said, and that one word said it all.

'I know, I know. But y'all were talking too loud and he heard everything and now he's threatening to go to the Feds,' I said, letting the information rush out of my mouth.

Dewayne, who must have been listening with half an ear, let out a wail like a tribal woman in a National Geographic special. 'You're killing her! You're killing her!' he screamed.

Jean came back in the room with Max's cup of decaf and said, 'Dewayne, please be quiet. My son is trying to sleep.'

Dewayne looked up at her with red-rimmed eyes and said, 'Sorry.'

Jean handed Max the coffee and sat back down, setting her crutches next to her chair. 'That's OK, Dewayne, I understand the need to grieve. Just try to keep it down.'

He nodded his head and began to blubber again. Although he did it real quiet-like.

'Well, he's right,' Charlie said, nodding his head toward Max Hardy. 'We need to call the Feds.'

'You trust those two to get LaDonna back alive?' I asked him, while Dewayne's sobbing grew stronger.

Charlie sighed. Finally he said, 'No. But...' Again he looked at Hardy. 'Milt, we got no business dragging another civilian into this. Bad enough we're gonna have to deal with Dewayne here,' he said, pointing over his shoulder at the slobbering bank president. 'And besides, what are we going to do about this anyway?'

'Well, I got a plan,' I started.

Charlie rolled his eyes. 'This I gotta hear,' he said.

'Did you bring your new toy?' I asked Charlie.

'Yeah, but what are you gonna do with a GPS locator? You gotta have something to stick it to,' he said.

Jean motioned for me to follow her into the kitchen,

and I went and helped her bring in a tray laden with some homemade bread she'd baked earlier that day in her bread machine. It was cinnamon with raisins and nuts—serious good eating. 'I'm beginning to see where you're going, Milt,' she said, taking a seat. 'And you can just forget it.'

'No, no,' Dewayne said, finally having quit the blubbering and wiggling his butt on the ottoman, real excited-like. 'I think I get it. Milt, this could work! It really could!'

'What?' Charlie said, his voice kinda loud in the room.

Jean and I both looked at him and said 'Shhh' at the same time. I mean, after all, even if this was police work, our son was still asleep upstairs.

So I told him the plan about being in the back of Dewayne's Lincoln when he pulled up close to the mimosa tree next to the well, slipping out and hiding, and then sticking the GPS thingy on the underside of the kidnappers' car.

'And what if they don't drive up close to the mimosa tree?' Jean asked. 'What if they don't drive up at all? What if they're hiding in the old Maxwell house and just walk up? Are you going to stick that thing on their butts, or what?'

Have I mentioned that my wife has made the fine art of sarcasm her own? Refined it and honed it to razor-sharpness?

'She's got a point,' Charlie said. Then he looked at the bottom of the locator. ''Sides, this thing doesn't have any stick-um on it, far as I can see.'

'Jean, where's that Crazy Glue I used to fix Johnny Mac's toy truck last week?'

Jean threw up her hands. 'You're out of your mind, Milt! Best case scenario, someone drives up—next to the mimosa—you crawl under the car, get out the Crazy Glue and that *thing*,' she said, pointing at the GPS monitor, 'and try to glue it on. Except you do like you did with John's truck and get the glue all over you, stick yourself to the device and the car drives off with you dragging behind it!'

I heard a slight sound and looked to my left where Max Hardy was sitting on the couch. His hand was covering his mouth, but I could tell he was suppressing a laugh. This I could do without.

OK, so it wasn't the best plan I'd ever had, but it was better than anyone else was coming up with.

'We need to call the FBI,' Charlie said.

'No!' Dewayne yelled. Me and Jean 'shhh'd' him. 'No,' he said more quietly. 'Look, I understand where you guys are coming from. But this is my wife! You're gonna get her killed if you call the FBI! Do you trust those two to do this right?' he asked, looking from me to Charlie and back again.

Charlie and I looked at each other. 'No,' he said.

''Sides,' Dewayne said, frowning, 'have you noticed how those two look like "X-Files" clones?'

Finally, someone else got it, and it had to be Dewayne. I hated to think that my mind worked anything like his.

'OK,' Charlie said, rubbing his hands together. 'We go with Milt's idea, but we refine it a bit.'

Jean rolled her eyes, Dewayne and Max Hardy both looked excited, and I started getting nervous.

EIGHT

IT TOOK ALL THE STRENGTH both Leon and Patch had to drag Jasmine away from the vent opening.

'I threw him the .357, Jas,' Leon whispered. 'He knows what to do with it. He'll be OK!'

'We can't leave him!' she whispered back, trying to get past the two men to get out of the vent.

'You think he'd want you to go down there, Jasmine?' Mr Thomas whispered to her. 'You think he'd want you to endanger yourself and the baby?'

Jasmine stopped struggling. Mr Thomas reached beyond Patch and took Jasmine's hand. 'My dear, he's alive. Better than my Naomi. And he's an armed policeman. He can take care of himself better than we can. You know that. We have to go somewhere to find help. That's all we can do for your Emmett now.'

Jasmine nodded, a giant lump in her throat. But she wasn't going to cry, hormones or not. She wasn't going to cry. She took a deep breath and said, 'OK, Patch, Leon, where to?'

Leon crawled over Mr Thomas to lead the way. 'I'm thinking the kitchen for food first, then they'd do the office for cash. They should be through there by now. If we get to the office, maybe the phones are back up.'

Jasmine said, 'Let's go,' and followed, with Leon and Mr Thomas ahead of her, Patch behind.

She noticed another thing that was different about these vents from the ones in the movies. Not only were they much smaller, they were dirty. The ones in the movies were all shiny aluminum; the one she was in had cobwebs, dust mites, sticky unidentifiable stuff, and the occasional roach.

Jasmine moved on with the others, until Leon stopped, holding up his hand like a traffic cop to indicate they all stop. He pointed in front of him at the vent and mouthed, 'We're here.'

Jasmine motioned for Patch to back up, which he did, allowing her to lay down on her side and rest. She was nauseous again, and the last thing she wanted to do was vomit in these vents. Not only would it be worse than gross, she thought, the way she wretched she'd call attention to them. So she lay there, breathing in through her nose and out through her mouth, closing her eyes and picturing her baby in its little room she and Emmett would build for it, all pink and white with ballerinas and fairies if it was a girl, all brown and blue with footballs and cowboys if it was a boy.

She heard a noise at the front of the line and looked up. Leon was taking the vent off. 'It's clear,' he whispered.

'It's clear,' Jasmine whispered back to Patch.

He nodded. Jasmine could see the sweat beading the man's face and bare chest, hear his ragged breathing. 'You OK?' she asked him.

Again he nodded, then said, 'Got a little problem with small spaces.'

'We'll be out of here soon,' she said, reaching back to touch his hand.

Patch squeezed the hand she extended. 'Yeah, pretty soon,' he said.

Jasmine looked back to the front where Leon was squeezing his small frame through the vent.

'Oh, Lord, it looks tight,' she said to Patch. 'I'm not sure if Mr Thomas will fit through.'

'I'll rip out the fuckin' wall if I hafta,' Patch said, and she knew he was serious.

Leon disappeared through the vent opening into the hotel office, then it was Mr Thomas's turn. He got his feet and legs out, but his butt and stomach weren't going through. Jasmine moved closer to Mr Thomas, trying to shove him through the opening. It didn't work. She said, 'Excuse me, George, but I've gotta do this,' and reached around to his front and pushed his stomach in. Getting the idea, Mr Thomas sucked in his gut and slid out, Leon barely catching him below. Jasmine went through easily, with Patch so close behind her that he kicked her in the head on his way out.

But they were free. Free of the vents at least. Patch turned the flashlight to lantern light and they could see it was a large inside room with no windows. Leon moved to a desk and turned on a desk lamp, and it worked. They all breathed a sigh of relief.

'Try the phones,' Patch whispered.

Leon picked up the phone, listened for half a second, pushed the on/off switch several times, then shook his head. 'Dead as a doornail,' he said.

Jasmine looked around the room. There were three desks, each with a credenza and a bookcase. All three had computers. She moved to the computer on the nearest desk and turned it on. 'Dial-up or broadband?' she asked Leon.

'Huh?' he said.

'Never mind,' Jasmine said, as the computer screen came to life. She saw the icon for the web and clicked on it. Nothing happened. She was just about to turn the computer off, when it started going through the gyrations and all of a sudden 'Yahoo' filled the screen. 'Broadband!' she said, grinning.

'What does that mean?' Patch asked, leaning one hand

on the back of her chair, the other on the desktop, staring at the screen.

'It means I can contact somebody,' Jasmine said. 'Anybody know the email address for the nearest police department?'

There were blank stares all around and Jasmine mumbled, 'Man, you know we're in trouble when I'm the computer hacker in the group!'

Not knowing who else to email, she decided, when in doubt, call home.

'LET ME SEE THAT THING,' Jean said, sticking her hand out for the GPS monitor. She looked at it, turned it over, looked at its backside, then picked up the butter knife off the bread tray. She stuck the butter knife to the backside of the monitor and let go. The knife stayed. 'Have you guys ever heard of magnets?' she asked, the whole sarcasm thing very evident.

'Well, shit,' I said grinning. 'That takes care of that problem. Now, our next big problem is: how do we get the money out of the bank?'

'I just tell my guys to leave for a few minutes—'

'And they're not going to wonder why?' Jean asked.

I was beginning to rethink this whole idea of involving my very smart wife—she's a bit of a buttinsky.

'They'll do what I tell 'em,' Charlie said a bit stiffly.

'Better idea,' Jean said, raising herself up on her crutches. 'It's almost ten o'clock. They've been at this for a while, right?'

Charlie nodded.

'They need a break,' Jean said, smiling. 'I've got some home-made soup in the freezer and another loaf of this bread. Why don't you and Milt take it to them and stand in their places while they take a meal break?'

Charlie nodded again, this time with a grin on his face. I smiled too and stood up to kiss my wife. 'You're a genius,' I said.

'No, just a woman. You guys just never think along the nurturing line.' With that she left for the kitchen and Charlie pulled me aside, out of earshot of Dewayne and Max Hardy.

'OK, so what do we do with the civilian?' he asked.

'You mean Dewayne or Max?' I asked.

Charlie just glared at me. 'OK, Max,' I said. 'Take him along, I guess. I'm not about to ask my wife to keep him prisoner here. And if he's loose, there's a good chance he'll turn us in to the Feds.'

'Do you realize how much trouble we're going to be in if something happens to this guy?' Charlie asked.

'More trouble than just robbing the bank?' I asked.

'Oh, fuck a duck,' Charlie said, which just about summed up the situation.

JEAN PACKED THE picnic basket with bowls, spoons, napkins, bread knives, butter, a big covered heater bowl of soup, and a loaf of bread in foil, along with a thermos of coffee, some cups, sugar and cream, and two chocolate bars I didn't know we had, and me and Charlie put it in the backseat of his personal car—one of those big four-door pick-ups that cost about as much as my house. Dewayne was going to follow us as far as downtown, then park on the back side of the courthouse and wait for us to show up with the money. Max was to ride with Dewayne to the courthouse and wait for us.

It was cool enough outside for us to wear jackets without causing suspicion, so me and Charlie donned two old hunting jackets I had lying around from the days when I used to hunt. We couldn't very well come out of the bank with a laundry bag full of money, so the hunting jackets, with all the pockets inside and out, were going to work as well as anything I could think of.

My wife stood at the door. I couldn't see her face as she was backlit from the lights of the house, but I could tell by her stance that she wasn't happy. I knew she was worried. I walked back to the door where I could see her, touch her.

'You be careful,' she said, her face stern.

'I will,' I said. I kissed her. She put her arms around my neck, her crutches falling on the floor, and hugged me.

'If you get yourself killed, Milt Kovak, I'll never forgive you!' she said, breathing it softly in my ear.

'I won't,' I said. 'Too much to live for.'

I let her go, picked up her crutches and handed them to her. 'I'll call you every step of the way,' I said.

'If I don't hear from you in an hour, I'm calling the Feds!' she said.

'Ooh,' I said, 'you play mean.'

'I will!'

I kissed her again and went back to Charlie's huge pickup, crawled up to the shotgun side and said to Charlie, 'Let's roll.'

'Y'ALL WILL PROBABLY kill me,' Emmett said, 'but I'm taking one of you down as I go.' He brandished the .357 as he said this.

'Do him,' the Mexican said, pointing at the Aussie. 'Never did like that dude.'

'Naw,' the Aussie said, pointing at the Brit. 'Do Kev. He's a bleedin' asshole.'

'Bugger ya both!' Kev said. 'Other words, Yank, we don't really care, now do we? Point is, bloke, you're gonna be dead, ain'tja?' He shrugged. 'One more body's no biggie.'

Emmett looked at the faces before him. A motley crew,

to be sure. But the one thing he believed beyond a doubt was they didn't really care if he killed one of them, as long as it was the *other* one. He turned the .357 around and handed it to them. Kev took the gun, handed it to the Mexican and reached down for Emmett's hand.

'Upsidaisy,' he said, jerking Emmett to a prone position. The Aussie opened the door and Kev pushed Emmett outside. 'Here we go, Yank. Gonna go see the cap'n, ain't we? See what he wants to do with you. Tell you now, though, it ain't gonna be pretty!'

The other two laughed as they led Emmett through the kitchen and out into the dining room. There were about ten men in that room, all scruffier looking than the last. Food was on every table, trash on the floor. China and crystal lay broken on the floor, and as he passed through the men, one farted and another burped. Emmett couldn't help wondering if he'd landed in a bizarre reality TV show.

His three captors led him to the middle of the dining room where one man sat alone at a table. He was older than the others by a good ten to fifteen years. His matted hair was streaked with gray and his grizzled beard was almost white. He wore a yachtsman's cap, running shoes, plaid Bermuda shorts and a T-shirt with the inscription, 'If God didn't mean for us to eat pussy, He wouldn't have made it look so much like a taco'.

'Whatja got?' he asked Emmett's three captors. His was the only American accent Emmett had heard yet from the pirates.

'We found this bloke hiding in the walk-in freezer,' Kev said.

'Whatja doing in there?' the captain asked, his voice friendly.

'Hiding from y'all.'

'Who are you?'

'Leon McKerry,' Emmett said. 'I'm the skeleton crew the staff left behind.'

The captain laughed. 'Well, you're not a skeleton yet, but we can fix that.'

The room erupted in laughter.

'Who are you?' Emmett asked.

'I'm the Dread Pirate Roberts,' the captain said.

That sounded familiar to Emmett, and he wondered where he'd heard the name before.

'Or, if you prefer,' the captain said, 'I'm Captain Hook.'

'Oy, Cap'n,' Kev said, 'be Cap'n Jack Sparrow!' and he laughed.

The captain laughed too. 'OK, Kev. That's who I am, Mr Leon McKerry, I'm Captain Jack Sparrow.'

OK, Emmett thought, he's making movie references. That Dread Pirate Roberts was in a movie too, he was pretty sure. But pirates watched movies? He had to wonder about that.

'So, Leon McKerry, where are you from?' the captain asked.

Thinking he'd screw up less if he told as much of the truth as possible, Emmett said, 'Oklahoma.'

The captain sat up, grinning from ear to ear. 'No shit? I'm from Ardmore! Played football for OU until I busted my knee! Jeez, small world!' He held out his hand to shake Emmett's. Emmett took the calloused, roughened hand and shook. 'Where in Oklahoma?' the captain asked.

'Longbranch,' Emmett said.

'Oh, man! Played ball with a guy from Longbranch. Dooley Hightower! Know him?'

Emmett smiled. 'Sure do. He's got a ranch outside Longbranch now. Runs cattle.'

Still holding Emmett's hand, the captain said, 'Never could stand that asshole.' The smile turned mean as his hold on Emmett's hand tightened. 'Never could stand Oklahoma.' The squeeze tightened more. 'Always said if I met an asshole from Oklahoma out here, I'd gut 'em like a chicken.' The feeling in Emmett's right hand was leaving. 'Didn't I always say that?'

A chorus of 'yep, Cap'n', 'sure did, Cap'n' came from around them.

'I guess I'm gonna have to kill you,' the captain said, the smile once again benign.

Damn, Emmett thought, I shoulda said I was from Texas.

IT WAS A QUIET NIGHT, stars shining like diamonds in a navy blue sky, little sliver of a moon. I rode shotgun while Charlie drove his big rig into Longbranch. The streetlights were lit up, and there were security lights in the businesses along the square, but other than that it was dark and quiet. Only the bank was totally bright. All the lights were on, our way of letting the bad guys know we were taking care of business. But they sure saw a way around that.

I was halfway thinking this was gonna be too easy, that something had to go wrong. You know, Murphy's Law: what can go wrong will go wrong. I'm a big believer in Murphy's Law, since it's been following me like a psycho stalker most of my life. And that's when I saw the black sedan parked in front of the bank.

'Oh, shit,' I said.

'What?' Charlie said, jerking the wheel and almost landing us in the front yard of the courthouse.

'Mulder and Scully,' I said, pointing at the sedan.

'Oh, shit, the Feds,' he said, slamming on his brake. 'What the hell are they doing here?'

We stayed where we were, mostly hidden by the courthouse, watching the front of the bank and the black sedan parked there.

'What do we do now?' Charlie said, almost whispering.

'They can't hear us, Charlie,' I said. 'Though I'm a little worried about Dewayne. He's too nervous to sit back there behind the courthouse for too long. Should we go tell him what's going on?'

'What if they've already seen us sitting here?' Charlie said. 'Hell, my damn lights are on. They're gonna come over and see us! We back up and go look for Dewayne, they're damn well gonna follow us.'

'Shit,' I said. I sighed. 'Look, there's nothing we can do but go on up there. Take the food like we were gonna. Then go get Dewayne and go back to my house to come up with a Plan B.'

Charlie put the truck in gear. 'I think it's Plan C or D by now,' he said.

We drove up and parked next to the black sedan and got out of the truck. The passenger side window of the black sedan came down and Mulder—I mean Whysmith—leaned across from the driver's side. 'Hey, guys, what's up?'

We both walked up to the open window, me carrying the picnic basket. 'My wife made a midnight snack for the boys,' I said, proffering the basket. 'Want some?'

Whysmith smiled in a superior way. 'No, I'm on a low carb, high protein diet.' He held up a can of something like it was proof he was a better man. 'Thanks, though,' he said, maybe remembering his mama's teachings. 'As long as you guys are here, I'll go on back to the hotel.'

'The reason my guys are here is to guard the place,' Charlie said. 'They don't need a chaperone.'

'Five hundred thousand is quite a temptation,' Whysmith said.

Charlie bristled. 'And my guys are trained, professional law enforcement personnel. And I resent you implying they'd take the money!'

Whysmith held up both his hands and smiled at Charlie. 'No implication meant, Chief. Just a little nervous is all.'

'Well, why don't you go back to your hotel and get some shut-eye? My department has this under control.'

Whysmith shrugged, rolled up the window, started the car and drove off. Charlie and I both breathed a sigh of relief. 'Hell, he's afraid my guys are after the money. He'd shit a brick if he knew the police chief and the sheriff were taking it.'

'All for a good cause,' I said, slapping Charlie on the back. 'All for a good cause.'

The two policemen guarding the bank were happy as clams to take a break in Charlie's truck with the picnic basket while Charlie and I stood guard at the vault. Dewayne had given us the override to the automatic timer and the combination to the vault. We did both, opening the thing like the top on a bottle of ketchup. It was that easy. I kept watch while Charlie filled his hunting jacket with cash, then he kept watch while I did the same. Then we looked at each other. Here we were, two reasonably honest officers of the law, sworn to uphold the laws of our town, county, state, and country, robbing a bank.

But it was for a good cause.

We gave the guys half an hour, then went back out to the truck. 'Y'all feeling better now?' Charlie asked, smiling at his boys.

'Yes, sir,' Donnie Metcalf said. 'Sheriff, please tell your wife thank you. That was some good soup, and that bread was awesome.'

'Yes, sir, Sheriff,' Dave Porter said. 'That was real nice of her to think of us.'

'Yeah, well, women are like that,' I said, nervous and ready to get in Charlie's truck and get the hell out of there. I could feel that money against my body and couldn't help wondering how these two boys couldn't tell something was up.

'Well, my wife's waiting, and so's Milt's, so you guys get on back to duty. The Feds catch us all standing out here, there'll be hell to pay.'

Donnie and Dave waved bye, said thanks again, and went inside the bank. Me and Charlie crawled in his truck and drove away, slipping behind the back of the courthouse where Dewayne Dickey and Max Hardy waited in Dewayne's Lincoln Town car.

Dewayne was shaking like a leaf as he got out of his car and rushed to my side of the pick-up. I had to shove him aside with the door to get out.

'Did y'all do it? What took y'all so long? I saw the Feds drive by and I thought I was gonna have a heart attack! Jesus, did you get the money?'

I put a hand on each of Dewayne's shoulders, looked him in the eye, and said, 'Dewayne, shut up. We got the money. Everything's OK. Calm down. Got that?'

He nodded but his entire body was still trembling. 'OK, OK,' he said. 'Can we leave now? It's twenty minutes to midnight! They're gonna cut off LaDonna's ear—'

'Shut up, Dewayne.' I looked at Charlie. 'I guess we're outta here,' I said. 'What's your plan?' I asked as I emptied the money out of both jackets and into a duffel bag.

'Anywhere around there I can hide this thing?' he said, pointing at his behemoth truck.

I thought for a minute. 'The Tracys live about half a mile from the Maxwell place. They took the kids to Disney World on vacation, left yesterday. They got a big old shade tree by the entrance to their driveway. Should work.'

'This side or the other side of the Maxwell place?' Charlie asked.

'We gotta go!' Dewayne whined.

'Shut up,' I said to Dewayne. 'Other side,' I said to Charlie.

Charlie sighed, squared his shoulders and said, 'OK, let's do it.'

'What about me?' Max Hardy asked.

We all just looked at him, me at least having forgotten he was there. Charlie said, 'You ride with me.'

I zipped up the duffel, threw it on the passenger side of Dewayne's Town car, and we got in our respective vehicles, me lying down on the back floorboard of the Lincoln. It took Dewayne two tries to get the Lincoln started again.

Charlie took off first and I told Dewayne to give him a three-minute head start. Dewayne sat there in the driver's seat, shaking so bad I could feel it where my rump rested against the back of his seat.

'Dewayne, we got everything under control,' I said, trying to calm him down. 'You need to loosen up a bit, Dewayne. Just relax. No way anything can go wrong now,' I said, wishing I didn't have to say it because that was just an invitation for old Murphy (as in Murphy's Law) to screw things up.

'I'm scared, Milt,' he said, his voice soft.

'Yeah, I know, Dewayne. Me, too. But that's OK. It'd be dumb not to be scared. But we just do what they say, and follow our own plan, everything's gonna be OK.'

Finally I told him to take off. Let me tell you, time slows down a lot when you're riding on the floor of a car. Seemed to take forever just to get out of town, and Longbranch is a pretty small town. But finally the street lights disappeared and Dewayne speeded the car up some, meaning we were out of downtown and the thirty-mile-per-hour limit, push-

ing up to forty-five. I felt the turn on to the highway, and
Dewayne taking the speed up to the sixty-mile-per-hour
limit. Finally, we turned on to the county road that led to
the Maxwell place, and let me tell you, that county road is
about as rough as any paved road could possibly be. Pot-
holes the size of small swimming pools. I never appreciated just how bad County Road 714 was until I was lying
on the floorboard of Dewayne Dickey's Lincoln.

Then, too soon, we pulled off County Road 714 on to a
dirt road, which could only be the driveway to the Maxwell place.

'Go slow now, Dewayne,' I said. 'See the well?'

'Yes,' he said.

'See the mimosa?'

'Yes,' he said.

'Pull up where the passenger side back door is as close
to the mimosa as you can get. You see anybody around?
Any vehicles?'

'No,' he said, his voice shaking.

The car stopped.

'How close am I to the mimosa?' I asked him.

He took a gulp of air. 'You slide out your side, you'll be
about three feet from the trunk,' he said.

'OK,' I said. 'You open your door then I'll open mine.
Don't shut yours for a count of ten, so I can get out without leaving the interior light on, OK?'

'Yeah,' he said.

'Then take the duffel and put it in the bucket like they
said, and lower the bucket, then get in the car and leave.'

'Yeah,' he said again.

'OK,' I said. 'On the count of three. One, two, three.'

Dewayne opened his car door and I opened the back
door, belly crawling out of the car and holding the door
slightly ajar until I heard Dewayne shut his, then as close

to the sound of his as I could, slammed the back door. Chances were somebody was watching. I crawled on my belly to the base of the mimosa, crawled into a ball, mostly hidden by high grass and the drooping branches of the tree. I couldn't see Dewayne, but I heard him place the duffel in the bucket, and heard the sound of the rope and pulley as he lowered the bucket into the well. Then I heard his footsteps as he walked back to his car, got in and drove off.

Leaving me all alone, hiding under the mimosa tree.

From: Sanisabel333
To: Prophesy911 (Sheriff Milt Kovak) PRIORITY
Milt—In trouble. Need help immediately. Hurricane hit island—everybody evacuated except us and skeleton crew. Pirates—yes, I said pirates—have attacked island. Have taken Emmett prisoner! Need help!!!!
Jasmine

Jasmine crossed her fingers and hit send. Now it was praying time. She looked at the rest of the bunch and said, 'I think we need to turn the light off. Someone may see it shining from under the door.'

Leon and Patch looked at each other. 'Gonna be dark in here,' Patch said.

'You got a thing about the dark, too?' Jasmine asked.

'Well, not a *thing* per se,' Patch said. 'But I don't exactly love it, know what I mean?'

'I don't love it either,' Jasmine said, 'but I think I'd prefer the dark over quality time with those yahoos out there,' she said, pointing toward the door.

'Yeah,' Leon said. 'Their idea of quality time and mine I think are kinda different.'

Patch walked over to the lamp and switched it off. The room was pitch black. 'Now what?' Mr Thomas asked.

'Now we wait,' Jasmine said.

PICK-ME WEBSTER woke up in the wee hours of the morning. The mother was asleep under his left arm, the daughter under his right. Or vice versa. He was never actually sure which was which, and didn't care in the least. They didn't speak English and he didn't speak Spanish, so very little about them, other than their warmth in his bed, mattered.

Pick-Me spoke four languages: English, as his mother tongue—if you could count the prep-school, New England upper-crust style of communication *English*—French, of course, plus German and Russian. The CIA, in their wisdom, had of course never sent him to any country speaking those languages, but exclusively to Spanish-speaking countries. Although he'd spent most of his thirty-odd years of service to the CIA in Spanish-speaking countries, he had refused, out of sheer bloody mindedness, to learn the language, hoping that his inability to speak the tongue would somehow translate into a transfer to Paris, or, at the very least, Berlin.

The transfers he had received, instead, had been from his first assignments in Vietnam and Cambodia to Buenos Aires, from Buenos Aires to San Paulo, from San Paulo to Mexico City, from Mexico City to Nicaragua, from Nicaragua to Panama City, from Panama City to Belize, from Belize to Madrid (which wasn't bad—at least it was the *Continent*!), and from Madrid to San Juan. He'd been in San Juan now for seven years, his longest stint anywhere. He thought there was a distinct possibility that the Company had forgotten about him. Except for the fact that a direct deposit check appeared in his bank account the second of every month, for all intents and purposes, the Company *had* forgotten about him. Pick-Me Webster had not had an assignment in thirty-two months.

Pick-Me sat up on the side of the bed, moving aside the feet of one of the hookers, and rubbed his face. He was afraid he was sobering up, which was a state of affairs Pick-Me was not excited about. He stood and roamed around the hotel room that had been his home for the past seven years. A largish room, by hotel standards, it held a double bed, a love-seat-sized sofa, a table and two chairs, and had a balcony that overlooked the outdoor market of downtown San Juan. Since the market sold fruits, vegetables and fresh flowers, its operation began every morning at five a.m. Pick-Me usually awoke every morning at five-oh-five a.m. Which was enough to drive any man to drink, as far as Pick-Me Webster was concerned. But this morning he had awakened before the market, a sad state of affairs, to be sure. He searched the room for a bottle and found several; unfortunately all of them were empty. He doubted room service, even at this hotel, would send up a bottle of Chivas at this hour. Or even a lesser brand.

The truth of the matter was that Pick-Me was bored. He had joined the CIA because his nature was to cause trouble. He figured if he was a spy, his natural tendencies could be useful. Unfortunately, he hadn't been able to use these natural tendencies in thirty-two months and he was itching for action. Any kind of action. The nastier the better. Pick-Me Webster was in for a real treat.

THERE WAS A BUG crawling on me. A big one. Didn't know if it was a biting bug, a stinging bug, or just your plain old ordinary creepy-crawly. Any way you wanna look at it, though, I really don't like bugs. Really. I mean I really, really don't like bugs. No big trauma from my childhood or anything; no stuck in a cellar with a colony of roaches (if roaches go for colonies, which I really don't know, nor do I care to find out); no tied to an anthill by my playmates; no being force-fed grasshoppers by a weird uncle. Nothing like that. I just don't like bugs. Really.

So to say I was uncomfortable, lying there in the tall grass under that mimosa tree, not being able to move because the kidnappers could be—probably would be— watching, while a giant bug crawled around on my defenseless body, is a bit of an understatement. I gritted my teeth, squinched my eyes shut, and prayed for the best.

Finally, I heard crunching through the tall grass. I opened my eyes and could just make out some boots coming up to the well. Great. No car. Nothing metal to stick the GPS to. Now what? I thought. Then some ambient light gleamed off of something and I could see that the fella at the well was wearing steel-toed boots with matching heel backs of steel—or something that at least looked like steel. I took out the little GPS and looked at it. It wasn't much bigger than a shelled peanut. Would he notice a peanut-sized something dragging on his heel? Would it peel off as he walked away? All I could do was try.

I carefully reached out and stuck the magnetized side of the unit to the heel of the right boot. And, wonder of wonders, it stayed there! Hooray! Something had finally gone right.

I heard the whine of the pulley as the bucket came out of the well. Heard the man grunt with satisfaction, then heard the bucket as he let it go and it bounced against the sides of the well as it went back down. No reason for this guy to be quiet. As far as he knew, he was totally alone. Little did he know…yada, yada, yada.

He crunched back through the tall grass, whistling. And why not? He not only had the loot from the first bank robbery, but he had the insurance replacement loot as well. He was thinking it was a good day. I was thinking, I hope to hell that GPS thingamabob actually works.

I lay there in the tall grass waiting, feeling the bug now going into my hair, or what was left of it, and finally heard a car start up, heard the guy rev the engine, then heard the crunch of dirt and gravel as he pulled out of the driveway of the abandoned house, switching on the head-lights as he did so. That's when I sat up and swatted at that goddam bug!

Using the side of the well for support, I got my stiff body up, stretched out the kinks I'd gotten from laying in one position on the wet grass for God only knows how long, and walked toward the road. I'd no sooner gotten there than Charlie Smith pulled up in his oversized pick-up truck. Max Hardy was riding shotgun.

'Get in the back,' I said, not too friendly like.

'Yes, sir,' he said, a little too sarcastic for my taste, but I climbed aboard anyway.

There's something to be said for living in the country. Out here we were a long ways from any highway, any town lights. There was none of that underlying noise you get so used to living in a city or a town with a highway running through it. The stars were so bright you could almost read by 'em, the quiet so absolute you could hear individual crickets and katydids.

'How'd it go?' Charlie asked me.

'Had to put the GPS thingy on his boot heel,' I said.

'Shit,' he said.

'The boot heel had metal on it,' I said.

'Think it'll stay there?' he asked.

'Don't know,' I said. 'Which way did they go?' I asked Charlie.

'They passed my hiding place going east,' Charlie said, turning the big truck around in the driveway of the aban-doned house. 'Get that little box there and open it up.'

I did as he told me. 'What is it?' I asked.

'The GPS locator thingy,' he said. 'You see a flash-ing light?'

'Yeah,' I said.

'Which way is it going?' Charlie asked.

'Hell if I know,' I said, studying the thingamabob real close.

Charlie pulled over to the side of the road. 'Here,' he said, 'you drive, let me navigate.'

'I'll do it,' Max Hardy said from the backseat. Charlie and I both just shot him a look. 'You are here under duress,' Charlie said. 'Don't even pretend to think you're part of this, Mr Hardy. And if you ever tell anybody about this, the last thing I'll do as chief of police is arrest your ass for anything I can think of.'

'Hey, I was just trying to help!' Max said, hands up in the air like he was surrendering.

'Well, don't!' I said, shooting him my own look.

I got out of the truck and got into the driver's seat, Charlie riding shotgun. I got the truck going about fifty, which was fast for this stretch of road in the dark, especially with me driving a truck I wasn't used to, and such a big one to boot. I took a sharp turn too fast and skidded a little. Slowing down, I said, 'Sorry about that.'

'Let's don't wreck this thing, 'K?' Charlie said. 'I still owe a shitload on it.'

We came to a crossroads and I asked Charlie, 'Which way?'

Studying the read out, he said, 'Right.'

I turned and headed down FM410, going north. FM410 was lined on both sides by giant oak trees, oak trees that spread their branches like soldiers arching their rifles at a wedding. In the daytime it's real pretty; at night it's scary as shit. Somewhere in these trees I knew there was a body of water, and that body of water wasn't covered by a bridge, but only a low water crossing. It hadn't rained in a couple of days, and run-off is usually pretty quick in our neck of the woods, but you could never be sure with a low water crossing. I slowed the truck down to about twenty miles an hour as we cruised through the over-hanging branches.

'Can't you go any faster?' Charlie asked.

I told him about the river or stream or brook or creek or whatever it was coming up.

'Yeah, OK,' he said, holding on to the chicken bar on his side of the truck. Man didn't trust my driving, that was for sure.

The asphalt started downhill and I slowed as we came to the cemented portion that was the low water crossing. It was dry. I went over it, up the asphalt on the other side, gaining speed. Suddenly Charlie yelled, 'Stop!'

I did. 'Shit,' he said. 'Back up. They turned! Do you see a road?'

I slowly backed up, all three of us looking out our windows of the truck for a turn-off. 'It's gotta be this side,' Charlie said. 'This thing says east again.'

'That side east?' I asked, totally turned around now.

'East, west. Hell if I know. They went that a-way is all I know for sure,' he said, pointing out his window.

From the backseat, Max Hardy said, 'There it is!'

We were nearly back at the low water crossing, and there it was: a dirt road heading to the right, following the creek, which seemed to have only a trickle of water in it. I turned down the road, going slowly, unsure where we were or where we were going.

'They've stopped!' Charlie said.

I put on the brake.

'They've stopped, Milt! Not us! Keep going!'

'Oh, yeah, right,' I said, putting my foot to the gas once more, going no more than twenty miles an hour down the old dirt road.

'Still not moving,' he said.

'How far up?' I asked.

He searched the screen then said, 'About a quarter mile.'

I turned off the lights and slowed to a crawl. If they were just sitting in their car, as the GPS monitor indicated, then they'd see us if we came in with lights blazing. This particular job required a little stealth.

'I can't see shit, Milt!' Charlie groused.

'Yeah, well, neither can they!' I shot back, which got me a shrug from the city police chief.

As my eyes got used to the darkness, I could make out a house ahead, a couple of lights shining in the windows. A pick-up truck was parked in the driveway. 'That them?' I asked Charlie.

'Looks like it,' he said, his voice quiet.

I pulled the big truck along the verge of the road and turned off the engine. We sat there for a minute, then I turned to Charlie. 'Any movement on the monitor?' I asked.

'Nary a thing,' Charlie answered.

I could see bodies moving around inside the house—looked like two people. 'Would the monitor show if he was just walking around like that?' I asked, pointing at the silhouettes on the window shades.

Looking at the monitor, Charlie said, 'Hell if I know.'

'Any way to keep the inside lights off when we open the doors?' I asked him.

He showed me where the switch was and I turned it off, then we gingerly opened the doors, not closing them all the way as we got out.

Max Hardy pushed his way out of the backseat.

'No!' I whispered, forcing him back toward the truck. 'You stay here!'

'And miss all the fun?' Max said.

'You got kids?' I asked him.

'Yeah, two,' he said, puzzled at my question.
'You want them to have a daddy?' I asked.
'Oh,' he said, and stayed where he was.

NINE

'I'LL PROBABLY KILL YOU in the morning.' That's what the Dread Pirate Roberts had said. Emmett remembered now. *The Princess Bride*. Funny movie. Well, it had been. Now it didn't seem so funny. He was trussed up in a cabinet in the kitchen. Somehow the pirates thought that was really funny, to stick him a cabinet. Fortunately, or unfortunately, they'd taken everything out of the cabinet, pots, pans and the rolling pin that had looked interesting to Emmett. He could only pray that Jasmine and the rest of their group were safely in the hotel office, and that the pirates had looted the office sufficiently so they'd have no reason to go back there.

He wasn't sure how long he'd been in the cabinet, since at some point he'd fallen asleep. He was rudely awakened by the cabinet doors flying open and two goons grabbing his trusses and pulling him out.

'Cap'n wants to see ya,' one of them said.

'Ain't gonna be pretty,' said the other.

They pulled him so quickly he didn't get a chance to get his feet on the ground, and ended up being dragged into the dining room. The captain was still sitting at his table alone. Unfortunately on an empty table next to him lay the body of Naomi Thomas.

The captain pointed at Mrs Thomas's body. 'Now who would this be?' he said, his tone genial.

'Mrs Thomas,' Emmett said.

'Mrs Thomas,' the captain said. 'Not *the* Mrs Thomas?'

Emmett shrugged. The captain stood up and walked around the table, coming to stand in front of Emmett. With a slight smile on his face, he raised his right hand and slapped Emmett hard across the jaw.

'You mentioned you were the only one here. Seems you lied to me, Leon McKerry,' said the captain.

'Since Mrs Thomas is dead, I didn't think to mention her,' Emmett said, licking at a trickle of blood at the side of his mouth.

'And where is *Mr* Thomas?' the captain inquired, still in that genial tone.

'Got on the boat,' Emmett said.

'Without his wife? Not a very loving husband,' the captain said.

'They got separated,' Emmett said.

'Uh huh,' the captain said, walking back around the table to sit down. 'Why is it I don't believe you?' he asked.

Emmett shrugged.

The captain inclined his head and one of the goons holding Emmett hit him hard in the ear. Emmett's ear rang and he felt disoriented for a moment. 'I don't know how they got separated,' Emmett said, breathing hard from the pain. 'When it started storming, the old lady just showed up at the door, blubbering her eyes out, said she missed the boat and she thought her husband was on it. That's all I know.'

'Did you kill her?' the captain asked.

'No, of course not. We were hiding from y'all in the freezer and it came on while we were both asleep. She either froze to death or just had a heart attack. I'm not a doctor. I don't really know,' Emmett said.

The captain smiled. 'You have an answer for everything, don't you, Leon McKerry?' he said.

'I'm just telling you the truth,' Emmett said. His head

hurt, and his arms, still tied behind his back and being held in a hard grip by both goons, were throbbing.

'I'm not sure if I believe you,' the captain said, which Emmett felt was a better state of affairs than the captain's earlier remark that he didn't believe Emmett at all.

'It's the truth,' Emmett said, holding his head up high.

'Uh huh,' the captain said. 'Take him back,' he told the goons, who turned him around quickly and pulled him back toward the kitchen. This time Emmett was able to keep his feet under him. He felt it was much more digni-fied that way.

IT WAS ABOUT FIVE HUNDRED yards to the house, and we bent double as we made our way through tall weeds and grasses to the front of the small forties-style bungalow. As we neared, I could tell the windows were open, and I could hear voices coming from inside.

'You know how much trouble you're going to be in when my husband finds me?' I heard a woman's voice say. After twenty years of listening to her it was fairly easy to tell it was my ex-wife, LaDonna. I breathed a sigh of relief that she was still alive.

'Shut up,' a man's voice said.

'I will not have you talk to me that way, you cretin!' La-Donna said. 'I'm the wronged person here, not you! This tape is entirely too tight! You're cutting off the circula-tion to my hands! If I lose a hand because of this, there will be hell to pay!'

'Shut up!' said another male voice, a little louder, a little more desperate.

'Obviously both your mothers forgot to teach you any manners! I can't imagine what kind of upbringing either of you must have had… Don't you raise your hand to me!'

'Stop, man!' said the first male voice. 'Don't damage the merchandise!'

'You haven't been here with her alone for over an hour, man! You've got no fuckin' idea—'

'Watch your language around a lady!' LaDonna said.

'See?' the second man yelled. 'Do you see what I've been going through?'

The first man laughed. 'Yeah, man, she's a pain in the ass all right!'

'How dare you…?' LaDonna started, but stopped suddenly and let out a squeak.

I peeked through a small opening in the window shades and saw one of the men stuffing something in LaDonna's mouth, then taping it in place with duct tape. I couldn't help thinking I might have stayed married to her longer if I'd ever thought about doing that.

They were normal-enough looking guys. One tall and thin, the other tall and very skinny. The thin one had dark brown hair cut in a short, businessman's cut; the skinny one's hair was longish and kinda stringy. Both wore blue jeans and T-shirts. No distinguishing marks that I could see.

I felt Charlie nudge me. 'You smell that?' he whispered.

I sniffed the air. I'd been so engrossed in seeing my ex-wife being manhandled that I hadn't noticed the smell. But I recognized it.

'Shit,' I said, 'they're cooking meth!'

'And I think they're burning it,' Charlie said.

We looked in each other's eyes, each of us knowing what was going to happen.

I sighed. 'We gotta get her out,' I said.

We crawled up on the porch and positioned ourselves on either side of the front door, guns drawn. 'On the count of three,' I whispered, then held up three fingers, one at a time. On the third finger, we both kicked the front door and it flew open.

The two bank robbers/kidnappers were nowhere near their weapons, but both made a dive for them. Instead of worrying about them, I left that to Charlie as I grabbed LaDonna, chair and all, and headed for the front door. The smell was getting stronger and nastier and just as I reached the front door, I heard a shot ring out. I threw LaDonna and her chair off the porch and as far into the front yard as I could, not paying that much attention to the 'umph' sound she let out upon landing. Instead I whirled around to see who was shooting and caught Charlie as he stumbled to the front door.

'You hit?' I asked.

He nodded but said, 'She's gonna blow!'

I could hear a hissing sound over the screams of the two men inside, both yelling things like, 'Get the money! She's gonna blow! Get the fucking money!'

Charlie and I headed out the front door to the front porch just as the house blew. The concussion blew us off the porch into the yard. Unfortunately my fall was broken by LaDonna and the chair she was still tied to.

EMMETT WAS RUDELY AWAKENED a second time, and again dragged into the dining room for an audience with the captain. He was happy to see that Mrs Thomas's body was not there. He hoped they'd be able to retrieve it, once this was all over, so Mr Thomas would have something to bury for himself and his kids.

'You got a reason why I shouldn't kill you?' the Dread Pirate Roberts, a.k.a. Captain Hook, a.k.a. Captain Jack Sparrow, a.k.a. the Ageing Pirate King, said to Emmett.

'I don't wanna die?' Emmett suggested.

The captain shrugged.

'I have a wife and two kids on the mainland?' Emmett offered.

'I got a wife and three kids in San Juan. A wife and two kids in Bermuda. A wife and one kid in Singapore, and a wife and four kids in Ardmore.' Again the captain shrugged. 'Not a big deterrent.'

Thinking fast, Emmett said, 'I have information you don't have.'

The captain narrowed his eyes and squinted at Emmett. 'And what information is that?' he asked.

'If I told you,' Emmett said, 'then I'd have no bargaining chip and you'd just kill me.'

The captain laughed. 'That's true enough,' he said. 'What do you propose we do?'

'I propose that y'all get back on your ship and as you sail off, I'll call out the information to you,' Emmett suggested.

The captain laughed and the rest of the crew joined in, Kev laughing so hard he slapped the Mexican on the back. The Mexican took umbrage to this and hit Kev in the mouth with his fist. Kev drew back to hit the Mexican when the captain stopped laughing and said, 'Enough.'

Kev lowered his fist. Looking back at Emmett, the captain said, 'First, we got us a right awful storm brewing out there. Nearly hurricane status, I hear. Second, we like this little island and its pretty little hotel. Don't we, boys?'

The crew vehemently agreed.

'Third, I'm not as stupid as you look, Mr Leon McKerry. I sail off and you tell me some story and I don't get a chance to prove it one way or the other. Or you tell me something that means nothing to me. No bargaining chip at all. I think we're at an impasse, Mr Leon McKerry. So I think I'll just kill you.'

'Why add murder to your rap sheet when you can just tie me up or stick me in a locked room?' Emmett said.

'Won't be my first murder,' the captain said.

'Well, every murder counts,' Emmett tried.

The captain shrugged. 'Not really. After you hit ten or eleven, the authorities stop counting. And if you're dead, then you can't tell 'em it was me anyway, get where I'm going with this?'

Emmett nodded. 'Yeah, I see where you're headed. But what good will it do the authorities if I tell 'em I was held captive by the Dread Pirate Roberts?'

The captain laughed. 'Yeah, that would be fun. See wanted posters with that actor's face on it!' He laughed loud and long, the rest of the crew again joining in. Emmett noticed Kev didn't slap the Mexican's back this time.

'I like you, Leon McKerry,' the captain said. 'You've got a sense of humor. You don't see that a lot in people you're getting ready to kill.'

'I suppose not,' Emmett agreed.

'Usually there's just a lot of blubbering and begging. Gets on my nerves.'

'I suppose it would,' Emmett agreed.

With a look on his face that in a cartoon would have warranted a light bulb overhead, the captain said, 'Say, Leon McKerry, you got any marketable skills?'

Thinking about it, Emmett finally said, 'Well, I'm a good shot. And I got some book learning.'

The captain nodded his head. 'Got me a few good shots. But I gotta admit that overall this is a pretty stupid bunch. Ain't you, boys?'

The crew laughed, most agreeing with the captain.

'You ever do any accounting?' the captain asked Emmett.

Emmett nodded his head. 'Used to do a lot back on the

mainland,' he lied. 'Had a job where I did the books for a small company.'

'Well, hell, Leon McKerry, that's all we are, right, boys? Just a small company.'

The crew again laughed good-naturedly and agreed with their captain.

The captain stood up and said, 'I'm gonna get me some shut-eye. You boys keep an eye on Leon McKerry here. And, Leon, I'll think about you coming on as my accountant. Or, as the Dread Pirate Roberts would say, maybe I'll just kill you in the morning.'

To SAY MY EX-WIFE was not happy is like saying Britney Spears is not gonna get any mother of the year awards. An understatement. For some dumb reason the first thing I did was take the gag out of her mouth. Shoulda been the last thing I did.

'Milton Kovak! I swear you broke my arm! Oh, it hurts! It hurts! What in the hell did you think you were doing? Throwing me on the ground like that! I could have fallen on something horrible, like a…I don't know, a…'

'LaDonna, the house was fixing to blow up,' I said. 'I did you a favor.'

'A favor? Oh, my arm! Untie me, for God's sake! I can't believe you're just standing there keeping me tied up—'

I got up from my prone position on the ground to my knees. 'As a matter of fact, LaDonna, I wasn't standing. I was on my ass just like you—'

'Don't be vulgar! Does that new wife of yours let you be vulgar like that?'

I attempted to untie her hands from the back of the chair. She screamed. I went for her legs instead. The minute they were untied she kicked me.

I got to my feet. 'That's it!' I said, walking away. 'Charlie, if you want that woman untied, you're gonna have to do it.'

At that point Max Hardy came jogging up to us. 'Need any help?' he asked.

I just glared at him.

Sometimes it was hard to remember that when I met LaDonna in high school, she was such a quiet, demure little thing. Like they say, butter wouldn't melt in her mouth (which is something I never did understand but feel is appropriate at this juncture). I'm not sure when she turned into the churlish, shrewish woman now sitting on the ground outside a meth lab—I think it must have been a gradual thing—but she's certainly no longer the woman I married.

Charlie walked up tentatively to LaDonna. 'Mrs Dickey, if you'll allow me—'

'Of course, young man,' LaDonna said, trying out a weak smile. 'But please be careful of my arm. I think it got broken when your assistant threw me out of the house like a bag of dirty laundry.'

'He's not my assis—'

'Whatever,' LaDonna said. Then screamed. 'I said be careful of my arm, for God's sake!'

Charlie stood up. 'Milt, there's a tool box in the back of my truck. Got a box cutter in there. Can you get it for me?'

'Can't let you slit her throat, Charlie, much as I'd enjoy it...' I started.

'Milton Kovak, you're just an old fool!' yelled my ex-wife.

'It was just a joke, ma'am,' Charlie said.

'Well, it wasn't very funny!' LaDonna said and started to cry.

'Milt, could you hurry up, please?' Charlie said, his teeth gritted. 'And there should be a first-aid kit in there, too.'

LaDonna's crying dried up. 'I won't have either of you

fools giving me first aid! I don't want to die right now, thank you very much!'

'It's not for you, ma'am,' Charlie said. 'It's for me. I've been shot.'

'Oh,' LaDonna said, finally seeing the blood on Charlie's sleeve. 'Well, don't bleed on me, for God's sake!'

I found the box cutter and first-aid kit and handed the box cutter to Max Hardy who took it over to where Charlie and LaDonna were. Max took over cutting LaDonna free, while I opened the first-aid kit and found some scissors and some gauze and tape. Ripping off Charlie's shirtsleeve, I saw a bloody mess, and reached back in the kit for some antiseptic wipes.

'How bad is it?' Charlie asked, wincing as I cleaned the wound.

'Looks like a through and through,' I told him. 'Pretty close to the outside, so chances are good there's no real damage.'

'Thank you, Dr Milt,' he said.

'Well, hell, man, you asked!' I said, putting on the gauze and taping it liberally.

Then we both turned and looked at LaDonna. The seat and legs of the chair she'd been tied to had broken off, but the back was firmly affixed to her back. Max finished cutting the ropes that bound her and the two of us helped her to her feet.

Once she was standing, she knocked my hand away. 'You know I'm going to sue you for every dime you're worth, don't you?' she said, glaring at me.

'Ma'am,' Charlie said, a sad look on his face, 'if you insist on such a route, I'm afraid your husband's involvement in a conspiracy to rob his own bank is just gonna have to come out.'

LaDonna glared at Charlie, glared at me, glared at Max, then started walking toward the truck.

PICK-ME WEBSTER had been thinking for about a year now of giving it all up. He was the last of his branch of the Webster line, and he had inherited the very large house in Providence, and had a comfortable trust fund, which would keep him in Chivas for the rest of his days. The balance of his parents' estate had gone to various charities, the bulk of it going to his mother's favorite, a program that taught inner-city kids manners and etiquette. His mother's money was earmarked for recruitment, as they always had a hard time getting ghetto children interested in manners and etiquette, as they were too busy dodging bullets in their project homes to worry about table service or which fork for which dish.

His days in San Juan were dull and boring, and if it weren't for his evenings spent discussing past exploits with members of other alphabet agencies, he'd have given it all up a long time ago. He loved the excitement of a good contract, of going undercover and pretending to be someone he wasn't, of flying a plane dangerously low through a jungle to extradite a fallen comrade. He loved to talk about his early days with the agency, when he *wasn't* in Cambodia, ha, ha, ha. There were new recruits from different alphabet agencies coming into San Juan all the time, and for a while they'd listen to him with rapt attention, until someone older and wiser gave them the skinny on poor Pick-Me Webster, who hadn't had a contract with his agency in thirty-two months.

Yes, Pick-Me Webster was thinking about giving it all up. Of going home where people spoke the same language, where he'd be invited to this and that, and would be able to hang out at the country club because he had a legacy membership that could not be revoked, no matter how drunk he got at the Nineteenth Hole. At fifty-nine, he still had time to find a young woman, settle down, maybe breed.

He'd never thought of becoming a father until lately, but it had a certain appeal. Carrying on the Webster line. Passing the elegant mansion in Providence on to yet one more member of the Webster clan.

But before he did that, dear God, just one more mission, just one more adventure. Just one more. As has been said often and with fervor, be careful what you wish for.

WE WERE BACK YET AGAIN at Longbranch Memorial Hospital. This time in the ER while they were redoing my handiwork on Charlie's arm and checking out LaDonna and, of course, giving Dewayne Dickey a shot of oxygen 'cause he kept passing out.

You know when you been married to somebody for a really long time, like I was to LaDonna, and you finally make an escape (either her idea or yours, it doesn't really matter), there's some things you'd like to forget. And I did. I'd completely forgotten about the aprons. Until I saw her on the ground outside the meth lab, chair tied to her backside, maroon-colored stretch pants, penny loafers, a loose-fitting maroon-colored top, and the apron.

Now, we're not talking about a little ol' apron you tie around your waist to keep your slacks clean while you're cooking or cleaning up the kitchen. No, LaDonna's aprons were those full body ones that go over the chest and around to the back and hang down below the knees. With ruffles. You know, the kind nobody's worn in this country since *I Love Lucy* was new. LaDonna's grandma, her mama and her all three made 'em. She had aprons for every season, every holiday, and every hobby. She had twelve aprons just for Christmas (as in 'The Twelve Days of Christmas'), and one of them even had the annoying words to that annoying song written on them—or hand-embroidered or whatever.

There was a slew of Halloween aprons, a plethora of

Fourth of July aprons, and more bunny and Easter egg aprons than you could shake a stick at. She even had a George Washington's birthday apron, although I wasn't sure if she wore it on the actual day, Presidents Day, or both. She made one for barbecuing that said, 'He makes the meat, I make everything else!' and a matching one for me that said, 'Man of Meat'.

Now, as any man who's ever been married to a woman can attest, if your wife makes you dinner you better say, 'Yum, yum'. And if your wife makes you an apron that says 'Man of Meat' on white sailcloth with big red letters, you better damn well wear it. She *had* given me a choice for my apron, either 'Man of Meat' or, gag me, 'A Meating of the Minds'. As you can see, I took the lesser of two evils. (After the divorce, I sold that apron in a garage sale for seventy-five cents to a woman, of course, who bought it for her husband. If I knew his name, I'd go apologize to him.) The one she had on when she got kidnapped was what she referred to as a 'working apron', since she'd actually been in the kitchen when she was abducted. It was white with pink flowers and green stems, bordered in the same color of maroon as her pants. You can see she takes them very seriously.

Yes, I know, I got off on a tangent, but better a tangent than thinking about what happened at the hospital. Which was LaDonna alternately yelling at me and giving me the cold shoulder. The cold shoulder was OK; the yelling got out of hand.

'I can't believe you threw me off the porch!' she yelled.

'OK, next time I'll leave you there!' I said, getting my back up.

'There wouldn't have been a *this* time if you and him—' she said, pointing at Charlie Smith '—woulda done your jobs right! Dewayne and I leave town for one afternoon and you let the bank get robbed! Then, just to prove how *really* incompetent you both are, you let me get kidnapped!'

'Well, forgive me, Miss LaDonna, I forgot to put three deputies up your ass!' I said.

'You are *so* vulgar! You haven't changed a bit!' she fairly spat out.

'Well, you have!' I yelled back. 'You're an even bigger pain in the ass than you used to be!'

'Milt, now stop,' Dewayne cut in, in one of his lucid moments. 'Y'all both need to stop or somebody's gonna say—'

'You stay out of this, Mr Bank President!' LaDonna shouted. 'You're the one who brought this idiot in on this, right? You couldn't even handle getting me back yourself! You had to go get *him*!'

'Mrs Dickey,' Charlie cut in, 'give your husband some credit. He did the right thing going to the authorities—'

'Who decided to rob the bank,' came a voice from the door. All heads swiveled in that direction. Michael Whysmith, a.k.a. Fox Mulder, stood in the doorway. I hardly noticed when Max Hardy slipped out a side door.

I do believe that, with the exception of LaDonna, there was but one single thought in that room: 'Oh, shit.'

TEN

Jasmine woke up in pitch-blackness. She had no idea where she was and felt panic setting in. She breathed deeply, in through her nose, out through her mouth, four times before the panic began to subside and she remembered where she was. It helped a little, but the total lack of sight, the almost absence of sound, kept her slightly disoriented. She remembered being at a desk, typing on the computer, sending an emergency email to Milt. She thought she was probably still at that desk. She felt around, felt the computer, the edge of the desk, the chair under her. Yes, she decided, she was still where she had been. She could smell something near her, then recognized the cloying scent of body odor and sickness that emanated from Mr Thomas. She reached out her left hand and touched his shoulder. He started.

'Jasmine?' he asked.

She smiled in the dark. 'Hey, George. How you doing?' she asked.

'Been better,' the old man said.

She squeezed his shoulder and dropped her hand. 'Please don't,' Mr Thomas said.

'Don't what?' Jasmine asked quietly.

'Don't remove your hand. I feel less alone that way,' the old man said.

Jasmine put her hand back on Mr Thomas's shoulder and patted him. 'It's going to be all right, George,' she said. 'We're getting out of this.'

'Yes,' he said, his voice lighter than it had been in some time, 'I believe we will.'

EMMETT WASN'T SURE what time it was when he woke up, still trussed up like a turkey for roasting, still in the empty cabinet in the hotel's kitchen. It was quiet, though. No sound of the storm raging outside the hotel, the sound that had accompanied all conversation, all quiet, all rest, all sleep all night long. Was the storm over? Or were they in the eye of the hurricane? Emmett, being from Oklahoma, a land-locked state, knew nothing about hurricanes, except that they did total and often irrevocable damage, killed people, left people homeless, and were even worse than Oklahoma's many dangerous tornados. He closed his eyes and prayed, something he hadn't done since J.R.'s death, prayed that his wife and the child in her belly were both alright, and that they'd all make it out of here, somehow, someway.

When the goons came for him, he looked first to the windows of the kitchen. It was daylight, but a gray, overcast sky; no sun, just clouds moving faster than normal. Is this what the eye of a hurricane looked like?

'Is the storm over or are we in the eye?' he asked.

One of the goons said, 'Shut up,' and the other just pulled his arm harder.

Emmett couldn't really feel the arm the goon pulled. He'd lost all feeling in his arms and shoulders, although his neck throbbed like there were tiny daggers sticking in at several places. He hoped that wasn't the case, but with these guys, he couldn't really be sure.

Again he was brought to the captain, who was sitting at the same table, wearing the same clothes he'd been wearing before, except, instead of the yachting hat, now he had on a baseball cap—Emmett's baseball cap, the one that said 'Prophesy County Sheriff's Department' right on the crown.

'Lookie here what I found,' the captain said, taking off the cap and throwing it across the table to Emmett. Emmett, still having his arms tied behind him, did not, of course, catch the cap.

Emmett looked down at it, then lifted his head to look the captain in the eye. 'Where'd you find this?' he asked, casually interested.

'In one of the rooms,' the captain said. 'One of my boys found it.'

'Um' was all Emmett could come up with.

'Where you think the body that goes with this hat may be?' the captain asked.

'Probably left on the boat with everybody else. Not everybody got all their stuff, I'm sure,' Emmett responded.

'Too bad they left *this* behind,' the captain said, tossing a picture at him.

The picture was of Emmett and Jasmine, just minutes after the wedding. The wedding that seemed to have taken place weeks ago, rather than just days.

'Um,' Emmett said. 'Yeah, that's me and my wife.'

'Sorta thought that. Guess where we found the hat, vis-avis the picture?'

'No idea,' said Emmett, again looking the captain in the eye.

'Same room,' the captain said. 'The hat and these pants,' he said, reaching under the table and throwing Emmett's slacks from the day before onto the table, his wallet landing on top, 'and this wallet here, were on one side of the bed, and this picture and some womanly stuff was on the other side.' He smiled genially at Emmett.

Emmett had begun to think that the captain's genial smiles were a slight bit more dangerous than his mean looks. Although the mean looks were sorta dangerous too.

'Um,' said Emmett.

'Emmett Hopkins,' the captain read from his wallet. 'Deputy, Prophesy County, Oklahoma.'

He looked up from his reading and smiled again at Emmett. 'Looks like you,' he said, holding the picture ID out for Emmett's inspection.

'Yeah,' Emmett said. 'It does.'

'You know what I think, Leon McKerry?' the captain asked.

'Got no idea,' Emmett answered.

'I think your name ain't Leon McKerry. I think your name's Emmett Hopkins, and I think you lied. I think you're a deputy for this Prophesy County, Oklahoma. That's the county Longbranch is in, if I remember correctly,' the captain said.

'Believe it is,' Emmett responded.

'And this lady you was with, your wife you said?' the captain asked.

Emmett didn't respond.

'I take it she's somewhere in this hotel?' the captain asked.

Still Emmett didn't respond.

'She's a pretty little thing,' the captain said.

He held up the picture for his men to see. 'Ain't she a pretty little thing?' he asked the group in general.

There were lewd remarks in response, the kind that set Emmett's teeth on edge and made the little daggers in his neck dig deeper.

The captain smiled his genial smile at Emmett. Still looking Emmett in the eye, he said to his men, 'Go find her.'

AFTER ABOUT A MINUTE and a half of sleep, I headed back to the station. It had been a long night. Mulder and Scully had kept us up way past anything proper, alternately reading us the riot act and threatening to send us all to prison. We explained fifty ways from Sunday what had happened, how we really didn't have any choice, yada, yada, but mostly they weren't having any. What with the money being blown up with the bad guys, our position didn't look so good.

I went back to the office not knowing if I was gonna be going about business as usual, or tying up my personal business for my years of imprisonment. But my first order of business was going to be to call Max Hardy, Neal Hardy's son, and find out where he'd disappeared to the night before. I'd barely walked in the door when Anthony said, 'Milt, you got something on your email.'

'Don't have time for that,' I told him.

'Looks like it's from Emmett or Jasmine and it's marked urgent,' he said.

'I'm sure they both think it's important to rub my face in the fact that they're having a good time in paradise,' I said.

Anthony shrugged. 'Just thought I'd tell you it's marked urgent,' he said, then got back to doing whatever it is he does on the computer.

I moseyed into my office and sat down, rubbed my face a few times, called out to Gladys for a cup of coffee, said please real pitiful like, and waited while she brought it. She brought me a steaming mug, threw a couple of Sweet & Lows at me and said, 'Jean said no sugar.'

Looking at my desk gave me a headache. I finally decided that reading an email from someone happy was preferable to doing anything there was to do here, before I, you know, got hauled off to the slammer. And, to be truthful, I really didn't care what had happened to Max Hardy the night before. He was out of my hair, and that was all that mattered. I had to wonder, though, if the Feds would hold me over in my own jail, or put me in Charlie's and Charlie in mine, just to be different.

I booted up the computer, which is what you call it when you turn it on, according to Anthony, and waited while everything came up, then hit the icon (that's the little picture on the screen) for the Internet, then connected myself to my email. Other than doing that, I could get Google, and look up things there, and find the icon for certain grafts and crap I needed. And find Free Cell. That's a computer game. I'm real good at it; so good, in fact, I think I'm becoming a computer nerd. I just hoped I'd get access in prison.

There were about twenty emails in my box, but I clicked on the one from Sanisabel333 first, saw it was from Jasmine, and read it.

That's when I bolted from my chair and ran to the front door, not exactly sure where I was going.

JASMINE FELT ANOTHER HAND on her arm. 'Jas, it's me, Leon,' he said.

'Yes?' Jasmine answered.

'Think we've been in here too long. These guys are pretty stupid, they might forget they've already come in here,' he said.

'So where do we go?' she asked.

There was no answer. Finally, she said, 'Leon, did you shrug? Nod, shake your head? I can't see you, you know.'

'Oh,' Leon said, then giggled. 'I forgot. I shrugged. Hey, Patch!' he whispered.

'What?' Patch said from a distance away, his voice heavy with sleep.

'Where you think we should go?' Leon asked.

'I like it right here,' Patch said.

'Man, I just know they're coming back!' Leon said. 'I can feel it!'

'You a mind reader all of a sudden?' Patch asked, his voice sarcastic.

Silence from Leon, then he said, 'Oh, forgot. I shrugged. No, I dunno. I just, you know, feel it. Like real hard. Like we gotta get out of here, and I mean fast.'

Mr Thomas touched Jasmine's hand, bringing it down to hold in his. 'I say we do what Leon says,' he told her softly.

'Why?' Jasmine asked.

'Because I believe in feelings. I told my Naomi I didn't want to come on this vacation, but she talked me into it. I had a feeling. I didn't go with it. Now I say we go with Leon's feeling.'

'I'm comfortable for the first time in two days,' Patch said. 'I ain't moving!'

Jasmine felt Leon's hand on her shoulder. 'Jas?' he said.

'Where do we go?' she asked him.

'Back in the air-conditioning vent?' he suggested.

'No way in hell,' Patch said.

Jasmine reached out her hand for the lamp and turned it on. They all squinted their eyes, adjusting to the brightness of the tiny-watt bulb. She looked over to the corner where Patch was stretched out, a woman's cardigan sweater laid over his chest.

'We're going, Patch, with or without you,' she said.

'Without,' Patch said.

'Man, come with us!' Leon said.

'No!' Patch all but yelled.

'Then when they catch you, don't tell 'em where we went, 'kay?' Leon said.

Patch just looked at him for a long minute, then said, 'I won't rat you out, man. You know better'n that.'

Leon walked over to Patch and did a complicated handshake, then headed for the wall with the air-conditioning vent, still open from their escape from it.

I WAS IN CHARLIE'S OFFICE, pacing back and forth in front of his desk. I'd called the only number me and Charlie could find for San Isabella, but a recorded voice had simply said, 'All circuits are down.' Then Charlie found a number for the Coast Guard in San Juan and I called them.

After finding someone who would actually talk to me, I identified myself and said, 'My head deputy and his new wife are on their honeymoon in San Isabella—'

'That island has been evacuated,' the Coast Guard guy said to me.

'Well, not real well, because I got an email from there dated yesterday, and timed at around ten p.m., from the wife—who also happens to be one of my deputies. She said there were pirates on the island and that they'd captured Emmett, my head deputy, and that they were in serious danger. Now I don't know about pirates—'

'Oh, yeah, lots of pirates around these waters,' the Coast Guard guy said. 'They love the little islands, especially during a storm. The islands get evacuated, just have a skeleton crew left, they can loot all they want.'

'So go out there and get 'em!' I all but shouted.

'And how do you propose I do that, Sheriff?' the Coast Guard guy said. 'The eye of the hurricane just passed over and we're getting the other side really hard right now. Surprised you even got through to us on the phone! No way I'm sending a helicopter or a boat out in this! If these deputies of yours know their business, they can take care of themselves,' he said.

'One of 'em's captured and the other one's pregnant! They need help!' I shouted. OK, yes, I was definitely shouting this time, but I could hear the storm and I'm gonna go with that as an excuse, not the panic I was feeling.

'Tell you what, Sheriff,' the Coast Guard guy said, 'as

soon as this storm lets up, I'll get a helicopter out there ASAP. How's that?'

'How long'll that take?' I asked.

'Oh, I dunno,' the guy said, real casual like. 'A few hours, maybe a day. No way it'll take more than two days.'

I hung up.

'What was that?' asked Scully—excuse me, Carmody—as she walked in the door.

'A totally useless Coast Guard captain,' I said. I explained the situation Emmett and Jasmine had found themselves in.

'I'd be worrying more about my upcoming arrest, trial and incarceration, if I were you, Sheriff,' said Whysmith/Mulder from behind Carmody.

'San Isabella?' Carmody said. 'That's near Puerto Rico, right?'

I nodded and she brought out her cell phone. 'My boyfriend's with the DEA and he's working an operation in San Juan,' she said. 'Let me call him and see what he can do.'

I fell into a chair while she dialed.

'Hey, baby,' she said, then laughed. After a moment, listening, she said, 'Yeah, I heard about the hurricane. Look, honey, I'm in Oklahoma…' Again she laughed. 'Yeah, tell me about it. Anyway, we got two law from here down in your neck of the woods on their honeymoon.' Listening again. 'Sheriff's deputies.' Listening again. 'They are too law!' she said and laughed. 'Anyway, they're on San Isabella…' Listening again. 'I know, but they didn't get evacuated somehow. They say there are pirates…' Listening. 'Really? Gross. Anyway, the female—who's pregnant, by the way—emailed here and said the male's been taken prisoner by these guys…' Listening. 'Well, God, I hope not. Anyway, we still got the woman…' Listening. 'Yes, that's what the Coast Guard said.' Listening. 'Anything you can do?' Listening. 'Uh huh.' Listening. 'Well, whatever you can do, babe…' Listening. 'Uh huh.' Listening. 'OK, sweetie. Miss you too!' She made a kissy sound and hung up the phone.

I jumped up from my chair. 'Well?' I demanded.

Carmody shrugged, then said, 'I'm sorry, Milt, but Jason said if they took your guy prisoner he's probably already dead.'

I fell back into the chair, feeling like I'd been suckerpunched in the gut. I'd known Emmett Hopkins as long as I'd been with the sheriff's department. We'd been best friends almost that long. He'd been through hell for so long, what with his boy, J.R., dying of leukemia, and then, years later, his wife, Shirley Beth, committing suicide with his police weapon. And now, finally on the verge of happiness, finally finding himself a new life, a wife and a baby on the way, he dies for no reason a million miles from home. I wondered if we'd even find enough to bury. I ached for Jasmine, happy herself for the first time since I'd known her, a widow on her honeymoon, having to raise a child on her own. If she survived. If she and the baby survived.

I covered my face with my hands and wept for the first time in my adult life.

'HEY, PICK-ME,' Jason Carstairs said, sitting down next to Pick-Me at the bar of the Casa Con Aqua.

Pick-Me looked up from his scotch, and smiled. 'Jason, me boyo. How doth they hang?'

'Always to the right,' Jason said. 'Helluva storm, huh?'

Pick-Me looked toward the one window of the bar. 'Well, would you look at that?' he said.

'It's a hurricane, Pick-Me,' Jason said, trying for patience. He, a minority in not only his alphabet agency, but

in most, liked Pick-Me Webster. There was something en-
dearing in the longer than regulation salt-and-pepper hair,
the silly ascots he always wore with his Hawaiian-style
shirts, the cuffed slacks and rubber-tire sandals adorning his feet.

Pick-Me always picked up the check, for two drinks at
the bar at the Casa Con Aqua, or for dinner for twelve at
the best restaurant in San Juan. His stories, to be honest,
got old after a while, but Jason believed them. He knew
for a fact that most of them were true, as he'd checked
Pick-Me out a couple of years ago when they'd first met,
and discovered that yes, he had flown cocaine out of the
poppy fields of Cambodia in 1971, and yes, he had saved
three American pilots shot down in Nicaragua by flying so
low through the jungle that they found leaves stuck in the
wheel wells of the plane once he landed. And it was also
true that Noriega had put out a hit on Pick-Me for sleeping
with one of his married cousins, a contract that, thank-
fully, had been nullified by Noriega's arrest just months
later. There were rumors that Noriega hadn't really been
in the drug business, but had been set up by Pick-Me in
order to get the hit revoked. But those were only rumors,
and Jason was pretty sure they weren't true. Not totally
sure, but pretty sure.

To Jason, Pick-Me was the real deal. A bona fide, old-
school spy, almost, but not quite, in the James Bond cat-
egory. Jason knew that as a DEA agent he'd see lots of
action, but not the caliber of action Pick-Me had seen over
the years. He doubted there'd be much history in taking
a drug mule here, a fourth in command of a minor car-
tel there. He envied Pick-Me his Cold War memories, his
Cambodian shenanigans, his never-quite-by-the-book exploits.

'Yeah, this hurricane is playing hell out on the islands,'

Jason said, sipping the fresh tequila shooter the bartender had placed before him.

'Hurricane?' Pick-Me said, once again glancing out the window.

'Yeah. Just got a call from this FBI agent I know. She said there's a couple of county deputies on their honeymoon got stuck on an evacuated island, and now they got pirates up their asses.'

'Really?' Pick-Me said, glancing at the bartender for a refill.

'Yeah, she wanted me to do something about it but, hey, it's a hurricane, ya know?' Jason said.

'Hurricane?' Pick-Me said, again glancing out the window.

Jason sighed. 'Yeah, Pick-Me, a hurricane. You know, big storm, lots of wind?'

'And these two county deputies on their honeymoon are stuck on an island with pirates, you say?' Pick-Me said, downing his fourth scotch of the hour.

'Yeah, that's what she said, my FBI friend,' Jason answered.

Quietly, as if to himself alone, Pick-Me Webster said, 'I've never flown in a hurricane.'

ELEVEN

'THE MONEY WAS INSURED, correct, Agent Whysmith?' said Judge Slater.

'Well, yes, your honor, but—' Whysmith started.

'And it did save Mrs Dickey's life, correct, Agent Whysmith?' said Judge Slater.

'Ah, yes, your honor, but—' Whysmith started.

'And what would you have had them do, Agent Whysmith?' said Judge Slater.

'Well, your honor, they should have—'

'Sat on their behinds while Mrs Dickey was being violated by these hooligans?' said Judge Slater.

'Of course not, your honor, but—'

I almost felt sorry for Mulder/Whysmith. He, of course, didn't know that Judge Jefferson Davis Slater was La-Donna's mama's sister's husband's brother, and I for one wasn't about to tell him. There was no real legal relationship there, either by blood or marriage. You can't help who your kin's husband or wife is related to, now can you? When anybody in Prophesy County wants to play the Six Degrees of Kevin Bacon game, we change it to how you're related to someone you just met. 'Cause chances are real good that you are.

LaDonna sat in the row behind us—that is, me, Charlie Smith, and Dewayne Dickey. The hand of her good arm was touching her husband's shoulder, and her broken arm was in a bright pink sling for all the world to see. She looked downright pitiful. And me and Charlie, with his arm in a matching sling, and even Dewayne, well, we just looked heroic.

'All I can say,' Judge Slater said, 'is it's a damn shame those hooligans let the money burn up, but what's the law to do when you're messing with meth freaks, know what I mean?'

Me, Charlie, and Dewayne all nodded our heads. Whysmith didn't.

'Agent Whysmith,' Judge Slater said, obviously losing his patience with the entire enterprise, 'I just don't see where these men did anything wrong. How you gonna lock up the sheriff of a county and the police chief of a city, not to mention the bank president of the only bank in town, for saving somebody's life? 'Specially somebody like poor Mrs Dickey,' he said, smiling at his brother's wife's sister's daughter. 'Lord knows what those men would have done to her if these three courageous citizens hadn't done their duty and gone to her rescue.' He shook his head. 'I don't see any charges here.' He banged his gavel. 'Next case.'

JASMINE WAS FEELING BAD—physically, mentally, emotionally, and spiritually. She wasn't sure if she was going to be able to contain the nausea this time, as she crawled her way through the air-conditioning ducts, and she felt sick about Emmett and guilty about Patch. And the thought of herself and her unborn baby being captured by the pirates somewhere below them in the hotel was enough to cripple her emotionally.

Leon was again in the lead, taking them further away from the kitchen and the office.

'Where are we going?' Jasmine finally asked him, whispering.

'There's a section of the hotel that's closed,' Leon whispered back. 'Got hit by the last hurricane and never fixed back up. If the pirates ever even looked in there, they wouldn't go far. It's a real mess and everything worth anything's already been taken out.'

'Then why didn't we go there to begin with?' Jasmine demanded.

Leon shrugged and grinned. 'Forgot about it,' he said, which Jasmine didn't doubt. Leon's short-term memory did seem to be a bit negligible.

All of a sudden Jasmine heard a noise and felt the air conditioning duct sway. She and Mr Thomas fell prone in the duct. 'What was that?' she demanded of Leon.

He too was lying in a prone position. 'Looks like the storm's back. Think we were in the eye there for a while.' With a dreamy look on his face, he said, 'I knew Annie was going to make it! Full-blown hurricane! Listen to her! I swear she's at least a force three, if not a four!'

'Yeah, well, bully for her,' Jasmine whispered, 'but let's get the hell out of these vents before the entire hotel comes down, OK?'

'Yeah,' Leon agreed. 'I wanna get to a window! I gotta see this!'

Jasmine envied the delight in his voice. She wished she had something, anything, to make her feel something less than totally undone. Closing her eyes, she said a quick prayer, asking for Emmett, her husband, to still be alive, and for her baby to make it through.

'SO WHO'S LEON MCKERRY?' the captain asked.

Emmett shrugged. 'Don't know,' he said. 'Just made it up.'

'Hum,' said the captain, the genial smile on his face. 'You know, I was arrested once in Prophesy County,' he said, 'back when I was a kid.' He laughed. 'Shooting out street-lights.'

His men laughed good-naturedly at the captain's youthful indiscretion.

'They put me in a cell. Reeked of pee,' the captain said.

Emmett wondered how that would offend this man, who reeked of odors much more pungent than pee, but he said nothing.

'The jail cells still reek of pee?' the captain asked.

'Not so much,' Emmett said.

'I've decided to kill you, Deputy Hopkins,' the captain said.

'I hope you've given that decision all due consideration,' Emmett said.

The captain laughed, followed quickly by the laughter of his men.

'All due consideration,' the captain repeated. 'I like that. Fact is, Deputy Emmett Hopkins, I like you, but I'm afraid you lied about your skill as an accountant.'

'Little bit,' Emmett said.

'That is a shame,' the captain said.

'Though, like I said, I am a good shot,' Emmett said, smiling at the captain.

'And I bet if I gave you a gun right this minute you could put a bullet straight between my eyes,' the captain said, smiling back.

'No doubt about it,' Emmett said.

'How about right between his eyes?' the captain asked, pointing at one of his goons, a scruffy-looking guy with big, greenish teeth and one eyebrow.

'No problem,' Emmett said.

There was a tittering of laughter from the men, although the green-toothed pirate wasn't finding it all that funny.

'Collin,' he said, addressing the green-toothed pirate, 'you and Kev and Mick go look for the wife.'

'Leave my wife out of this,' Emmett said, the smile gone from his face.

The captain made a 'tsk, tsk' sound. 'What? And separate you two on your honeymoon? That's just cruel, Deputy Hopkins. I hate coming between a man and his wife, don't I, boys?' he asked and his men all laughed in agreement.

'Now, when we find her,' the captain said to Emmett, 'we'll see what she has to say about how good a shot you are.' He clapped his hands with delight. 'I think we'll play a little game! You know, like William Tell and the apple on his son's head!' He looked at his men. 'What do you think?'

As one, they looked baffled by his allusion. Looking back at Emmett, the captain said, 'I really do hate not having anyone to talk to, Deputy Hopkins. At least, with you on board, you'd get my drift, wouldn't you?'

'Drop dead,' Emmett said and the captain laughed.

I WAS WALKING OUT of the courthouse with a gleeful Charlie Smith and a hen-pecked Dewayne Dickey, who was getting chewed out by LaDonna as we walked, when I got accosted yet again by Agnes Shorewalter.

'Sheriff! Sheriff!' she yelled from the open window of her Toyota Long Bed pick-up, which was illegally parked in a handicap zone, motor running. It wasn't the VW van anymore, but it *was* still painted with flowers and such. She jumped out of her truck and ran to the sidewalk to meet me. Charlie went one way and Dewayne and LaDonna went the other, leaving me alone in the middle with Agnes.

'Hey, Agnes,' I said, sighing. 'Sorry I don't have any new information—'

'Well, I do!' she said, hands on ample hips as she glared at me. She obviously hadn't had much time that morning to get herself ready. The muumuu was on backwards and inside out, the tag sticking out the front, and the ton of gray hair was loose and hanging down her back, almost to her bottom. 'They did it again!'

'Who did what again?' I asked.

She pulled her right arm back, and for a minute there I was afraid she was going to bitch-slap me. But then she put the hand down and said, 'I am not a violent person.' She closed her eyes. 'I am not a violent person. I am not a violent person.'

'Agnes?' I said.

She opened her eyes. 'The Satan worshippers were back last night. They tore up half an acre of organic kale and left a fire ring pentagram in the middle of it!' She bit back a sob as she said, 'In the middle of my organic kale!'

'Follow me to the station, Agnes. I'll get somebody on this right away.'

As I turned to head for my Jeep, she grabbed my arm. 'I don't want one of your deputies, Milt! I want you!'

'Agnes, I got some real trouble brewing and I don't have the time—'

'You never did like me, did you?' she said.

'What?' I said.

'I know what people around here think of me. That old hippy chick! Well, I'll tell you something, Mr I'm-the-Sheriff-and-I-think-I'm-hot-shit! My silly organic vege-tables and hippy do-dads can buy and sell the lot of you! You know what my bottom line is? And I'm not talking my hip measurements here, Mister! So get your eyes off my butt! I'm talking half a mil last year and I'm not talk-ing gross! I'm talking net! Pure profit! And yeah, Buddy, I'm laughing all the way to the bank! But not the bank that you let get robbed either, Mr I-couldn't-find-my-ass-with-a-map-and-a-flashlight! I go to a real bank in the city and I've got my own VP who looks after me like I'm Heidi-Frigging-Klum! And my stock portfolio would make you lose your lunch! So, I think it's about frigging time you started treating me like I'm a real person and not just that old hippy chick everybody laughs at!' By the time she finished the tirade, her face was the shade of a ripe eggplant and I wondered about calling for EMS.

'You through, Miz Shorewalter?' I asked.

She took a deep breath then said, 'Yes.'

'The bank got robbed, yeah. And a city policeman got shot and later murdered. I got a temporary deputy murdered in my own jail cell. My ex-wife got kidnapped by the bank robbers and I just barely walked out of that courthouse behind us without having to spend my golden years in prison. And my best friend just got murdered by pirates on a Caribbean island and his pregnant wife, one of my deputies, could end up with the same fate. So, no, to tell you the truth, I don't give a flying shit about your frigging organic kale, Miz Shorewalter! I got bigger fish to fry. I will, however, get one of my deputies to follow you back to your place and see what can be seen. Other than that, honey, you are shit out of luck.'

With that I turned and headed for the Jeep. Once I got in, I noticed Agnes Shorewalter get in her pick-up and follow me. I doubted if I'd get her vote next election.

I WAS IN CHARLIE'S OFFICE, pacing. 'We gotta get Jasmine out of there!' I said for at least the hundredth time.

'I don't know how,' Charlie said.

'We can't just leave her to those—those…'

'Pirates?' said Agent Carmody, coming in the room.

'Whatever,' I said, glaring at her.

'Well, I just got a call from my boyfriend. The reception was really bad. I guess because of that hurricane they're having. But I think he said they were going to take care of it,' Carmody said.

I stopped pacing. 'They? Who's they?'

Carmody shrugged. 'I have no idea.'

FINALLY LEON STOPPED. The air conditioning duct was still swaying, and the rush of wind outside the hotel was still sounding like a freight train heading in their direction. But at least they'd come to the vent Leon had been looking for.

'This is it!' he whispered. He looked through the vent, waiting for any movement in the room below. Finally, after what felt to Jasmine like an eternity, he kicked out the vent cover and dropped down. Jasmine helped Mr Thomas through the hole, pushing on his belly as she'd done at the earlier vent hole, then followed him through.

Leon had been right. The place was a mess. There was a hole in the ceiling about a hundred yards in, with rain blowing in at, well, hurricane strength. They moved away from the hole, further into the wing and found a room with a door still attached and no holes in its ceiling. A broken desk lay on its side in the room, and Jasmine and Leon dragged it over to block the door, then they all found spots on the floor, no one saying anything. This was, they all knew, their last-ditch effort. They had no place to go from here.

Jasmine lay on her back, her mind going places she'd rather it not go. Places like what she would do if she and the baby made it out, but Emmett didn't. Places like what he would do if Emmett made it out, but she and the baby didn't. And, of course, her mind traveled back, to the past, to the life she wanted to forget, to the life she thought had changed when she found Emmett.

Basically to her life with Lester Bodine. They'd started going steady in the fall of the seventh grade, and he'd been true to her until the spring of that school year, when he'd lost his virginity to a tenth-grader from the high school.

Since she'd refused him her favors, he'd felt it only fair that he see other girls for *that*, and Jasmine had felt she had to agree. So, from the seventh grade until their senior year in high school, Lester Bodine had had his pick of the girls in their school, and he'd picked often if not quite well.

Jasmine had had no intention of giving it up until her wedding night, but, after the senior prom, when Lester gave her a tiny diamond engagement ring, all bets were off.

She'd been confident then that, since she was his emotionally *and* physically, his exploits with all the other girls in school would cease and desist. And to her absolute knowledge, they did. Rumors were just that: rumors. The pitiful looks other girls gave her from that day to her wedding day were just sour grapes on their part.

When the looks didn't stop after the wedding, Jasmine put it all down to plain old jealousy. Here she was, a married woman, with her own home, although it was just a single wide trailer in Lester's parents' backyard, and all these girls still lived at home with their mamas and daddies and didn't have one ring on their fingers.

Her friends, the few she had that she felt had never, at least not more than once, slept with her husband, carried tales of this girl saying she'd been with Lester, and that girl saying she'd been with Lester, but Jasmine never believed them. Just because Lester worked at his daddy's feed and grain store, which was open from six in the morning until five in the afternoon, and still had to work until the wee hours of the morning (doing inventory three to four nights a week, fifty-two weeks a year), didn't mean she had to believe these rumors that these girls were spreading just because they were jealous of a real loving relationship.

It wasn't these rumors that made Jasmine stay on the pill long after Lester decided it was time for them to have a baby. It wasn't these rumors that kept her hiding the pills from her husband and suggesting maybe there was something wrong with his equipment when she failed, every month, to wind up pregnant. It was just the feeling that she wasn't ready, for whatever reason, to bear Lester's child.

And it certainly wasn't the rumors that ended her up in the sheriff's office in the wee hours of the morning, ten years into the marriage, pretty damn close to being arrested. No, it wasn't the rumors this time. It was actually coming home and finding Lester in bed with Maryanne Sergeant, a girl she'd always despised. Maryanne had fled the scene in one of Jasmine's good towels, and Jasmine had decided that it was time for Lester's much needed and much overdue circumcision. Using a steak knife and no anesthetic for the procedure was possibly what ended her up in the sheriff's office.

She never did know what Milt had said to Lester to keep him from pressing charges, but that had finally been the end of the marriage.

Was this now the end of her second marriage? Now that she'd finally found the right man, the man of her dreams, the love of her life, was this it? Was it all over?

TWELVE

PATCH WAS FAST ASLEEP in his corner, huddled under the blossom pink rayon sweater he'd found on the back of one of the computer chairs. His dreams were spotty and not pleasant, but better than the reality that woke him.

Two goons had his arms and were dragging him out of the room. 'Hold on! Hold on!' Patch shouted, but nobody held on and nobody answered. 'What's going on here, gents?' he asked, but still received no reply.

So he settled down and allowed himself to be dragged through the hotel, seeing as how there seemed to be no alternative to his situation. He ended up as a heap on the floor in the dining room. The first thing he noticed was Emmett, Jasmine's husband, standing right by him, arms behind his back, a shocked look on his face.

Then he heard someone say, 'What piece of crap have you brought me now?'

Patch sat up and looked toward the speaker. A grizzly-haired white guy sitting at a table by himself.

'No offense, Tyrone,' the man said, glancing behind him at a large black man with a diamond star in his front tooth.

'None taken, Cap'n,' the black man said in an English accent.

'Well, this piece of crap don't like you none, either,' Patch said from his perch on the floor of the dining room.

The captain, or whatever he was, inclined his head slightly and one of the goons who had dragged Patch through the hotel smacked him on the side of the head.

'I especially don't like back-talkin' from such as you,' the man said, again turning to the large black man behind him. 'No offense, Tyrone.'

'None taken, Cap'n,' the large man answered.

'You notice I ain't calling you no names?' the white man said to Patch. 'In deference to my man Tyrone's feelings.'

'Thank you, Cap'n,' Tyrone said.

'But I gotta ask you, Tyrone, you remember that guy ran on Captain Rory O'Shannon's ship, called himself Patch?'

'White guy with one eye, Cap'n. Sure I remember him,' Tyrone said.

'See, two things different between him and this here Patch. That one being white and only having one eye, while this one is black and has two eyes.'

'That he do, Cap'n,' Tyrone said.

'That just don't seem right, Tyrone. Him having two eyes yet calling himself Patch. What do you think about that?' the captain asked.

'Don't seem right,' Tyrone said.

The captain finally stopped staring hard at Patch, and turned to look at Tyrone. 'Why don't you even things up some?' he said.

'Whoa, now, wait a minute,' Patch said, putting up both hands to ward them off. 'I don't reckon that's a good idea, Captain, sir.'

'You don't reckon, do you?' the captain said, looking back at Patch, a small smile playing across his chapped lips.

'No, sir, no, sir. Look here, anything you want. Anything,' Patch said.

'Where's the woman?' the captain asked.

Patch said, 'What woman?'

The captain inclined his head and the goon standing next to Patch smacked him on his ear.

'Where's the woman?' the captain demanded again.

Rubbing his head and whining, Patch said, 'Man, I don't know what you're talking about! I don't got no woman!'

'*His* woman,' the captain said, pointing at Emmett. 'You were with her, right?'

'Oh, her,' Patch said. 'She dead.'

'Then where's her body?' the captain demanded.

'Outside. I drug her out there, 'fraid she might start stinking up the place, know what I mean?'

'And how did this woman die?' the captain asked.

Patch looked at Emmett then back at the captain. 'See, weren't my fault none, really, but when you guys got Emmett here, she got to carrying on something fierce, and I thought y'all was gonna hear her, so I tried to shush her, and well—'

Emmett lunged at Patch, but two of the pirate goons pulled him back. The captain laughed, his men following suit.

'I'm not sure which of you is more full of shit,' the captain said. 'You, Emmett, with all your lies, or your two-eyed Patch here, telling his lies. You don't really think he killed your wife, do you?'

Staring daggers at Patch, Emmett said, 'If he did, he's a dead man.'

'Oh, he's a dead man either way,' the captain said.

'Now, Captain, sir…' Patch said, getting to his knees in a pleading position.

The captain rolled his eyes. 'Say "please, massa",' the captain said. 'That's what you people say, right?' Turning his head at a slight incline, he said, 'No offense, Tyrone.'

'None taken, Cap'n,' Tyrone said.

'Please, massa, sir,' Patch said, his hands up in a prayer-like position.

The captain laughed uproariously at this, as did his men.

And while they were so occupied, Patch took a quick look at Emmett, then used his untied right hand to knee-cap the goon on his right, while using his left leg to trip the goon on his left.

Emmett simultaneously swung around, taking down one of his goons with his taped-together hands, and using his leg to kick the other goon in the nuts. Both went down. Of course, that was only four, and as there were at least ten men in the room, not counting the captain, even less the four they managed to knock down, the odds still weren't all that good. Before either man could take a step towards freedom, they were both flat on their faces, staring at the dining-room carpet, arms painfully pulled behind them and tied.

JASON CARSTAIRS HAD three more tequila shooters before he began to see the wisdom of Pick-Me Webster's plan.

'We fly low,' Pick-Me said, 'close to the water. Water's going to be rough, but we stay above it, above it and below the clouds. We can make it to San Isabella in less than an hour in the right plane.'

'Where you gonna get the right plane?' Jason asked.

'Oh, I have my ways,' Pick-Me said, a large grin on his face. 'You up for a real adventure, me boyo?'

'Ah, hell,' Jason answered, 'why the hell not?'

And so it began.

JASMINE'S PLIGHT HAVING cleared my mind of any other responsibilities, it was a good thing Max Hardy called me that afternoon, because I sure as hell forgot to call him.

'Sheriff?' he said. 'Max Hardy.'

'Mr Hardy,' I said. 'Where'd you run off to last night?'

'Figured you didn't need me hanging around. Thought

you and the Chief might be in enough trouble without having taken a civilian with you into the fray, so to speak.'

'So to speak,' I said.

'Hard to explain your position vis-a-vis the blackmail,' Max Hardy said.

'You making fun, Mr Hardy?' I asked.

'Little bit,' he said.

'Glad you can see the humor in all this, and, by the way, since you *asked*,' I said, which he didn't, 'the judge dismissed all charges.'

'Well, that's good to hear,' Max Hardy said. 'And since you *asked*,' he said, obviously copying me, 'I had a long talk with my sister.'

'How's she doing?' I asked.

'Better than I would have thought,' he said. 'She was pretty upset when you told her what you did, but I think it was because it confirmed suspicions she already had about him. Seems Wilson had already hit her up for money, several times, as a matter of fact. She never gave him a cent.' He laughed. 'Seems Elise is a little more...um, worldly, I guess that's the word, than I thought.'

'How so?' I asked.

'She said she never had any intention of marrying Wilson.'

'Really?'

Max Hardy laughed. 'She wouldn't tell me, but she told my wife. She said she realized the only thing she liked about the relationship was the sex. She'd just about decided to dump him when you came to see her.'

I shook my head. 'Well, good for her,' I said. 'I think next time she'll know what to look for.'

'According to my wife, all she's looking for is a cute ass and...' He paused. 'To quote my wife, "some staying power".'

'Well,' I said, still shaking my head, 'I guess that's, well, liberated?'

'I guess so,' Max Hardy said. 'Look, Sheriff, I'm sorry about busting your chops last night, making you take me along, but I was half thinking Wilson Everett was involved.'

'What makes you think he wasn't?' I asked.

'Well, the bad guys got blown up last night, right?' he said.

I agreed that they had.

'Wilson called me this morning, begging me to intervene with Elise on his behalf. I told him to take a hike.'

'So he probably wasn't involved,' I said.

'Probably not,' he agreed. 'But thanks again, Sheriff. And no hard feelings, I hope?'

I laughed. 'None on my part. And, please, give your sister my best,' I said as we rang off.

I heard a commotion from the lobby and got up to see what was going on. In the big room I saw Gladys standing behind her counter wide-eyed, with Agnes Shorewalter standing in front of her. In her right hand she held a blonde girl about twelve by the neck of her T-shirt, and in her left hand she held a dark-haired girl about twelve by the arm.

'Guess what, Sheriff?' Agnes said upon seeing me.

'What's that, Agnes?' I said.

'Found me some Satan-worshippers in the act!' At which point she let go of both girls and they flew into Gladys's counter.

'Dawn Marie Meadows!' Gladys said, staring at one of the girls. 'What is going on?'

'I didn't do nothing!' the little blonde said.

'It was all her idea!' the dark-haired girl said, pointing at the blonde.

'No, it wasn't!' the blonde screamed at the dark-haired girl. 'You wanted to do it, too!'

I whistled and everybody shut up. 'In my office,' I said to all three females.

With quiet dignity, Agnes Shorewalter led the parade.

Once we were all seated, I said, pointing at the blonde girl, 'OK, you're Dawn Marie Meadows. Who are you?' I said, looking at the dark-haired girl.

She shrugged.

'You don't know your name?' I asked.

At which point she burst into tears. The blonde said, with some disgust in her voice, 'Her name is Lindsey Adams and she's a big old baby!'

At which point Lindsey Adams hit Dawn Marie Meadows, while Agnes Shorewalter sat back, her arms folded across her chest, and just glared at everybody.

I got up and separated the two girls, then called Gladys on the intercom. 'Gladys, would you please call the parents of Ms Meadows. The other girl's name is Lindsey Adams and her parents live on—what street, Lindsey?'

The question just brought more wails of agony from the dark-haired girl, but Dawn Marie, being the well of information she was, said, 'Her father's name is Robert and they live on Fourth Street.'

I repeated the information to Gladys and hung up. Turning to Agnes, I said, 'Miz Shorewalter, I cannot interview these juveniles without their parents present, so instead, I'll just ask you to state what you saw with your own eyes.'

'Of course, Sheriff,' she said, glaring at the two girls. 'I just got back from my stand this afternoon, and I saw these two in the woods behind my house. So I walked around the other direction, so that I could come up behind them, and I caught them building another pentagram-shaped fire ring. When they saw me, they tried to run off, but I'm faster than you might think,' she said, glaring at me.

'And did they say anything to you?' I asked.

'Other than rude comments about my lifestyle and weight? No, not much,' she said.

'We didn't do nothing!' Dawn Marie Meadows said.

'Anything,' Agnes corrected. 'If you're going to be a felon, at least try not to sound like a stupid felon.'

'Shut up, you old fat hippy!' Dawn Marie fairly spat at Agnes.

I'd had about enough of Prophesy County's next generation. I got up and yelled out to the bullpen for Dalton. He came quickly and I said, 'Take these two young ladies, and I use that term loosely, to the interrogation room, please, Deputy.'

'Yes, sir,' Dalton said, and held the door open for them to proceed him. Dawn Marie just glared at everyone, while Lindsey burst into a new bout of tears.

Once they were gone, I said, 'Good work, Agnes. Want me to deputize you?'

'Since I'm doing your work for you, might as well,' she said, but she smiled when she said it.

At that point Anthony Dobbins came in the back door from checking out an alarm gone haywire out in the county, and I gave the case over to him, since it was his to begin with. Agnes and me shook hands, so I guess we were friendly acquaintances again.

Basically, it had been a hell of a day.

LATER THAT NIGHT, I lay in bed, unable to sleep. I had no idea if Carmody's boyfriend was going after Jasmine or not. Carmody hadn't been sure of exactly what he'd said. All I could do was pray, and that I did, over and over. I had to get Jasmine back, and I'd help her raise her and Emmett's child. I'd be Uncle Milt, and when he or she was old enough, I'd tell him (or her) about his (or her) daddy, what a great guy he was, and how much he'd loved him (or her), even though he (or she) wasn't born yet.

I'd tell him (or her) stories about going fishing with Emmett and how he fell asleep in the boat sometimes, once almost falling in the water. I'd tell him (or her) about weekday lunches at the Longbranch Inn, and how Emmett had loved his chicken-fried steak with cream gravy. I'd tell him (or her) what a great cop his (or her) daddy had been, and what a wonderful police chief, glossing over him leaving the department. I'd tell him (or her) how much I relied on Emmett as my second in command at the sheriff's department. I'd tell him (or her) how much his (or her) daddy had loved his (or her) mommy, and how his only thought was to start a home with her and their baby. I'd tell him (or her) what an outstanding man his (or her) daddy had been, what a loss he was to me, and to everybody who knew him.

And then I started bawling again, which woke up my wife. It certainly wasn't on purpose, but I did find something new that got my wife frisky. Who knew tears worked on a woman that way?

THIRTEEN

PICK-ME WEBSTER dragged the unconscious body of the mechanic further into the hangar. This was the mechanic who had refused to allow Pick-Me to take his own twin-engine Cessna out in the storm. It had gone something like this:

Pick-Me: 'Millard, my man, taking the plane for a spin.'

Millard: 'The hell you say.'

Pick-Me: 'This is my friend Jason. He'll be flying with me this evening.'

Millard: 'Ain't no way, Jose.'

Pick-Me: 'I'm on a mission, Millard.'

Millard: 'I don't give a fuck. These planes is my responsibility and ain't no one taking one of 'em out in a hurricane! Even you, Pick-Me.'

Pick-Me: 'So sorry, Millard.'

At which point Pick-Me let go with a left hook to the side of Millard's head, which knocked Millard unconscious but allowed less damage to Pick-Me's hand. At which point the following conversation took place:

Jason: 'Shit, man! Why'd you do that?'

Pick-Me: 'Because he wouldn't have allowed me up in the plane otherwise, Jason.'

Jason (looking at the raging storm): 'So maybe he's right, Pick-Me. Maybe we shouldn't go up.'

Pick-Me (laughing): 'Don't be silly! I can fly the ass off a hurricane! Help me drag him some place comfortable, would you, my man?'

Jason took Millard's feet while Pick-Me took his head

and they half-carried, half-dragged the mechanic to a cot in a corner where they deposited the top half of his body, leaving the lower, heavier half dragging the ground.

The wind was howling, the rain coming down almost horizontally, the one little, dwarf palm tree next to the hangar was bent double in the wind, half of its fronds gone. Jason stood at the hangar door, gaping at the hurricane.

'Now,' Pick-Me said, stepping out of the hangar and becoming instantly soaked with rain, salt-and-pepper hair hanging long down his collar, pink-tinged face and bulbous, red-veined nose turning dark from the wet. He clapped his hands with delight, headed toward the Cessna, and said, 'Climb aboard!'

'ALL I CAN THINK ABOUT is Jasmine,' I told Agent Whysmith, who was not happy.

'I'm very sorry about your deputy, Sheriff,' Whysmith said, while his demeanor said he really wasn't. 'But we've got work to do right here. The FDIC, in their wisdom, has decided to replace the replacement money. Which I guess is fine since the bad guys are dead. But I still want to be very careful. God only knows how many of your assholes around here have decided the bank is easy pickings.'

'So talk to Charlie Smith. He's the town police. I'm the county. Bank's got nothing to do with me,' I said, still pacing and watching the phone, willing it to ring.

'Chief Smith is in place, Sheriff. But I need you and your men as back-up,' Whysmith said.

'Yeah, well, last time we did that all hell broke loose,' I countered.

'Leave someone in place,' Whysmith suggested. 'I just need you and a couple of your people at the bank.'

'I'm already two down with Jasmine down there and Emmett—' I couldn't even say it. I didn't want to start bawling again in front of Whysmith. Crying in front of my wife was one thing; crying two times in front of an FBI agent was quite another.

'OK, you and one, just one of your guys. Please, Sheriff.'

He said please. An FBI agent said 'please' to me. What's a guy to do?

I agreed and Whysmith left. I called Anthony and Dalton into my office.

'OK, here's the deal,' I told them. 'The money's coming in to replace the replacement money, so the FBI thinks they need more of a presence, which means they want some of us down there. As strapped as we are for staff right now, I can't afford more'n me and one other guy going, so, Anthony, I'm gonna leave you in charge here and, Dalton, I need you to go with me.'

'Yes, sir,' said Anthony.

'Yes, sir,' said Dalton. Then, 'Milt?'

'Yes, Dalton?' I said with a sigh. That's the thing about Dalton. It's gotta be all spelled out. In the dictionary, under the definition of 'big and stupid', there's a picture of Dalton Pettigrew. OK, maybe that's a little over the top. Maybe just under 'big and not as bright as a forty-watt bulb'.

'They bringing the money in rather than just a wire transfer?' he asked.

'That's the way I understand it, Dalton.'

'Why they doing that, Milt?' Dalton asked.

'I don't know,' I said slowly. 'It's just the way they're doing it. A cash flow thing or something, Dalton. You think you can handle this?'

'Oh, yes, sir,' Dalton said, grinning. 'Just wondered.'

So me and Dalton got ready to leave, getting shotguns together, Kevlar, all those things a cop needs to protect and serve.

'SOMEBODY SHOOT Two-Eyes,' the captain said.

'No!' Emmett shouted, almost simultaneously with Patch.

'You two!' the captain said, laughing and shaking his head, as a parent might to two quarrelling children. 'OK, somebody shoot the deputy.'

Somewhere in the group, somebody started singing 'I Shot the Sheriff', and everybody laughed—everybody except, of course, Emmett and Patch, both of whom still lay face down on the floor, arms behind them, noses deep in the hotel's dining-room carpet.

'Captain,' Emmett said, trying to turn his face toward the man in charge, only to get a kick in his neck in response. He turned back, his nose back in the carpet, and tried again. 'Captain, listen. Patch here's as good as they come. Real smart. You want an accountant, Patch here is your man. He's been doing the books here at the hotel for two years now, right, Patch?'

One dark brown eye was studying Emmett, then Patch said, 'That's right, Captain. I handle the books for the hotel.'

'Yeah?' the captain said. 'What's a debit?'

'When you pay something off,' Patch said.

'OK. What's a credit?' the captain asked.

'When somebody pays you,' Patch said.

'How much is four-hundred and twenty-four times sixty-four?' the captain asked.

Patch thought for a minute and said, 'Thirty-two thousand, eight hundred and forty-eight.'

Emmett stared at Patch and mouthed, 'That right?'

Patch shrugged in return.

The captain looked at his men. 'That right?' he asked the room in general.

Lots of shrugs, a couple of, 'sounds good'. and 'might be'.

'OK,' the captain said. 'You can be my accountant. For a few days anyway. Probably kill you in the morning.'

And everybody laughed.

Patch's one eye got wide as he looked at Emmett. Emmett whispered, 'It's a Dread Pirate Roberts thing.'

Somehow, Patch didn't seem reassured.

THE THREE OF THEM huddled together, a piece of the broken desk their only cover. Only Mr Thomas was dressed. Jasmine was still in just panties and a T-shirt; Leon in nothing more than his Tweety Bird boxers. Leon's bare feet were bleeding from having stepped on glass and nails on the floor of this abandoned part of the hotel. The hurricane had brought lower temperatures with it, and Jasmine's body was covered in goose-flesh and she trembled from the cold.

Mr Thomas began unbuttoning his Hawaiian-style shirt.

'What are you doing?' Jasmine asked.

'You're freezing,' Mr Thomas said. 'Take my shirt.'

'No, sir,' Jasmine said. 'I won't do it. Keep it on. Stay warm.'

'Not while a young pregnant woman is suffering, child. I won't do that. Now take it,' he said, having gotten the shirt off. 'Besides,' he said, smiling slightly, 'I'm wearing an undershirt.' He draped his shirt over Jasmine's chest, pulling the tail of it down over her knees, which she had pulled to her chest.

Jasmine immediately felt warmer, but wasn't sure if the guilt would be worth it. Maybe for the baby, she thought. For the baby I can handle the guilt.

'How long are we just gonna sit here?' Leon demanded.

'Long as it takes,' Jasmine said.

'Long as what takes?' he asked.

'As long as it takes for the pirates to find us, or for the cavalry to come,' she said.

'Ah, Pick-Me,' Jason said, sobering up as the Cessna twin engine warmed up. 'I'm wondering how good an idea this is.'

'Jason, my boy, when was the last time you did something reckless?' Pick-Me asked.

'Ah, when I asked my girlfriend to marry me?' Jason answered.

'Oh, my Lord, and you're afraid of simply flying through a hurricane? Much less dangerous than that, my boy,' Pick-Me said, beginning his taxi down the short runway of the private airport. 'Besides,' he said, grinning, 'if things don't go well tonight, you'll have an excellent excuse to get out of the wedding!'

Pick-Me pulled back on the stick, only to have the Cessna come up, then fall back down. Again he pulled back on the stick, and the Cessna bucked like a rodeo bronco: up and down, down and up.

'Ah, Pick-Me,' Jason said, holding on to the door on his side of the small aircraft. 'I'd like to get out now.'

'Don't worry, son. This is a good little ship. She'll make it. She's a sweetheart, aren't you, dearie?' he said, patting the cockpit dials of the Cessna.

As if all she needed was a few endearments, the Cessna pulled up and stayed up, climbing through the rain and the wind, rocking wildly but staying up. 'See?' Pick-Me said. 'I told you she was sweet!'

Jason barely heard him from the roar of the engine, the roar of the wind, and the roar of his mother's voice saying, 'Jason, you get down from there this minute!'

'Do you have windshield wipers?' Jason asked, his voice softer than he thought.

'Wipers?' Pick-Me shouted. 'Oh! Used to! Lost 'em somewhere in Ecuador! Just reach out the window and wipe your side off occasionally! Here!' Pick-Me shouted, handing Jason a red mechanic's towel. 'Try this!'

Jason looked at the towel, looked at Pick-Me, and threw up on his shoes.

'I CAN'T BELIEVE I'm doing this!' I groused as I drove my car into town to the bank.

'How you think Emmett and Jasmine are doing?' Dalton asked.

I hadn't shared the information about my deputies with any of the staff. They had work to do and lives to live; they didn't need this worry on top of that. It would all come out soon enough, I thought.

'Fine,' I told Dalton. 'Just fine.'

'I'm real glad Emmett got married,' Dalton said. 'Aren't you, Milt?'

'Yeah, Dalton, I'm real glad,' I said.

'I been thinking about it a lot lately,' Dalton said.

'About Emmett and Jasmine?' I asked, not really caring, just talking to keep him from asking too many questions.

'No, about getting married,' Dalton said.

That got my attention. 'Well, Dalton, I didn't know you were dating anyone special.'

'Oh, I'm not,' Dalton answered, 'just thinking about getting married. You know my mama's getting kinda old, Milt. Can't keep on living with her forever. Figure maybe I should get married. Maybe give Mama some grandkids. She'd like that.'

Oh, brother, I thought. 'Yeah, I bet she would, Dalton,' I said, pulling into a parking place in front of the bank.

We got out and joined the crowd inside the bank. It was closed, but still crowded, what with police personnel, FBI personnel, bank personnel, and then me and Dalton, or I guess I should say sheriff department personnel. We all stood around waiting for the armored truck to arrive with the replacement money for the replacement money. Not sure how many times the FDIC was gonna do this, but insurance is insurance, right?

I couldn't help noticing how fidgety Dewayne Dickey was. Katy Monroe kept patting him on the back, saying what appeared to be reassuring words. Glad it was her job this time and not mine.

'WELL, THEN, IF I keep Two-Eyes, I guess I kill you, huh, Deputy?' the captain said.

'Don't see the point of that,' Emmett said from the carpet.

Patch had been pulled up from the floor and was sitting at a table with some scary-looking dudes, three of whom were patting him on his bare naked shoulders and grinning. Patch had some doubts about his welcome.

'The point?' the captain said and shrugged. 'No point, really. Just don't need two more guys, and I'm not leaving you here. Not unless you wanna tell me where that cute little wife of yours is.'

'Patch already told you,' Emmett said.

'Oh, yeah,' the captain said, grinning. 'She's dead.' He looked over at Patch. 'You really kill a white woman, boy?' he asked.

'It was an accident,' Patch said, his voice shaky.

'And you threw her body out in the rain, that right, boy?' the captain asked.

'Didn't want her stinking up the place,' Patch said warily. 'Didn't know how long I was gonna be there.'

'Now how'd you get outside, Two-Eyes?' the captain asked. 'All the outside doors are guarded, right boys?'

There was a chorus of affirmative answers. The three

men touching Patch bore down a little harder on his shoulders and arms.

'Not all of 'em,' Patch said.

'Oh?' asked the captain.

'Yeah,' said Patch. 'There's a door by the office, goes to the back by the kitchen.'

'Take him,' he said to the three men guarding Patch. 'Bring the deputy here his little wifie. Sure he'll wanna cry over the body.'

As the three men stood up, bringing Patch to a standing position with them, Patch said, 'Ah, you know, there's a hurricane blowin' out there, Captain.'

'Really?' the captain said. 'Hadn't noticed.'

'Mighta blown the body away,' Patch offered.

'My, my, that would be a powerful storm, wouldn't it?' the captain said. 'Take him,' he told his men.

The three men dragged Patch out of the room. Emmett closed his eyes and prayed that Jasmine was somewhere where they wouldn't find her.

'Something tells me that boy's lying,' the captain said. 'What do you think, Deputy?'

Emmett said nothing.

'You just don't seem all that upset about your little cutie wife being thrown out with the trash. Seems to me you'd be a little more upset. Seems to me you wouldn't be taking up for that boy if you thought he killed your wife, accident or not.'

Emmett said nothing. 'Cat got your tongue, Deputy?' the captain asked.

Still Emmett said nothing. The captain nodded to one of his men standing by Emmett and the man kicked Emmett in the ribs.

The pain was excruciating, indicating to Emmett that he already had a problem in that vicinity, but he tried to hold his tongue. Anything he said at this phase, he figured, was going to be the wrong thing.

'Ah, hell, Deputy, you're no fun.' He waved to the man standing over Emmett. 'Take him on back to the kitchen. Let him stew for a while in there. I'm tired of him.'

Two men grabbed his arms and dragged him toward the kitchen, not even letting him get a chance to get to his legs.

FOURTEEN

IF ANYTHING THE STORM was getting louder, Jasmine noticed. And colder. She huddled close to Mr Thomas and waved Leon over.

'Come sit with us,' she said. 'All we have is our body heat.'

Leon came over, arms crossed over his skinny, hairless chest. 'Wish I'd thought to put some clothes on,' Leon said, ''fore I came and woke you guys up.'

'Yeah, wish I had too,' Jasmine said.

Mr Thomas pointed through the gloom of the unlighted room. The heavy clouds and rain from outside lent the indoor setting the light of dusk. 'That a tarpaulin?' Mr Thomas said.

Leon got up and walked to where Mr Thomas had pointed. 'Yeah. Old canvas one.' He shook it, dust and debris flying around them. 'Sorry about that.' He brought the tarp over and draped it across Mr Thomas and Jasmine, settling in next to her, with enough tarp left to cover him.

'Well, hell,' Leon said, grinning, 'this is better than home.'

'Do me a favor,' Jasmine said, 'don't ever invite me over, OK?'

THE ARMORED CAR pulled up in front of the bank and three uniformed police went outside to usher the guards in. Two men came in carrying bags, a third guard, a woman, pulled up the rear, holding a shotgun across her chest.

The guards handed the bags over to Dewayne, who took them, two in each hand. His shoulders bent with the weight of them. And that's when all hell broke loose.

Katy Monroe grabbed Dewayne by the hair, pulling his head back, a very sharp-looking knife at his throat. 'Move back!' she yelled, and we all did. 'OK, back further. Keep moving. OK. That's good. Now your weapons. Everybody drop 'em. You too, Milt! Drop your damn gun.'

I did as she said.

'Dalton!'

'Yeah, Katy?' Dalton said.

'Pick up all the guns, slide 'em over here to me,' Katy said.

Dalton just stood there.

'Dalton! Did you hear what I said?' she demanded, the knife pricking Dewayne's skin and a trickle of blood oozing down his neck.

'Yeah, Katy, I heard you!' Dalton said, a whine in his voice. 'But it don't make sense! You want me to pick up the guns or you want me to slide them to you? Which? If I pick up the guns, then I'd have to toss them to you; if I slide 'em, I can't pick 'em up!'

'Oh, for God's sake! Dalton, just kick 'em over here, OK? With. Your. Foot,' she said distinctly.

Dalton did as she said. With all the law enforcement in that room, there were a lot of guns to kick.

'Now all of you, back up to the vault!'

The vault hadn't been opened yet; Dewayne had put in a new timer and it was ten minutes until the vault door would automatically open. So we all just huddled in front of it.

Katy began walking backwards toward the front door of the bank. 'I'll send Dewayne back to you, probably in one piece,' she said.

She wasn't looking behind her. All of us at the door of

the vault were. We saw the door open, saw LaDonna take in the situation. Saw LaDonna realize that Katy Monroe had a knife at Dewayne's throat. Saw LaDonna jump on Katy's back and start pummeling her with her casted right arm. Katy dropped the knife and Dewayne as she tried to remove the she-devil from her back. It just wasn't gonna happen.

'PICK-ME,' JASON SAID, now totally sober, 'we gotta turn back.'

'Can't,' Pick-Me said, 'we already passed the point of no return.'

'We just left the fucking airport!' Jason shouted over the noise of the storm, the engine, and Pick-Me's tuneless whistling.

'If I'm in the air, that's *my* point of no return,' Pick-Me said, a stern look on his usually pleasant, if pickled, face.

Jason took off his seatbelt and fumbled in the small back part of the Cessna for a flotation device; hell, something made of wood, foam rubber, whatever. Something that would float!

'If we get out of this alive,' Jason shouted, 'remind me to kill you, OK?'

Pick-Me laughed. 'Don't worry, son,' he said. 'You won't have to. There's no way we'll live through this!'

Jason sat back down in the co-pilot's seat, a small, inflatable children's duck-shaped floaty in his hands. 'Oh, shit,' he said under his breath.

'WHAT WAS THAT?' Leon said.

'What?' Jasmine asked.

'Shhh!' Leon whispered, pulling the tarpaulin over their heads.

The door to their hiding place opened, the broken desk moving easily away from its job of blocking the door.

'OK, boy, this is as far as you go,' said a voice that reminded Jasmine of the one they'd heard in the freezer—yesterday? Or only hours ago? She had no idea.

'Captain said I was to be his new accountant,' said Patch. Leon grabbed Jasmine's hand and they both squeezed.

'Can't tell when the cap'n's kidding, now can you, boy?' said the pirate voice. 'He don't like coloreds none. Real racist he is. Only reason he's got Tyrone aboard is 'cause the bloke's so big I think he scares even the cap'n!' The pirate laughed long and hard.

'What have we got?' Leon whispered in Jasmine's ear.

'You mean weapon-wise?' she whispered back.

'Yeah,' Leon said.

'Just the shotgun. Is it loaded?' Jasmine whispered.

'I think so,' Leon said.

From the other side she felt Mr Thomas's hand on hers. She opened her palm and he laid something in it. Squinting through the gloom of the storm and the cover of the tarp, she saw a Swiss Army knife resting in her hand.

'And we got this,' she said, holding the knife up for Leon to see.

'And this,' Leon said, bringing a two-foot copper pipe from his other side.

'And this,' Mr Thomas whispered, proffering a good-sized piece of two by four.

'So I guess we're rescuing Patch?' Leon asked.

'Can't see any way out of it,' Jasmine said.

EMMETT WASN'T SURE why they hadn't killed him yet, but he had a sneaking suspicion that the captain actually liked him; maybe he missed having an American to talk to; maybe he didn't hate Oklahoma as much as he claimed.

Maybe the poor guy was homesick. Whatever the reason, Emmett was now sitting at a table by himself, hands still tied behind his back, feet tied, and a plate of food in front of him. He could do no more than smell it, of course, since his hands were tied behind his back.

'Oh, now, Deputy,' the captain said from his private table across from Emmett's, 'forget what your mama taught you and eat!' He laughed and his men joined in.

It was true Emmett was hungry. The last he remembered eating was the night the storm broke out and Leon had that nice spread in the bar. He had no idea how long ago that was, but his stomach was telling him it had been a good bit of time. So Emmett leaned forward, nudged the plate with his chin, getting it a little further toward the center of the table, then stuck his face in it, grabbing bits of food with his teeth.

There was general laughter from the room.

'Look at him go!' the captain said, clapping his hands with glee. 'He'll make a right fine pirate, don't ya think, boys?'

There were choruses of 'Oh, yeah, Cap'n', and 'you bet-cha, Cap'n', and 'right-o, Cap'n'.

'Hate to kill a man on an empty stomach,' the captain said.

Emmett looked up from his plate, food smeared on his face. 'You gonna let me digest at least?' he asked.

The captain laughed long and hard. Finally, wiping his eyes, he said, 'Oh, Deputy, you play a good game! I'm gonna miss you!'

LEON PEEKED FROM under the cover of the tarpaulin, and saw that the two pirates holding Patch had their backs to him. Getting back under cover, he looked at his team. 'OK,' he said, 'they got their backs to us. My idea is we just charge out of here swinging. Whatja think, Deputy Jasmine?'

'As good a plan as any I could think up,' she said, patting Leon on the back. 'Mr Thomas, you up for it?'

'I think I've had about enough of this shit!' the old man said.

'Amen, brother,' Leon said.

'On the count of three,' Jasmine said. They looked from one to the other and Jasmine counted. 'One, two, *three*!'

They threw the tarpaulin off and charged.

FIFTEEN

CHARLIE AND HIS BOYS did their thing with Katy and took her off to the city jail, with the Feds in tow. I went back to the sheriff's office, glad that was over so I could concentrate solely on getting Jasmine and her unborn baby home. I got on the horn and called the Coast Guard station in San Juan again, getting the same rigmarole again. Losing my temper didn't help the situation, but it made me feel better. I slammed the phone down and sat in my chair fuming. After I got Jasmine back, I decided, I was going up the chain of command of the U.S. Coast Guard and heads were gonna roll! Of that I was gonna make damn sure.

Then the phone rang. Half expecting (or just hoping) it was the Coast Guard telling me they'd found Jasmine, I was a mite disappointed when it was just Charlie Smith.

'Milt?' he said. 'You gotta get down here.'

'I'm busy, Charlie,' I said. 'What's up?'

'Katy Monroe's clammed up and she won't talk to anybody but you,' he said.

'Why me?' I demanded.

''Cause we're all strangers,' Charlie said in a silly falsetto. 'That's what the girl said. Said you know her, you'd understand.'

'How am I gonna understand her killing two people and robbing the bank three times?' I demanded.

'Don't ask me. She hasn't lawyered up yet; just demands to see you or she's not talking,' Charlie said.

'Oh, for God's sake,' I said in disgust. I had better things to do, like worry about Jasmine, than waste my time baby-sitting Charlie's case. I figured I'd spent way too much time on that already. But what's a lawman to do, you know? 'Be there in five,' I said.

'OH, SHIT!' JASON SCREAMED as the Cessna dropped out of the sky like a carnival Tilt-A-Whirl, plummeting to the gray Caribbean below. At the last possible moment, Pick-Me managed to push the stick up and the plane's nose reached for the sky while a small section of the tail kissed the water below.

'Now isn't this more fun than sitting in a bar drinking?' Pick-Me shouted at Jason, laughing out loud.

'I hate you!' Jason shouted. 'I hate your mother! I hate your future children!'

Pick-Me made a 'tsk, tsk' sound. 'If I knew you were going to be such a spoilsport, Jason,' Pick-Me said, 'I'd have left you in San Juan!'

'You're insane!' Jason shouted.

'Not within any standardized testing scales!' Pick-Me shouted back. 'They keep checking.'

'How much further?' Jason shouted.

'Oh, a hop, skip, and a tumble,' Pick-Me said, and laughed.

THE TARP CAME OFF and Jasmine, Leon, and Mr Thomas jumped up and rushed the two men holding Patch. Seeing his rescuers before the pirates did, Patch lashed out at one of his captors, then fell to the floor, not wanting to be in the way of the tools of justice his rescuers were brandishing. One pirate had been carrying a shotgun, which he'd laid down on the broken desk when he entered the room. The other had a pistol jammed in his pants at the small of his back. Neither was able to get to a weapon before they

were being beaten about the head and shoulders with the
two by four and the copper pipe. Jasmine held her shotgun
by the barrels, wielding it like a club, and was using that
to inflict as much bodily harm as possible.

It only took a moment before both goons were out cold
on the floor of the room. Finally using the Swiss Army
knife, Jasmine cut Patch's restraints.

'Well, it's about damn time!' Patch said, grinning.

'Where's Emmett?' Jasmine demanded.

Patch rubbed his hands and feet then gingerly stood up.
'In the dining room with the so-called captain. We get Emmett, then give me just five minutes alone with that racist
pig-fucker!' he said.

'Who? The captain?' Leon asked.

'Don't get me started,' Patch said, still rubbing his
hands where the ropes had held him.

'Let's use Patch's ropes and tie up these suckers,' Jasmine said.

'May I?' asked Mr Thomas, as he kicked over one of the
pirates and roughly jerked the man's arms behind his back.
Under his breath, Jasmine heard him say, 'For you, Naomi.'

'TELL YOU WHAT I'm gonna do, Deputy,' the captain said.
'I'm gonna make it quick. Some of my boys like to play
with a guy a little bit before doing him, but I'm going to
do you myself. That way I'll make it quick and relatively
painless.' He grinned at Emmett. 'Please take note I did
say "relatively".'

'Can I leave a note recommending you for sainthood?'
Emmett said.

The captain laughed. 'See? That's what I'm talking
about! That's what I'm going to miss! None of these assholes has a sense of humor, do you, boys?'

The responses varied from 'not much' to 'little bit' to 'huh?'

'I figure I just shoot you between the eyes, that'll do the trick, and you won't feel a thing. How does that sound?' the captain asked Emmett.

Emmett shook his head. 'Hard shot,' he said. 'What if you miss? Just take an ear off? Shoot off my nose? Then you'd be no better than your boys.'

'Hum,' the captain said, touching his finger to his chin as if in deep thought. 'You have a point. I am, however, a pretty good shot. I'd say the chances are, hum, seventy/thirty that I'll make the kill shot.'

Again Emmett shook his head. 'So I have a thirty percent chance of extreme agony?' he asked. 'I really don't like the odds.'

'Not a betting man, are you?' the captain asked. 'Well, I have to admit, in your shoes I'd probably feel the same. You got any ideas?'

'A few,' Emmett said. 'One, you untie me and hand yourself and your boys over to my custody.' The captain laughed at this idea. 'Two, you untie me and leave me here when you and your boys leave.' The captain shook his head at this one. 'Three, you put me back in the cabinet and leave, and I take my chances on getting out.' Again, the captain shook his head. 'Now, listen,' Emmett said. 'This one has the added bonus that I might not get out and you and your boys can imagine me slowly starving to death and trussed up like a turkey in that kitchen cabinet.'

'True,' the captain said, 'that does have its own brand of charm.'

'Or four, and I think you might like this one, you and me pace off. Each with our weapon of choice. You know, Dodge City style,' Emmett said.

The captain grinned. 'I do like that. An element of

chance. A possibility of a surprise ending. Plus, a little American history lesson for the boys.' He nodded his head. 'But, if you do get me, what's to stop my boys from just blowing you away?'

'We make a deal,' Emmett said. 'You, me and your boys. If I win, I'm the new Dread Pirate Roberts.'

The captain laughed loud and long. Finally he said, 'It's a deal.'

SIXTEEN

KATY WAS SITTING in a cell on the top floor of the court-house when I got there. She was still wearing her work clothes, stuff she musta bought before she got so skinny: a gray woolish-looking skirt, a pale pink blouse with a ruffle down the front, and black patent-leather heels. A gray jacket lay neatly folded on the cot next to her. Both the skirt and the blouse looked like they belonged to a much larger woman.

Although the courthouse was a much prettier build-ing than the one that housed the sheriff's department, it was old, and the cells on the top floor proved that out. The bottom floor had been maintained like crazy over the years, even renovated a time or two; the jail cells not so much. The bars were probably original, the walls defi-nitely so. I figured you get a good-sized lineman in there for drunk and disorderly, one swift kick could take down the whole place.

But Katy wasn't gonna be the one to do that. One swift kick from Katy would probably just knock her on her own ass.

'Hey, Katy,' I said as the guard unlocked the cell door and allowed me in. He closed the door behind me and I felt a shiver when I heard the click as I was locked in with her. Never have gotten over that feeling of confinement when-ever I've gone in a jail cell with a prisoner. Always hav-ing been on the side of good rather than evil, I've always managed to get out of a cell with just a yell to a guard, but still and all, it made me uncomfortable.

'Milt!' Katy said, standing up and hugging me. I was glad I'd had to remove my weapon upon entering the cells.

'Sit down, Katy,' I said, disengaging her arms from around my neck.

She sat, patting the spot next to her and removing her jacket so I could sit down. I did, and she grabbed my hand. 'Milt, please help me! I didn't do this!' she pleaded, tears in her eyes.

'Didn't do what, Katy?' I asked, amazed at her audacity. 'Didn't grab Dewayne by knifepoint and try to steal the replacement money? Didn't threaten to cut him up in little pieces?' I shook my head. 'Honey, we got about a hundred-eleven witnesses saw you do that!'

Katy shook her head vehemently. 'No, not that! Of course I did that! I'm talking about Billy Johansson and Neal Hardy! I had nothing to do with their deaths! And nothing to do with the original bank robbery or Mrs Dickey's kidnapping!'

I disengaged my hand, scooting a little further away from her on the hard cot of the jail cell. It was true I'd known this lady since she was a little girl, but I hadn't known her well. Friendly acquaintances only, but even this little bit of history she seemed to be wanting to take full advantage of.

'You know those guys at the farmhouse?' I asked. 'The two cooking meth?'

She nodded her head. 'My husband, John, and his brother, Sam,' she said, a tear leaking out of one eye.

'I thought you were divorced,' I said.

She shook her head. 'No. I… Well, no. You see,' she started, and the story went something like this:

Katy Monroe's husband, John, had this brother, Sam,

who was a meth head. Sam got Katy strung out, which pissed off John, until he lost his job and discovered that meth was good business. So John and Sam went into the meth-making business, using the last of John's severance pay to buy a little farm in Prophesy County. Unfortunately, Sam and Katy snorted, shot, or what-have-you most of the profits, and John had to come up with a better plan to make money.

Then Katy lost her job. Because she was such a high muckety-muck with her company, they decided to let her resign rather than can her ass, which they shoulda done, once they caught her snorting meth in the ladies'. Now Katy swore it was John's idea to rob the Longbranch First National, but since he and Sam were both dead, looked like we'd never know for sure. But the fact was that Katy had worked at the Longbranch First National as a teller for three summers while going to college, and she certainly knew the layout. And the history of the vault and the vault door was well-known by anybody who'd ever worked at the bank.

Knowing that no one would believe that she and her fancy-pants husband would move from Tulsa to Long-branch for any reason other than dire straights, they made up the story of the divorce and Katy stayed in her parents' RV in their backyard while John and Sam stayed at the farmhouse where they cooked the meth, which they were still doing because they still had customers, not to mention the needs of Katy and Sam.

Since Katy was a vice president of the bank, she had her own key. They would sneak in the bank in the wee hours to do their dirty work. It only took one night using a jack hammer they rented from a hardware store in Oklahoma City to handle the cement of the vault wall. After that they just used shovels to dig out to the wall of Neal Hardy's mediator's office next door. They carried the cement and the dirt out in bags, schlepping them to the farm, where they put it in a supposed compost heap. The vault had a six shelf rolling rack that was kept at the back wall, and they'd just roll it out at night to do their dirty work, and roll it back for the daytime, with a rag covering the hole, and nobody could see through the boxes of files on the rack that there was a hole being dug.

They picked the day of Emmett and Jasmine's wedding to do the deed, knowing everybody was gonna be out of town and up on my mountain. They also knew in advance that Billy Johansson was going to be the only one on patrol in the city and that I'd asked Neal Hardy to guard the sheriff's department in the absence of all sheriff's department personnel. This information had been given to all businesses in the downtown area two weeks prior to the wedding. Dewayne Dickey had been a recipient of the flyer that had been put out. Easy enough for Katy to have found it, not to mention all the talk in town about the wedding.

Katy was adamant that she knew nothing about what went down with Billy and Neal. She swore she knew nothing about it, that it was all Sam and John's doing.

'Why'd they kill Billy?' I asked her. 'At the hospital, I mean.'

'Because he could ID them,' Katy said.

'How?' I asked. 'How would Billy know John or Sam?'

That stymied her for a minute. Finally she said, 'I don't know.'

'It wasn't Sam or John Billy recognized, was it, Katy? It was you,' I said.

She shrugged.

'Somehow Billy saw you. Was it when you shot him?' I asked.

'No!' she said, swinging around on the cot to stare into my eyes. 'I swear to God I didn't shoot him, Milt!'

'But you were there when he was shot, weren't you?' I asked. 'You were there with either John or Sam or both, and Billy saw you, and when he regained consciousness, he could tell Charlie you were involved. That right?'

'It wasn't my idea!' she whined.

'But why kill Neal?' I asked, getting my dander up. 'He wasn't even in town! He was all the way out at the sheriff's office! He didn't see diddly! So why kill him?'

Katy shrugged while I thought. Finally I said, 'Because he was y'all's scapegoat, right? The hole from the vault was going into his office. His death had to be planned from the beginning! How could you pin this on a retired highway patrolman if he was alive to dispute the claim? He'd probably be able to prove he had nothing to do with it, and then we'd be looking closer at that vault. Maybe figure out the shovel pattern showed which way the tunnel was being dug—not from Neal's office to the bank vault, but from the bank vault to Neal's office! Am I right?'

Katy shook her head. 'I don't know what John and Sam were thinking!' Katy said. 'I just did like I was told,' she claimed.

'Yeah,' I said, patting Katy on the leg. 'You're a good little German, Katy.'

'Huh?' she said.

SEVENTEEN

AFTER TYING UP the two pirates, Jasmine got their weapons and handed the extra shotgun to Leon, which Patch quickly grabbed away from him.

'I ain't going back in there without my own personal fire power!' Patch said.

Since Leon's copper pipe was severely bent from the beating he'd given the two goons, Mr Thomas handed him his still sturdy two by four. 'You take this,' he told Leon. 'I'll hang back.'

'No,' Jasmine said. 'You'll stay here. I don't want you near these goons.'

Mr Thomas got his back up. 'Young lady, I've been in this from the beginning and I plan on seeing it through. For Naomi,' he said, his shoulders straight.

Jasmine sighed. 'Mr Thomas, I hate to say this, but you're our weakest link. You would be the most likely one they'd grab. And then Patch and I would be in the position of having to make a decision: put down our weapons or let them kill you. Please don't make me make that decision.'

Mr Thomas went back to the tarp and gingerly sat down on the ground. 'Just don't forget I'm here when this whole thing is over,' he said.

Jasmine grinned at him. 'Don't worry about that. I'll come get you personally,' she said.

Turning back to Patch and Leon, she said, 'OK, y'all ready?'

Patch hefted the shotgun to his shoulder while Leon whacked his hand with the two by four. 'Let's go get us some assholes,' Leon said.

'HELP!' JASON SHOUTED into his cell phone.

'—son? —you?' he heard, thinking it could be Luanne.

'Help!' he shouted again. 'This asshole's going to kill me!'

'—k? ear—e? —lo? Ja—? He—?'

'Luanne! Can you hear me?' Jason shouted.

'Oh, for God's sake, bucko, hang up. No one can hear you,' Pick-Me shouted.

'—nec—! Ca—ear—! —ack!' And the phone went dead in Jason's ear. A tear sprung to his eye. His last hope at rescue, and she couldn't hear him. He didn't even get a chance to say goodbye.

'I do believe I see San Isabella!' Pick-Me shouted to Jason.

'How do you know it's the right island?' Jason shouted back. 'All these damn things look alike!'

Pick-Me pointed out the window. 'I just have this feeling!' he shouted.

Below them Jason could see an island, and on a grassy knoll above the beach, spelled out in white rocks, he could see clearly, even through the falling rain, 'San Isabella.'

'Oh,' he said.

'Now to land this puppy!' Pick-Me shouted.

'Is there an air strip?' Jason shouted back.

'Air strip?' Pick-Me shouted. 'I don't need no stinking air strip!'

'I'M NOT SURE HOW involved Katy was in the murders,' I told Charlie Smith and the Federal Bobbsie Twins, 'and I'm not sure how much we can prove in a court of law. But the girl knew, she had to know, they were gonna kill Neal, and I'm pretty sure she knew they were gonna kill Billy in the hospital, too.'

'So the two guys at the meth lab were her husband and brother-in-law?' Whysmith asked.

I nodded my head. 'That's what she says,' I told him.

'Well, if this woman is a meth addict,' Luanne Carmody said, 'I doubt we can believe half what she says.'

'It just makes sense she had to know about Billy,' I said. 'Since she was the only one he could identify.'

Charlie Smith nodded agreement. 'She may not have injected the meth herself,' he said, 'but she's just as guilty.'

'Not that I don't want this collar,' Whysmith said, 'but seems to me this bitch will get longer time if this is tried as a state murder, rather than a federal crime. And I think a local jury will be happy to hand down a fairly harsh sentence.'

'You giving me a present?' Charlie Smith asked.

Whysmith shrugged. 'Just saving the American taxpayers a little money,' he said.

'Letting the Oklahoma taxpayers foot the bill, huh?' Charlie said.

Again Whysmith's shrug. 'Oklahoma victims, Oklahoma bad guys, Oklahoma crime scene. Why not?'

He stood and held out his hand for Charlie to shake. Which Charlie did. Then Whysmith turned to me and I shook his hand too. More than happy to shake the man's hand as he was leaving. Then we did the same thing with Carmody.

As she was walking out, I called to her. 'Agent Carmody?'

She turned. 'Yes, Sheriff?'

'If you hear from your boyfriend,' I said, 'you'll let me know right away?'

'I called him about twenty minutes ago,' she said. 'I couldn't hear a thing. That storm must really be bad. Sounded like an engine it was so loud.'

'He didn't tell you anything about my deputy?' I asked, crestfallen.

She shook her head. 'I'm sorry, Sheriff. The connection was so bad I couldn't understand a thing he said.'

'Thanks,' I said.

'I'll let you know if I hear from him,' she said and followed Whysmith out the door.

THE BIG BLACK MAN the captain called Tyrone untied Emmett's hands and feet. Emmett rubbed them, trying to get the circulation going. If he was going to kill the captain, he'd have to have *some* feeling in his hands. When the pins and needles came, he leaned down to rub his feet. He was going to have to stand up to kill the son-of-a-bitch, so he'd need some feeling in his feet, too.

'You ready?' the captain asked, still sitting at his table.

'As I'll ever be,' Emmett said.

The captain stood and held out one hand. Without the captain having to look in that direction, one of his boys handed him a long box, which the captain took and set on the table.

'Bought these a while back. Always had a fondness for pretty pistols,' the captain said.

He opened the box, revealing twin dueling pistols with long, silver-plated barrels and pearl handles. Real beauties, Emmett thought.

The captain took out a small case in the lid of the box and opened it, spilling bullets on the table top.

'Choose and load your weapon,' the captain said.

All the men in the room backed up, some pushing tables out of the way as they did so, leaving a long, empty swatch of floor from the door to the lobby to the door to the kitchen.

'You want a second?' the captain asked.

'Not if it means choosing from your men,' Emmett said.

The captain laughed. 'Ain't nobody else here.'

'Bring Patch back,' Emmett said.

The captain shook his head. 'Afraid I can't do that, Deputy. I'm afraid your friend Patch has met with a slight accident.'

Emmett's gut tightened. 'Then let's just do this,' he said. 'The sooner you're dead, the better.'

'Kev!' the captain called out. 'Can you count to ten?'

'Believe so, Cap'n,' he said.

'Then please do so!' the captain said, walking to the center of the cleared out space, facing the kitchen door.

Emmett took his stance with his back to the captain, facing the doorway to the lobby.

Kev stood off to one side. In a loud voice he began: 'One, two…'

I CALLED MY WIFE at the hospital where she works as a psychiatrist.

'Honey,' I said, once I got her on the phone, 'can you drive me to Tulsa?'

'When?' she asked. 'Why?'

'Now and because I gotta fly to San Juan,' I said.

I heard her sigh. 'Honey, they probably won't fly in there,' she said. 'Last I saw online the hurricane is still blowing strong.'

'The airlines said they might be flying that way. I can get as far as Miami for sure—'

'And sit in a hotel in Miami for how long, Milt? Doing what? Just waiting? You can do that here, and get some work done, and be with your family,' my wife said.

'Dammit, Jean, you always gotta be so damn *reasonable*?' I accused.

That was met by a stony silence.

I sighed. 'I gotta do something,' I said.

'Honey, there's nothing you can do,' she said. 'I'm so sorry, Milt. But it's the truth.'

'I gotta hang up,' I said.

'Milt, I'm sorry,' she said.

'Umm,' I said and hung up. Knowing she was right didn't keep me from being pissed as hell that she wouldn't drop everything and drive me to Tulsa. And that's the God's honest truth.

Rather than just sit there and stew about it, I decided to call up the mayor and see how he was doing.

His secretary, Bernice Eisenbach, answered the phone. 'Hey, Bernice,' I said. 'Milt Kovak. His Honor around?'

'Hey, Milt! How's that little boy of yours?' she said. Bernice is a nice lady, if a bit talkative.

'Growing like a weed and smart as the devil,' I said.

She laughed. 'I'll just bet! Takes after his mama I take it?' she said.

I said, 'Whoa, now don't go disparaging my contribution to his gene pool!'

'Oh, no,' she said, 'he's not balding already, is he?'

'Funny as a turd in the punch bowl, Bernice. Now where's His Honor?'

'Not here, and I didn't say yea. You never heard that.'

'Heard what?' I said.

'Actually, he called and said he was under the weather,' Bernice said. 'If it's important you can probably catch him at home.'

'I don't think it's all that important,' I said. 'Thanks, Bernice.'

I rung off and stared alternately at the paperwork on

my desk, and the silent phone. That's when I decided to get up and get out.

I drove over to the mayor's house, thinking checking him in person would let the both of 'em—the mayor and the Mrs—know I was serious about their earlier shenanigans.

I rang the bell and waited. Candy's Hummer was in the driveway, and I noticed the garage door was up, and the mayor's Cadillac was in there. Those were the only vehicles I knew them to have, so I rang the bell again.

Finally the door opened a crack and Candy Waylon stuck part of her head out.

'Oh, hi, Milt. May I help you?'

'Hey, Miz Waylon,' I said. 'Just coming by to check on you and the mayor. How's he healing?'

'Quite well, thank you,' she said, the door still only open a crack.

'Can I talk to him?' I asked.

'Ah, well, he's, ah, busy right now, Milt. Can I have him call you?' she said.

'I'd really like to talk with him, Candy,' I said.

'Now's really not a good time, Milt. How about he calls you in, say, half an hour?' she said, trying on a smile, which wasn't a real good look on Candy Waylon.

Something wasn't right and I didn't like it one bit. For all I knew, the mayor was bleeding to death on the living-room floor. 'Candy, I need to get in your house right now. Please open the door.'

'Do you have a search warrant?' she said.

'You really want me going to the judge and asking for a search warrant? Telling him what happened at the Motel Five as the reason for needing one?' I said.

Candy sighed and opened the door. At which point I kinda wished she hadn't.

The mayor's wife was dressed up, but not Sunday-go-to-meeting dressed up. She was wearing fishnet stockings with black stiletto heels, what we used to call hot pants, and a black bra with cones like that singer Madonna wore in that video. I gotta admit I was struck speechless. Finally, after a minute or two of staring at this woman who clearly didn't have the body for the outfit, I said, 'Ma'am, may I see the mayor, please?'

Silently she led me through the men's club living room to the master bedroom. It was a very large room, the walls painted blood red, and all the furniture a shiny, vinyl-looking black. In the middle of a bed that was larger than any king-sized I'd ever seen lay the mayor, all stretched out, naked as he'd been when I'd seen him in the motel, except for the black rubber mask over his head. He lay spread eagle on the red satin sheets, hands and legs tied to metal fixtures on the bed posts.

I sighed. 'Hey, Walden,' I said.

'Oh, hey, Milt,' he said.

'You OK?' I said.

'It's not what it looks like,' His Honor said.

'I just need to know if this is consensual, Walden,' I said.

'Oh, yes,' he answered.

'Milt, you and Dr McDonnell should try this some time,' Candy said, smiling shyly at me. 'It's lots of fun!'

'Uh huh,' I said. 'Mayor, how are your injuries?' I asked.

'Healing nicely, thank you,' the mayor said.

'Well, then,' I said. 'I guess I'll just leave y'all to it.'

Candy Waylon walked me to the door of the bedroom. 'You can find your way out, right, Sheriff?' she said.

'No problem,' I said.

She smiled a shy smile. 'Thanks for dropping by!' she said, and gave me a little finger wave.

I left the house quick as I could.

JASMINE HELD THE SHOTGUN against her breast, while Patch held his military-style. Leon held the two by four like a baseball bat, the pistol snug in the back of his Tweety Bird boxers. They'd made it out of the blocked-off part of the hotel and were heading down the hall in front of the office, walking slowly and listening for any sign of the pirates.

Then they heard it. Two men talking.

'I'm thinking about killing his bloody ass next time he does it,' said a deep voice with an English accent.

'Now, Tyrone,' said a voice laced with a Latino accent, 'he don't mean no harm.'

'The hell he don't!' Tyrone said.

'It's just his way,' said the Latino. 'He calls me "spic" all the time.'

'And that don't chap your ass?' asked Tyrone.

'Well, yeah, sure, but...'

'But what? Don't you want to gut him?' asked Tyrone, his voice a little whiny.

'Sometimes, sure. But mostly he's a good cap'n,' the Latino said. 'How much you got stashed away in the Caymans?'

'Some,' Tyrone admitted.

'More'n some,' the Latino said. '*Mucho dinero, mi amigo,*' he said and laughed. 'He done good by us.'

'Some things are more important than money, Oz,' Tyrone said.

'Name two!' Oz said.

'My pride!' Tyrone said, his voice getting strident. 'My

ethnic pride! I'm black and I'm beautiful! And I don't need that red-neck asshole constantly makin' racial slurs!'

'Well, at least wait until we split up this take before you do him,' Oz suggested. 'I think we gonna get some good bread from this haul.'

'So why not take him now, then we get the whole haul?' Tyrone suggested.

''Cause we don't know who his fence is!' Oz said, his voice losing patience. 'He holds that information pretty close to the vest, eh, *amigo*? You know who his fence is? No, I didn't think so! So what we gonna do with a bunch of computers and ain't really silver silverware, huh? You know who wants to buy that kinda shit, man, 'cause I don't!'

There was a slight silence, then the deep voice of Tyrone said, 'OK, I'll wait until we split this haul. Then I do him.'

'That's all I'm asking,' Oz said, then they heard what sounded like a slap on the back. 'So let's find this little wifie girl the captain wants so bad.'

Jasmine looked at the two men, who looked back at her. 'So let's let 'em find you,' Patch suggested.

'They'll rue the day,' Jasmine said, and grinned at Patch and Leon.

Handing Leon her shotgun and taking the pistol out of the back of his Tweety Bird boxers, she stuck it in the waist-band of her panties, her long T-shirt covering it, and walked to the corner of the corridor and around it, coming face to face with the two pirates.

'Well, lookie-here,' said Tyrone, a big smile exposing the gold tooth with the diamond star flashing inside it. 'If it ain't Mrs Deputy I'll eat your socks,' he said to Oz.

'Gotta be!' Oz said, smiling his own smile, which only exposed several holes where teeth should have been.

'Cap'n's been looking for you, little missy,' he said. 'And your husband, too. If he's still alive, that is.'

'Oh, no,' said Jasmine in a monotone. 'Are you big bad pirates going to ravage me before you kill me?'

'Huh?' said Oz.

Jasmine brought out the pistol from the waistband of her panties and blew off Tyrone's left big toe.

EIGHTEEN

'WHERE ARE YOU going to land?' Jason screamed.

'As close to the hotel as possible!' Pick-Me shouted back.

'Not that close!' Jason screamed.

'This'll work!' shouted Pick-Me as he lowered the Cessna over the beach, coming in low and fast toward the big plate glass window of the dining room.

'No!' Jason screamed.

'Yeehaa!' Pick-Me shouted and laughed out loud.

EMMETT WALKED HIS paces, praying as he did so. It had been a while, but since being on this island, he was getting the hang of it again. 'Dear Lord,' he thought, 'if you find it in your heart that I need to go, please just see to it that Jasmine and the baby make it out OK. Please let 'em get home and let the baby be OK. Jasmine's gonna be a good mother, Lord, you'll be real proud of her.'

'Seven, eight, nine, ten,' Kev counted out.

Emmett was two paces away from the door to the lobby; the captain an equal number of paces away from the door to the kitchen.

As both turned to fire, all hell broke loose.

TYRONE CURSED AND FELL DOWN, and Oz screamed. Patch and Leon came fast around the corner, brandishing their weapons.

'Oh, shit! I shoulda known!' Oz said. 'It's that nig—!'

Tyrone, still on the floor dealing with his missing toe, let go of it with one hand and knee-capped Oz. 'What'd I just say about that?' he yelled at the Latino.

'Take off your shirt,' Jasmine said to Oz.

'Do what?' Oz demanded.

'How many toes do you want?' she asked.

He took off his shirt. Jasmine handed it to Tyrone. 'Wrap up your foot so you won't bleed to death,' she said. 'Or not. I don't care.'

Tyrone took the shirt and wrapped his wounded foot gingerly. Near them was what appeared to be a closet with a lock on the outside.

'Any idea where the key is for that room there?' she asked her two companions.

Patch brought out a set of keys from his pocket. 'It's a closet. It'll be a little close for the two of them, but that'll be the fun of it,' he said, grinning.

Using the pistol, Jasmine waved the two pirates toward the now open doorway of the very small closet. 'Get in,' she said.

'Hey, I'm a big bloke and you shot off my toe!' Tyrone protested.

'Would you rather I shoot off your pecker?' Jasmine said. 'I have some expertise in that field.'

Tyrone hobbled toward the closet. 'When I get out of here, bitch—'

'I'll shoot you between the eyes,' Jasmine said with a smile on her face. 'And it will be a pleasure,' she added as she slammed the closet door on the two pirates.

Patch used the key to lock it, tried the handle to make sure it was secure, then said, 'On to the dining room, lady and gent?'

'After you,' said Leon.

'No, no, after you,' said Patch, and they both laughed, high from their first win of their little war.

SEVERAL THINGS HAPPENED at once. Jasmine, Patch, and Leon snuck up on the lobby entrance to the dining room, just as Pick-Me's twin-engine Cessna hit the sand of the beach, bounced once, and flew, at a slower pace, into the plate glass window of the dining room. Simultaneously, both Emmett and the captain had turned to fire their antique dueling pistols.

Emmett's pistol fired; the captain's, unfortunately for him but fortunately for Emmett, jammed. Emmett's bullet lodged in the right shoulder of the captain, bringing him to his knees, keening in pain and bewilderment. The plane came through the window, scattering the crew to hell and gone, while Jasmine ran inside and threw herself on her new husband. Patch and Leon started screaming at the running crew, brandishing their weapons and gathering them together.

Meanwhile, Jason fell out of his side of the plane, reverently kissing the carpet on the dining-room floor, while Pick-Me came out of his side, took a step to the wing of his Cessna and, brandishing his own weapon, a pristine World War II Luger his father had bought from someone who had actually fought in the war, yelled, 'You are all under arrest, by the authority of the United States Government!' It would have been more impressive if he hadn't burped at the end.

'OK, SO YOU WERE RIGHT,' I said to my wife. Lord, how I hate saying that to my wife. Or anybody else for that matter. But especially to her!

'I have no intention of saying "I told you so". But I did,' she said, her glasses resting on her pert nose, while she leaned back on a bunch of pillows, a medical journal in her hands that she was pretending to read. I knew she wasn't really reading it; I knew she was secretly gloating.

'I'm glad you're not gonna say it,' I said.

'Wouldn't dream of it,' she said. 'Although I did, of course.'

'What? Dream of it?' I said, grinning.

'No,' she said, stretching out the little word. 'I told you so.'

'Ah ha!' I said, sticking a finger in the air for emphasis. 'You said it!'

'Only because you forced me to,' Jean said, flipping a page of her journal, acting like the whole exchange was boring her to tears. I knew it wasn't. I knew she was gloating. I can tell when a woman's gloating. Which is most of the time when she's talking to a man. Why is that?

'Emmett and Jasmine'll be on the first plane out of San Juan tomorrow,' I told her. 'Should get into Oklahoma City around seven tomorrow night. Still got that lay-over in Miami.'

'Did a doctor check out the baby?' Jean asked, finally laying down the medical journal.

'Yeah. Emmett said everything's fine,' I said.

'Not much of a honeymoon,' Jean said.

'Yeah, Emmett said they're gonna finish their two weeks at home in bed,' I told her.

Jean laughed and leaned towards me. 'Now that's a honeymoon,' she said.

'You getting frisky?' I asked.

'Of course not,' she said, turning off the light. 'Just ignore me.'

NINETEEN

NOT MUCH OF A HONEYMOON indeed, Jasmine thought as they packed their bags for the ferry ride to San Juan. Strange, she thought, but she was going to miss this piss-poor excuse for an island paradise.

It had taken the Coast Guard another ten hours to reach them, which meant gathering up all the stray pirates, and the ones they'd left bundled or confined in various parts of the hotel, and getting everybody into the dining room. It also meant dealing with the captain's wound, which Patch insisted he wanted to do. After hearing the captain scream occasionally, Jasmine finally looked over to see Patch poking his finger in the captain's bullet hole, and saying, 'Call me boy again, you old fart! Come on!'

Jasmine and Emmett mostly just gave orders, which Patch and Leon seemed happy enough to take, and Jasmine had kept her promise, going to get Mr Thomas herself and bringing him into the dining room. During the long ten hours of waiting, he would get up occasionally to stretch his legs, at which point he would kick a nearby pirate and say, 'For Naomi.' Jasmine didn't mind. Wasn't her jurisdiction. And besides, she sort of wanted to kick a few of them herself.

Emmett had gone to the room they'd slept in that first night and found them some clothes, and she felt better now, with blue jeans and a bra, clean panties and a clean T-shirt. Leon had cleaned and bandaged his feet and gone to his room for clothes and shoes and seemed to be in a better mood. And, after eating what little was left after the pirates' banquet of the past however many hours, they all felt better, if not one hundred percent.

They'd found Naomi Thomas's body after the storm let up, tossed outside the door of the kitchen like so much garbage. Leon had found her, thank God, and didn't let Mr Thomas know what the pirates had done. No one wanted the old man to have to live with killing someone. Leon and Patch had wrapped the old lady up in plastic wrap, mummy-like, and left her on a counter in the kitchen for when the authorities showed up.

If Jasmine hadn't been a happily married woman, she thought she could fall head over heels for Pick-Me Webster. Now there, she thought, was a man! The little DEA agent, Jason, couldn't stop retching, but Pick-Me, after announcing the imminent arrest of anyone in the room he didn't like, had jumped down easily from the wing of his plane and taken command. And part of that command had been walking directly up to Jasmine, bowing from the waist, and taking her hand to kiss it European-style. Emmett, she could see immediately, didn't have the same opinion of Pick-Me Webster that she had, but that was so often the case with a man of Pick-Me's obvious charms.

But as interesting as Jasmine found Pick-Me, all she really wanted to do was go home with Emmett and start their life together, *sans* pirates. There was a baby on the way and the three of them had a life to begin.

SAD TO SAY A JURY didn't believe a word that came out of Katy Monroe's mouth. They decided that, although it really couldn't be proved, she'd been at least peripherally involved with the murders of Billy Johansson and Neal

Hardy, and totally involved in the bank robberies and kidnapping of my ex-wife, LaDonna. She got a life sentence, eligible for parole in twenty years. I personally doubted if the little lady would live that long. If she were to lose ten more pounds, she'd probably be dead.

Jasmine's working a desk now, as she's too pregnant to fit behind the wheel of a squad car, much less run down a perp. But she doesn't seem to mind; in fact, she's smiling all the damn time, which is such a far cry from the Jasmine Bodine of old that it's kinda spooky. My old friend Emmett does a lot of smiling himself when he's not thinking about it, but then he'll realize he's doing it and puts a frown on his face, which just looks plain phony, if you ask me.

I got a note in the mail about two weeks after Emmett and Jasmine got back from Luanne Carmody, the FBI agent with the DEA boyfriend. She said she and Jason had broken up when he left the DEA to go to work for his father's factory. According to Carmody, they manufacture the plastic covers for tampons, which she said was poetic since he turned out to be such a douche bag. Her words, not mine.

Jasmine got her own note, this one from the CIA guy who rescued them, and I wouldn'ta known about it if she hadn't left the note on top of her desk, under a pile of papers, a coffee cup, and some while-you-were-out slips. I swear I wasn't snooping. It went something like this:

My Dearest Jasmine,
What an appropriate name for such a vision. I am writing you to let you know that the company and I have decided to part ways. I will be going home to Providence where they have to take me in. But if

you ever need a flyboy who can come in low and
steady, I'm your man.
Sincerely,
Pick-Me.

I wasn't sure, but it sounded dirty to me. Needless to
say, I didn't tell Emmett.

* * * * *

REQUEST YOUR FREE BOOKS!

2 FREE NOVELS
PLUS 2 FREE GIFTS!

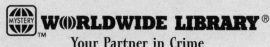

Your Partner in Crime

YES! Please send me 2 FREE novels from the Worldwide Library® series and my 2 FREE gifts (gifts are worth about $10). After receiving them, if I don't wish to receive any more books, I can return the shipping statement marked "cancel." If I don't cancel, I will receive 4 brand-new novels every month and be billed just $5.24 per book in the U.S. or $6.24 per book in Canada. That's a savings of at least 34% off the cover price. It's quite a bargain! Shipping and handling is just 50¢ per book in the U.S. and 75¢ per book in Canada.* I understand that accepting the 2 free books and gifts places me under no obligation to buy anything. I can always return a shipment and cancel at any time. Even if I never buy another book, the two free books and gifts are mine to keep forever.

414/424 WDN FVUV

Name	(PLEASE PRINT)

Address	Apt. #

City	State/Prov.	Zip/Postal Code

Signature (if under 18, a parent or guardian must sign)

Mail to the Harlequin® Reader Service:
IN U.S.A.: P.O. Box 1867, Buffalo, NY 14240-1867
IN CANADA: P.O. Box 609, Fort Erie, Ontario L2A 5X3

Want to try two free books from another line?
Call 1-800-873-8635 or visit www.ReaderService.com.

* Terms and prices subject to change without notice. Prices do not include applicable taxes. Sales tax applicable in N.Y. Canadian residents will be charged applicable taxes. Offer not valid in Quebec. This offer is limited to one order per household. Not valid for current subscribers to the Worldwide Library series. All orders subject to credit approval. Credit or debit balances in a customer's account(s) may be offset by any other outstanding balance owed by or to the customer. Please allow 4 to 6 weeks for delivery. Offer available while quantities last.

Your Privacy—The Harlequin® Reader Service is committed to protecting your privacy. Our Privacy Policy is available online at www.ReaderService.com or upon request from the Harlequin Reader Service.

We make a portion of our mailing list available to reputable third parties that offer products we believe may interest you. If you prefer that we not exchange your name with third parties, or if you wish to clarify or modify your communication preferences, please visit us at www.ReaderService.com/consumerschoice or write to us at Harlequin Reader Service Preference Service, P.O. Box 9062, Buffalo, NY 14269. Include your complete name and address.

WWLI3

REQUEST YOUR FREE BOOKS!

2 FREE NOVELS
FROM THE SUSPENSE COLLECTION
PLUS 2 FREE GIFTS!

YES! Please send me 2 FREE novels from the Suspense Collection and my 2 FREE gifts (gifts are worth about $10). After receiving them, if I don't wish to receive any more books, I can return the shipping statement marked "cancel." If I don't cancel, I will receive 4 brand-new novels every month and be billed just $5.99 per book in the U.S. or $6.49 per book in Canada. That's a savings of at least 25% off the cover price. It's quite a bargain! Shipping and handling is just 50¢ per book in the U.S. and 75¢ per book in Canada.* I understand that accepting the 2 free books and gifts places me under no obligation to buy anything. I can always return a shipment and cancel at any time. Even if I never buy another book, the two free books and gifts are mine to keep forever.

191/391 MDN FVVK

Name	(PLEASE PRINT)	
Address		Apt. #
City	State/Prov.	Zip/Postal Code

Signature (if under 18, a parent or guardian must sign)

Mail to the Harlequin® Reader Service:
IN U.S.A.: P.O. Box 1867, Buffalo, NY 14240-1867
IN CANADA: P.O. Box 609, Fort Erie, Ontario L2A 5X3

Want to try two free books from another line?
Call 1-800-873-8635 or visit www.ReaderService.com.

* Terms and prices subject to change without notice. Prices do not include applicable taxes. Sales tax applicable in N.Y. Canadian residents will be charged applicable taxes. Offer not valid in Quebec. This offer is limited to one order per household. Not valid for current subscribers to the Suspense Collection or the Romance/Suspense Collection. All orders subject to credit approval. Credit or debit balances in a customer's account(s) may be offset by any other outstanding balance owed by or to the customer. Please allow 4 to 6 weeks for delivery. Offer available while quantities last.

Your Privacy—The Harlequin® Reader Service is committed to protecting your privacy. Our Privacy Policy is available online at www.ReaderService.com or upon request from the Harlequin Reader Service.

We make a portion of our mailing list available to reputable third parties that offer products we believe may interest you. If you prefer that we not exchange your name with third parties, or if you wish to clarify or modify your communication preferences, please visit us at www.ReaderService.com/consumerchoice or write to us at Harlequin Reader Service Preference Service, P.O. Box 9062, Buffalo, NY 14269. Include your complete name and address.

SUS13